THE MARCH KINGDOMS
FEAST

STUART SIMMS

Stuart Simms is an aspiring Scottish author currently based in Denmark. In October 2021 he released his first book *Elementals*, a collection of fantasy short stories inspired by his experiences of mental health. He hasn't won any awards, but there's still time. Even if awards aren't forthcoming, he'd claim to be unaffected by it.

Email me at: **stuartsimms.author@gmail.com**

 @muse_bulletin

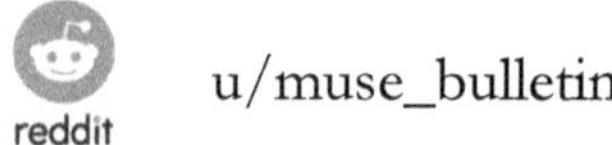 u/muse_bulletin

@thevikingworrier

Also by Stuart Simms

ELEMENTALS: STORIES OF THE FOUR ELEMENTS
A short story collection available from Amazon

Cover design by Stuart Simms
ISBN: 978-1-7397204-4-5

To my mum, my partner, my cousins, my friends, teachers, lecturers and all the other women who have ever guided, mentored and inspired me. I'm a better person because of you all.

'Warlocks and witches in a dance;
Nae cotillion brent-new frae France,
But hornpipes, jigs, strathspeys, and reels
Put life and mettle in their heels.
A winnock bunker in the east,
There sat Auld Nick in shape o' beast:
A towzie tyke, black, grim, and large,
To gie them music was his charge;
He screw'd the pipes and gart them skirl,
Till roof and rafters a' did dirl.—
Coffins stood round like open presses,
That shaw'd the dead in their last dresses;
And by some devilish cantraip sleight
Each in its cauld hand held a light...

...As Tammie glowr'd, amaz'd and curious,
The mirth and fun grew fast and furious:
The piper loud and louder blew,
The dancers quick and quicker flew;
They reel'd, they set, they cross'd, they cleekit
Till ilka carlin swat and reekit
And coost her duddies to the wark
And linket at it in her sark!'
-Robert Burns, Tam O'Shanter

1

The Seer of the Crossroads

Kenrig found her work on the road, though only rarely did she stumble across it. She had to seek it out. Ask questions. Follow trails. Root around in the dark corners everyone else overlooked.

Only rarely did she stumble across it, but sometimes the strangest of jobs fell into her path.

'Dandall, are you still listening?' she said over her shoulder.

When she didn't get an answer she turned in her saddle. The boy rode a short distance behind her, hunched miserably on the back of his equally gloomy grey mare. He was hidden from the rain in the depths of his cloak and hadn't looked up from the path when she'd spoken.

She pulled her own horse to a stop. 'Dandall!' she shouted.

He nearly startled out of the saddle and lost his grip on the mare's reins. Kelpie tossed her head and side-stepped from the dirt path, burying both of them in a hedge. When the boy regained control and caught up to Kenrig his scrawny, sun-starved face hung miserably out of his hood.

'If you want to learn from me,' she said. 'You have to keep up.'

On foot she stood a head taller than the boy. On the back of her own horse she towered over him. Stoic was an enormous beast, covered in a shaggy, russet red hide that made him resemble the hairy cows roaming the mountains of the Marches more than any horse. She had often wondered if she'd been mistakenly sold a hornless bull, but he was even-tempered and tireless so she supposed it didn't matter.

She took Dandall's sullen silence as acknowledgement and set Stoic walking again with a whistle. The grumpy teenager was a far cry from the talkative boy she'd met years ago. Back then she'd been grateful whenever he was quiet, not knowing how frustrating it would be to speak without answer. At least Stoic occasionally grunted in reply.

'Have I ever spoken to you about strange songs?'
Dandall shrugged.
'You can definitely hear singing, can't you?'
He tilted his head up and frowned. To Kenrig's ear the air carried the high, breathless voice of a child and she was relieved when he nodded to confirm he could hear it as well.

'Good,' she sighed. 'What to do when you hear a

song that doesn't exist is a lesson for another day. For now, if you only learn one thing from me, know that I've never found anything dull at the source of a strange song.'

The boy shrugged again, or he might have shivered. 'Seems like a good way to get killed.'

'Maybe, but I haven't died yet.'

*

Their next job came to them from a child playing at a crossroads. The child in question was a young girl dancing barefoot in a mud-stained dress. She skipped and span around the centre of the crossroads, singing a song of her own creation as far as Kenrig could tell.

'A child?' Dandall said. 'I'd say that's pretty dull.'

'We haven't even spoken to them yet. At least try to seem excited for once.'

She led Stoic to the crossroads and dismounted in the shade of an apple tree heavy with late autumn fruit. She left Dandall holding the reins of both horses and approached the girl.

'That was an interesting song,' she said, stopping a few feet from the girl. 'Did you make it up?'

At the sound of her voice the girl turned to face her and stood still on the broad parting stone that capped the crossing of four dirt tracks. The parting stone had been worn smooth by the passage of centuries of travellers, but ancient carvings were still visible in its surface. Intricate knotwork and stylised markings formed a map to mark the directions Karlan settlers had travelled after parting at the crossroads.

The girl looked briefly startled, then her face set with surprising indifference behind a curtain of matted brown hair. The girl clenched the hem of her dirt-caked dress, twisting it back and forth as she looked Kenrig up and down.

Kenrig realised she and Dandall were probably no cleaner than the girl after their travels through the hills dividing the North and Middle Marches.

There was no easy road across the border and they'd spent days riding the high ridges in an endless sea of clouds. Their world had been reduced to an impenetrable haze which diffused the sun all around them so that she could hardly bear to keep her eyes open. When she'd closed them to spare herself from blindness, and trusted Stoic to keep to whatever faint path existed, the light shone red through her eyelids and denied her any kind of rest.

Sounds and smells were dampened under perpetual rain and the passage of time was marked only by the shifting of colours within the cloud layer. The sun climbed across the sky and set behind the horizon without ever revealing its position. As it fell, blinding white gave way to honey and amber yellows, burning oranges and ruddy pinks, before night filled its absence with deep blacks made grey by the shifting clouds.

The paths had become mud under their horses' hooves and both of them were caked with filth that had refused to wash away under the rain. Water had saturated the amber wool of her cloak and slipped through her armour to soak the clothes beneath.

They'd descended after six days, following a trail that had wormed its way between the hills through narrow ravines and across sheer-sided cliffs, bringing them to the contested farmland that made up the disparate kingdoms of the Middle March.

'Can I have an apple?' the girl asked.

Kenrig had been staring down at the mud streaked across her trousers. 'An apple?'

She swept greying hair from her eyes and followed the line of the girl's outstretched arm to the tree. 'Alright.'

Her boots trampled rotted apples as she left the road to stand under the tree. Her stomach growled as she reached up into its branches so she plucked an apple for herself and the boy as well. She threw an apple to him and he dropped Kelpie's reins to catch it. The mare turned to wander away and he ran to give chase.

The girl took advantage of their distraction to approach Stoic and rummage in his saddlebags. She withdrew a copper coin with a shameless smile and held it up to the darkening sky. She ran her fingers over its surface, fascinated by the crow engraved on it until she was offered an apple and hunger became her immediate concern.

Kenrig waited until the girl had devoured the apple before speaking again. 'What's your name?'

The girl wiped juice from her chin with a sleeve. 'Lissi.'

'Nice to meet you, Lissi. I'm Kenrig.'

Lissi eyed the remaining apple Kenrig was holding. 'I know.'

Kenrig's hand paused as she brought the apple toward her mouth. 'What do you mean by that?'

For the first time the girl looked sheepish. 'I know things. Things I'm not meant to.'

Kenrig took a bite out of the apple and offered the rest to Lissi.

'What sort of things do you know?'

Lissi finished the second apple and dropped the core. Her face contorted with concentration and she was quiet for a few moments. One of her big toes unconsciously followed the lines of knotwork on the parting stone.

'Bad things my granny said,' she answered after a while. 'Things I'm not supposed to know. I get dreams.'

Kenrig dropped to one knee in front of her. 'And these dreams come true?'

Lissi nodded. 'I dreamt my granny died. She got mad when I told her. She shut me in the cellar all day.'

She hesitated and looked down at her feet. 'Daglan found me and said my granny was dead. Everyone thought I was playing down there, but I wasn't. I didn't say what my granny did. She always said I shouldn't say bad things about the dead.'

'That's sound advice in my experience. How did she die?'

'She fell and hit her head. Just like I told her she would.'

'Do you still have these dreams?'

She nodded again. 'I dreamt Yenna's dad was sick with fever. And Jan's foot would go bad.'

She started counting off dreams on her fingers. 'I dreamt the reeve fell off his horse because he'd had wine. I dreamt that Henya's dog ran off and never came back. And I dreamt that the smithy got hit by lightning. And I dreamt Sorley had a fancy woman in Vyland. I dreamt–'

Kenrig interrupted her, fearing Lissi would carry on for some time. 'And all of these dreams happened, just as you dreamt them?'

Lissi nodded so hard that Kenrig worried she'd do herself an injury. 'Every one!' she shouted. 'But no one ever believed me!'

'I bet you don't believe me,' she added sullenly.

Kenrig smiled and shook her head. 'I believe you.'

Her hand darted out and plucked the copper coin still held in Lissi's fingers. She held it out between them, then clicked her fingers as she swapped it for a silver coin so quickly it seemed like magic to the wide-eyed girl. She offered the silver coin to Lissi and pocketed the copper one out of sight.

'I've met other people like you, Lissi,' she said. 'Some of them have dreams. Others tell the future using raven guts.'

Lissi screwed up her face in disgust and Kenrig laughed. 'What are you doing out here alone?'

Lissi admired the silver coin as she had the copper one, watching it reflect the gathering yellow light of early evening. At Kenrig's question she ran to the eastern path and pointed across the intervening fields to a solitary hill a few miles distant. A collar of brown and purple heather clung to its slopes before giving way to a rocky crown at the summit.

'I dreamt you spoke to the eerie-folk,' she said. 'So I came to wait for you.'

Kenrig stood and studied the hill, straining her eyes for anything significant at its peak. 'Eerie-folk? What do you mean by that?'

Lissi turned back and frowned with concentration. 'Eerie-folk. You know, fairies, puckies, bogles, prowlies. Up on the hill.'

'And what do these eerie-folk want?'

'You ask a lot of questions.'

'Just a few more I promise. You said I spoke to these eerie-folk. What did I speak to them about?'

Lissi shook her head. 'Dunno. I dreamt they took everyone up the hill. That happened, so you have to speak to them because I dreamt that too.'

Kenrig felt goosebumps raise across her arms. Unconsciously, she ran a hand over the bandoleer of daggers strapped across her chest. As always her hand paused over the sixth sheath which had been empty for years.

She checked the action of her falchion in its scabbard, easing the blade out. 'They took everyone, but not you?'

Again Lissi shook her head. 'I didn't want to see my granny. So I ran here.'

'Your dead granny?'

Lissi began counting with her fingers once more. 'Mmm hmm. Yenna's dad too. And Ida's old husband. Henya's dog. Jan's wee brother. Lots of folk. All dead. The eerie-folk brung them.'

Kenrig turned her head to look at Dandall and check that he was listening. He was flushed from chasing Kelpie, but the red in his cheeks darkened at her attention.

'He wasn't in my dreams,' Lissi said.

Kenrig looked at her again and she continued. 'You spoke to the eerie-folk. Just you.'

Kenrig searched the summit of the hill and for a moment would swear that she saw a glimmer of light.

She stood. 'What did I say about strange songs, Dandall?'

'We have a job then,' he said, and she didn't miss the faint cheer in his voice.

'We have a job,' she said.

2

Uninvited Guest

Karstend village was spread across miles of farmland and dozens of isolated steadings, but a small collection of homes and a village hall were nestled on the southern slope of the hill, the Dullie Fell as Lissi called it.

The girl happily rode in the saddle ahead of Kenrig, kicking her feet back and forth against Kenrig's shins as she ate the apples bundled in her lap. In her role as guide Lissi took the odd break from eating to point them down one of the many identical paths that loosely divided the fields into squares, or to tell some story that had played out as she'd dreamt it whenever they passed a landmark only she could distinguish.

Kenrig for her part trusted that Lissi was steering them truly. She would've had no trouble finding her way to the Dullie Fell, the hill was so out of place in the flat landscape it looked as though someone had pinched the earth and pulled it up into a wide mound. Yet somehow Lissi navigated them through the confusing pathways onto a more direct route that brought them to the village before the end of the day.

Even so it was late into the night by the time they arrived at the hill. 'How long were you waiting for me, Lissi?'

'Dunno,' the girl said between bites. 'It was an awfy while.'

'You must've walked for a long time. It's a few hours ride to the crossroads.'

'Wouldn't have found you if I didn't.'

There were no lights in the village, but breaks in the clouds brought enough light to outline the buildings in dull moonlight. A ragged palisade surrounded the village, running in a tight semi-circle up to the southern slope. The outer buildings, squat drystone cottages, leaned against the palisade and followed its line around the hill, forming an informal marketplace with covered stalls pushed against their walls.

Taller two-storey homes were set at odd intervals further up the hill stacked onto foundations of cut stone, narrow boxes of ochre-stained planks that were a striking yellow even in the darkness. Each of these houses was connected to the marketplace by stairs of roughly sawn logs buried into the broad slope. Higher still was a wide hall built from the same yellow planks spreading out from a far older tower of rough drystone. Behind the hall the faint outline of a path wound its way up and around to the darker eastern slope and out of sight.

The gates to the palisade were thrown wide open despite the late hour. 'Before your eerie-folk arrived, were any strangers invited into the village?' Kenrig asked.

Though she couldn't see Lissi concentrating she could almost sense the deep furrow of the girl's brow. 'Dunno. Father Keld had lots of visitors.'

They tied their horses to one of the stalls and Kenrig helped Lissi down from the high saddle. 'Lissi, why don't you show us where you live.'

The girl skipped across the trampled mud to a cottage beside the opposite gate. The cottage had no stall set out in front, but instead had a fenced off yard housing a covered workshop. A clay forge sat beneath the canvas awning, filled with white charcoal that was cold to the touch. Racks were mounted from the sloped roof and hung with iron tools. Lissi skipped over a cracked ploughshare on her way to the door.

'Daglan and Etholie look after me now,' she said, cheerfully. 'Since granny died.'

The door to the cottage hung open with the key left in the lock and Lissi pushed her way inside easily, heedless of the dark interior. Kenrig paused at the door and lifted two lanterns from the smith's workshop. Their reservoirs were filled with oil and with a few whispered words from her they quickly flared to life. She passed one to Dandall.

In the light she could see Lissi staring at her from the doorway. 'Was that magic?' the girl asked.

Kenrig smiled. 'Just a little bit.'

Lissi studied Dandall. 'Can you do magic an' all?'

He kicked his toe against the ground. 'I'm learning,' he muttered.

'That's a no then.'

Kenrig held up a hand to cut off Dandall's reply. Her smile faded when she examined the wooden doorframe. A thick nail was embedded above the door, but where there ought to be a protective charm hanging from it there was nothing. She held the lantern close to the ground and found a copper sun charm lying in front of the door. Beneath the threshold a hole had been dug to unearth the copper sun's dark counterpart, a black iron moon. Both charms had been cleanly snapped, leaving the cottage without their protection.

She stooped under the doorway and suppressed a shudder at the chill inside the cottage. The interior was a single room centred around a firepit, cold and dark like the forge outside. A table and stools sat beside the pit underneath the roof beam which was hung with bundles of dried herbs and decayed flowers. Two beds occupied opposite ends of the cottage.

She followed the sour smell of rot to the firepit. A cast iron pot hung on a frame above it, full to the brim with a congealed broth hosting a layer of green mould.

She set the lantern down on the table and moved around the cottage lighting the stubs of candles. Lissi followed her, listening intently as she commanded the petty magic that ignited the wicks.

'It doesn't make sense,' Lissi said.

'What doesn't?'

'You're saying words, but I can't hear them.'

Kenrig lifted Lissi onto one of the stools. 'I said the same thing the first time I heard Hieratic spoken aloud.'

'What's that?'

Kenrig removed her necklace and held it up to the light. The heavy black iron chain grew darker the closer it came to the light, while the circular cage of golden knotwork hanging from it brightened until it was almost unbearable to look at it. Inside the narrow cage was an inscribed bone sliver.

'Can you see that?' she asked.

'See what?'

'Try looking out of the corner of your eyes and let them unfocus.'

When viewed directly the Hieratic characters inscribed into the surface of the gold knotwork were nearly impossible to see, even for her after years of training. Only by letting her eyes blur and observing the shifting script in her peripheral vision could she see them clearly. A familiar nausea rose in her throat the longer she looked at the spells crawling across the metal.

'Ummm...yes...no,' Lissi said, straining her eyes. 'I think I saw something.'

Kenrig set the necklace on the table and pushed it over to Lissi. 'Hieratic is the language of the Scriptures. I can't explain how, but only people who are trained to read it can truly see it, never mind understand it. That's why priests and mystics are the only ones who can read the Scriptures properly. They train for decades so that they can read them without using the technique I showed you.'

Lissi gently pressed her index finger to the necklace. 'Are you a priest?'

Kenrig shook her head, partly to clear the lingering dizziness that came with reading the script. 'No, but I trained with one. A man who had dreams like yours.'

She leaned across the table and lifted Lissi's hand onto the necklace. 'I need you to stay here and look after this for me, okay? Will you wear it for me?'

With the sun and moon charms removed from the cottage, the building lacked protection against whatever force had come to the village. She didn't want to be separated from the necklace's protection when dealing with an unknown threat, but also didn't want to risk bringing a child with her while she confronted whatever had taken residence on the hill. She'd made a mistake like that before.

Dandall made a choked sound behind her. 'You're going to leave that with her?'

'I am.'

'But-'

'Check the other houses. Look to see if their charms are gone.'

She didn't need Dandall to search the other houses to know they'd had their protections removed, but she'd learned that the boy was easier to deal with when he was kept busy. He hesitated on the cusp of saying something, then stormed out of the cottage.

It was a relief to remove the necklace, even for a

short while. Physically it wasn't heavy, but she felt as though she could stand straighter without it around her neck. A lingering itch remained on her neck and chest where the metal had rested, but the sensation of crawling across her skin had faded with the removal of the Hieratic spells from contact with her body. She almost shuddered to think of wearing it again.

Lissi turned her head to the side and made another attempt at reading the script on the necklace. 'I'm going with you,' she said. 'I want to see if my dream comes true.'

Kenrig moved so that she was in Lissi's eye line. 'Your dream was true. You found me, and I'm on my way to speak with your Eerie-folk.'

She held up a hand when Lissi tried to interrupt. 'You've done your part. I don't know how long you spent waiting out at the crossroads, but now it's time for you get under a warm blanket and rest. And keep that necklace close.'

· *

She stayed long enough to ensure that Lissi obeyed her, then left the cottage. Dandall's search of the other cottages confirmed her suspicions. The protective charms had been removed from all of them.

She searched some of them herself, finding that just like Daglan and Etholie's cottage, the remnants of untouched meals had been left to go cold in every hearth. Other than the destruction of the household charms there were no signs of any kind of disturbance. Keys were left in every lock and she found no signs that anyone had been taken from their homes by force.

The pattern was repeated at the houses on the hill, except that the larger homes had a number of narrow windows on three of their faces. On the east and south walls the windows were securely latched. On the west wall the window shutters had been left wide open. She checked enough of the houses to confirm that the same was true in each of them.

The log stairs to the village hall were slick with rainwater and most of the tracks left behind were indistinct, but where she could see complete footprints they were all travelling up toward the hall. The broad building was in complete darkness like all the others. No light crept out of the gaps in the shuttered windows or around the main door, and the hall was so wide that the light of her lantern couldn't reach all the way to its ends.

The main door rattled in its frame when she pushed against it and even with Dandall's help it didn't shift.

'Barred from the inside,' she said.

She moved around the front of the building toward the western windows, following the footprints that were now deeply etched into the wet path. The footprints continued around the side of the hall and joined the path where it turned to climb the hill.

As expected the two shuttered windows were open to the night. She scanned the ground beneath the windows expecting to see signs that someone had broken into the hall, but instead found several sets of deep prints where it seemed that a number of people had jumped down from the windows.

On the sill of one window only a single muddy print had been left leading into the hall. She held her lantern high overhead to light the interior, but couldn't see further than a row of long tables stacked to the ceiling.

She backed away from the building keeping her eyes on the windows in case the hall's intruder was still inside, though she suspected that they were long gone.

The path to the summit was rutted with the passage of dozens of people, but beyond their prints she saw no other trace of the village's population. There were no lights on the hill except their own and no sounds above the muffled fall of rain.

Dandall fidgeted with the body of his cloak as they walked, wringing water from the blue tartan. He sighed as the water fell across his boots.

'Something you'd like to say?' she asked.

He didn't meet her eyes, but she could see muscles working in his cheeks beneath the rough, dark stubble as he clenched and unclenched his jaw.

'You asked to come with me,' she said. 'And you've looked like a well-skelped arse for months.'

'Why did you leave your pendant with her?' he asked.

'She needs its protection.'

'More than us?'

'Maybe.'

She looked over at him, noting the tension in the stiffness of his shoulders. 'Better not to bring children when confronting dangerous beasties,' she said. 'I learned that a few years ago.'

'I was older than she is,' he said, his voice cracking. 'And you couldn't have killed that creature without me.'

'I also wouldn't have had to kill it without you either. You were a stupid, reckless child and you were nearly the death of us both.'

He was quiet for a while, long enough for her to hope in vain that the matter was ended.

'You should have brought it,' Dandall mumbled, then more loudly added, 'You don't even know what's up there.'

'Of course I do. Eerie-folk. Fairies, puckies, bogles and prowlies, wasn't it?'

He stopped walking and she turned to face him. Standing further up the hill only increased the disparity in their heights and made Dandall appear to her like the Cadogan child she'd first met. She banished the thought as unhelpful.

'You didn't know what you faced then either,' he said, knuckles white where he gripped his lantern. 'When my dad died. You didn't know, and he's dead now.'

She lowered her own lantern and the shadow of his

hood deepened the gaunt lines of his face. She prepared to speak, but decided against it. He'd barely said anything in the months since he'd joined her and if he chose to speak there and then she wouldn't stop him.

'You lied to him. You told him you knew what you were doing, but you didn't did you? We wouldn't have been on the road that day if we hadn't found you. We left Feidal early when we met you. If we'd left later, if we hadn't travelled that night-'

His next breath shuddered from his throat. 'He might still be alive.'

Years later she still remembered the drowning screams. 'It's foolish to think like that. Speculating won't bring him back.'

'I don't care,' he shouted. 'You lied. You didn't know what you faced then and you don't know what we're facing now.'

'I knew what I faced the second time I had to save you though, didn't I?'

She hated herself for the brief moment of satisfaction she felt, turning Dandall's accusations against him. There was something about that teenager who'd latched himself onto her mission which brought out the worst of her temper. Alone she hadn't needed to justify herself to anyone and now she was forced to answer the criticism of a boy less than half her age.

'I've made a lot of mistakes,' she said. 'Plenty before I met you, and plenty since. I can't apologise for them all. I won't apologise for them all.'

He opened his mouth to speak, but she cut him off.

'You followed me to learn, because you were going to get yourself and others killed doing this on your own. If you're going to learn, you'll benefit from my successes and my failures, and be grateful that you'll learn not to repeat the same mistakes.'

She turned around and started up the hill again. After only a few steps she stopped and spoke over her shoulder.

'I was getting tired of you staying quiet all the time, but if it's easier for you to learn by keeping your mouth shut and listening, then that's how we'll do this.'

*

They didn't speak for the rest of the climb. At first she was grateful to hear nothing more than the laboured sounds of their breathing, but after a while the tension hardened between them, dragging at them like iron weights.

The eastern slope was steeper and the path narrowed as it spiralled gradually toward the summit, bringing the villagers' tracks to a single file. Away from the village the grass grew wilder, hiding rocks and deep patches of clinging mud. The hill had looked small from a distance, but the climb was steep enough that they had to pause and rest as the summit appeared again, visible as a dark mass of shadow against the heavy night sky.

I need to leave Stoic and walk more often, she thought. She almost said it aloud in an effort to dispel some of the awkwardness that had settled over them, but she was stubborn, even when she didn't want to be.

Eventually, the path circled around to the shallower western slope and brought them to a wider path set with scattered patches of stones pressed into the mud. The low remains of drystone walls lay in the grass on either side of the path, divided into short sections by the absence of the carved pillar-like stones the Cadogan tribes had once used to keep paths safe from threats like these Eerie-folk. The finely worked stones had likely been uprooted and reshaped to build forts for the first Karlan settlers, or chapels once the Karlans joined the Hierat and became Marchers.

'This is a sithean,' Dandall whispered. 'A fairy hill.'

The path angled sharply upward to the summit. It passed through a rough channel formed by mottled rock on either side. In the flickering light of their lanterns the rocks loomed high overhead, split by shadows that stretched and turned to face her as she passed. She could easily imagine someone hiding in those shadows, yet no tracks deviated from the path.

The hill crested toward its wide, flat summit where the rocks abruptly stopped and circled outward to enclose the summit's edge. The summit itself was in a darkness so complete that the entire village could have hidden within it and they'd be none the wiser.

A chill shivered down her neck and her chest felt suddenly tight as she continued upward. The lantern seemed painfully obvious in her hand, but part of her was comforted by the warm light.

Around their feet the tracks of the villagers continued on to the summit. She held her lantern higher and crept forward with her eyes darting between the path and the darkness ahead. None of the footprints deviated from the path, even where she could spot children's footprints she saw no sign that anyone had walked in anything other than an orderly procession.

The footprints stopped abruptly as the path disappeared. She took another step forward, holding the lantern ahead of her, but no matter how close she held it to the edge of the summit its light failed to illuminate any further ahead. It pressed at the edge of the darkness, bending away against the summit's curve. The light shrank to a bright crescent as she approached the dark edge until she held the lantern directly before it. Light spread left and right, but none emerged ahead of her.

With a whispered command she snuffed both lanterns, knowing she could ignite them just as quickly if they needed them again, and waited until her eyes adjusted to the dark. Like the buildings of the village far below, the rocks around the summit were outlined with a faint silvery moonlight that gave them substance against the night. The summit lacked any shelter and was open to the sky, yet it was obscured by formless shadow.

'An illusion?' Dandall asked.

Holding her hand out to the darkness she felt the familiar itch of magic across her palm.

'Can you feel that?' she asked.

Dandall held out his hand a short distance from hers. 'I...think so. Yes. Yes, it...itches?'

'Now let your gaze unfocus like we practised.'

She followed her own instruction and scanned the dark surface through the corners of her eyes. The darkness blurred and separated into thin layers like the strata of sandstone, taking on shades of black differentiated by bands of blue, purple and green.

There was a texture to the drifting layers like the fine bristles of feathers, swaying at the direction of unseen force to create a dizzying pattern. She probed the outermost layer with her index finger, careful not to watch her own hand too closely in case she focused on the layers of magic and lost her ability to perceive them. Though she only touched it lightly she could sense the texture keenly against her fingertip.

She closed her eyes, choking down bile as her sense of the magic faded. The deep breaths she took in through her nose carried a cloying, sweet scent like the stink of perfume, followed closely by the acidic, sulphurous smell of rot. She was glad her stomach was empty as the nausea passed.

Staring directly into the darkness it was solid once more. She hadn't seen magic on such a scale for a long time, but amongst its layers there were none of the familiar symbols a mystic would need to construct such a powerful effect. Which meant the magic was an innate effect likely conjured through the presence of the Eerie-folk, whatever they were, without any conscious design.

Dandall lost his last meal beside the path, something she could easily sympathise with. At least it meant he'd succeeded.

The overlapping layers of magic presented an effective barrier she wouldn't simply be able to push her way through physically, but she had a simple solution for that. She drew one of the five daggers from the bandoleer across her chest. The blade was no longer than her hand, more of a needle than a dagger, but the steel gleamed against the dark barrier. The blade was etched with shifting Hieratic characters, though the metal was smooth to the touch.

'What are you doing?' Dandall asked.

He stood and wiped his mouth on the patched sleeve of his tunic.

'I'm going to cut the barrier,' she said. 'And you-'

He pushed his cloak over his shoulders and reached for the notched dirk shoved through his belt.

'-are going to stay here.'

He looked like she'd just slapped him. 'But, why?'

She pointed toward the summit with the dagger. 'As you said, I don't know what I'm going to face. Taking you might be a liability. Leaving you here might save me if everything goes wrong.'

She drew a second dagger and held it out to him by the hilt. He'd stolen the blades from her when they'd first met, but he seemed reluctant to take one as she freely offered it. He sighed then took it, stowing it beside the dirk.

She'd expected more of a fight from him, but was glad he didn't argue. 'This barrier will probably close behind me. I don't know if I'll be able to signal you on the other side, so I'm trusting your discretion in using that blade. Don't follow me unless you have to. Or I don't come back by morning.'

She turned to the barrier and pressed the dagger's tip against its immaterial surface.

'Find somewhere to hide. And make sure Lissi doesn't try and sneak through.'

Holding one of the rarest weapons in the March Kingdoms ahead of her she cut her way from one world to another.

3

The Eerie-folk

The darkness parted like cloth under the dagger's consecrated blade and she emerged onto the Dullie Fell's summit in the midst of a feast.

The silence of the night faded behind her, driven out by the staggering beat of drums and the skirl of bagpipes. The sheer volume of noise stunned her and she stood by the entrance she'd carved trying to make sense of what she saw.

Under the dark shroud she'd believed the summit was flat, but it was riddled with broad, circular pits. The walls of each pit were lined with stones pressed into the earth and on the grass above the worn ruin of larger structures wormed between the openings. Narrow, high-sided passages joined the pits together into a continuous spiral circling a larger central pit. Inside these ancient foundations the people of Karstend celebrated.

Fires burned in stone hearths piled with steaming plates of food and clay pitchers overflowing with wine and ale. Bright cloth streamers were hung from the ruined walls and each pit glowed with the warmth of long torches driven into the ground. Men and women gathered in groups, drinking by the cupful and laughing as their children raced through the passages. Drums were played out of rhythm across the celebration and on the grass above the pits a smaller group danced to the chaotic encouragement of pipes and drums.

The cold autumn rain was a distant memory, lost to the haze and pleasant warmth of a summer evening. The air was hot enough that Kenrig's damp clothes began to steam and for the first time in weeks she thought they might actually dry. Her leather armour felt suddenly stuffy and she could feel sweat forming on her brow as the heat set her skull throbbing.

With a start she realised that she'd already unfastened the buckles securing the armour across her chest, and looked down to find her cloak discarded on the ground beside her sword belt and the bandoleer of daggers.

She stared down at her weapons, reeling as if she'd just been dragged from a deep sleep. She tried to understand the time she must have lost as she unknowingly disarmed herself. Only her fear cut through the confusion and enabled her to lift her weapons.

She fumbled the belt and bandoleer back into place and re-secured her armour, struggling with the buckles as her fingers trembled. It took her minutes to set everything in order and she was seized by an overwhelming fear of discovery. But when she looked up nothing had changed.

The villagers danced and drank without interruption, none of them even glancing in her direction.

As her panic faded she wasn't certain why she'd feared being seen by the villagers. She'd come to that place to understand their disappearance, so surely she wanted them to notice her. Yet she had a lingering dread that if the villagers noticed her then whatever had conjured that place would be made aware of her as well.

A chill traced the line of her spine and she turned, watching as the gap she'd cut through the dark magic slowly knitted itself closed. On the other side was the autumn night she'd left behind, heavy with a constant rain and chilled by a wind cold enough to pierce the strange warmth of the world she'd crossed into.

She breathed in the cold of that wind, drawing it down into her lungs to drive out the fear and confusion of that false summer. Part of her wished she hadn't left her pendant behind.

When she turned, the world of the feast had changed behind her. She held the chill of the cold wind at the back of her mind, letting it cut through the delirious magic that she could already feel plucking at her focus. The celebrations continued without pause, but she watched them as if through a veil.

The bright cloth streamers revealed themselves to be rags dancing in the ghost lights of dead torches. Plates of steaming food chilled and greyed under her attention and discoloured water spilled from the pitchers down empty hearths. The structure of the ancient homes was unchanged, but without the warmth of lit hearths the pits were filled with a sinister gloom.

She crossed the summit and moved between the pits, standing over the people within them. They threw back cups of the dirty water heedlessly, as if it truly were wine and ale they drank. They crashed their cups together and shouted cheers, but their movements were strained and repetitive. Laughter echoed between their groups, carrying a humourless edge.

The villagers were dressed in their best clothes as though they'd gathered for a wedding or festival. The colourful linen of their clothes had become dull in the gloom and bore the stains of mud from their ascent to the summit. Gowns and shirts were torn as if by blades or claws, hanging limp from the emaciated bodies beneath. One of the women dancing on the grass above the pits skipped listlessly and bore bloody lashes across her naked back.

Everywhere she looked the villagers acted as though they were in a grand performance, weary from endless rehearsal. The drummers hunched over their instruments beating their hands bloody against the taut animal hides. A trio of pipers heaved air into the frayed bags of their pipes, straining until their faces were red enough to burst. In the discordant ceilidh the dancers twirled and skipped, stumbled and struggled to rise, lifted back to their feet by partners who had little strength of their own.

Those that stood and ate the spoiled banquet of food did so with eyes that were wide open to the horror of their involuntary consumption. The more that she observed the clearer the reality of the occasion became and her revulsion made it easier to keep her mind clear.

Amongst the helpless celebrants were individuals who seemed to find true enjoyment from the event. Where other participants faltered in the clashing of cups there were those who proposed new toasts, cajoling the others around them into refilling their cups. When a drummer slowed their beat, hoping to spare their raw palms, they were ridiculed and beaten until they took up a punishing rhythm once more. If a fallen dancer was too slow to rise, one among the ceilidh would appear with a willow switch and thrash them until they stood.

Kenrig paid special attention to these individuals, scanning their gleeful faces for some clue to their nature, but she saw little to distinguish them from the other villagers beyond their obvious enjoyment. She was reluctant to shift her focus to search them for signs of magic, out of fear that she would make herself susceptible to the power that had affected her at the threshold.

For brief moments she let her gaze slip into the blurred awareness necessary to observe the magic, counting only a few shallow breaths before she withdrew to the safety of mundane senses. In those moments she sensed the mind-altering power of that place pressing against her like the tide rushing against the coast, patiently wearing down her resolve.

The villagers blurred under her double-vision, flickering with the intermittent glamour that bound them. Languid auras waxed and waned around them, dull and heavy except for brief flares of pain and fear as they were goaded from exhaustion to manic activity.

Among them their tormentors burned like the ghost lights of the torches, radiating grim pleasure in sickly, pale waves. Between the waves their forms distorted and changed. When the white light was brightest they were flesh and blood, dressed in their finest clothes and smiling with demented joy. In the dim breaks from one wave to the next they were skeletal spectres of withered muscle and taut skin, clothed in scraps of funeral garb and leering with rictus grins.

Lissi had told the truth, the dead had come to the Dullie Fell.

*

She was kneeling in the central pit when she returned to her true, ordinary senses. Nausea and confusion roiled inside her, incapacitating both her body and her mind so that she could neither move nor think clearly. She realised with horror that the magic of that miniature realm had taken control again and brought her to her knees at the heart of the feast.

Long moments passed before she could make sense of her surroundings. Intense heat washed over her and worsened her nausea, but she forced her eyes to stay open in an effort to regain some control. A few feet in front of her a bonfire raged, spewing smoke into the sky, and she wondered how she could have failed to see it sooner.

She heard the roaring of the flames and the breaking of the birch saplings that fuelled them as though she was only remembering the sounds hours after they'd passed. Heat and light dimmed as the flames shrank and the birch frame collapsed into charcoal. Under her scrutiny the bonfire slithered down into the bed of spent wood, greedily drawing away its heat until she was left with only the memory of it. Embers lingered in the ashes and died in their own turn as the illusion faded.

The acrid smoke from the dead bonfire rose to join the false sky and in the clear air left behind she noticed the shrivelled body lain across the ashes. Its flesh was charred black and red down to the bones beneath, any recognisable features burned away into the shrunken mass that hardly seemed human anymore. The spicy scent of wood smoke transformed into the stink of burnt meat.

Across the body's chest was a smoke-stained necklace that was otherwise untouched by the flames. The chain was black iron and held a golden pendant set with the inscribed skull of a gorged-carrion bird. An answering itch tingled where her own pendant had hung and she realised with mounting dread that the body had once belonged to a priest. *Keld,* she remembered.

For a Hieratic priest to have their body burned was a grave insult. The traditions of the faith demanded that the temple's servants have their bones picked clean of flesh by carrion birds bred solely for the purpose. Even a village priest like Keld would have had his body conducted into a cathedral aviary so that his bones could be purified while his soul passed into the Otherworld.

Those that carried out the insulting funeral were arrayed around the pit. Six figures lounged above her on ruined walls, inhuman in the easy indolence they expressed toward the nightmarish scenes around them. Their bodies were lithe and long-limbed beyond human proportions. Tattered fabric loosely clothed their stained bodies and bore grisly ornaments of flesh and bone. They watched with disinterest from behind metal masks as a seventh figure tormented one of the villagers inside the pit.

The creature towered over the man who danced to the vicious encouragement of a short whip. Lashes covered the man's torso, staining his ragged shirt with blood.

'Put some mettle and life in those heels,' the creature screamed.

They cackled and howled, setting the metal of their leering mask screeching with their unearthly voice. Kenrig pressed her hands to her head as the sound rang sharp in her ears, bringing tears to her eyes. The other six creatures joined their own listless laughter in harsh chorus and she clamped her eyes shut against the pain.

An involuntary gasp escaped her throat and the laughter stopped. In alarm she opened her eyes wide and rushed to her feet. The creature with her in the pit stared at her with eyes that she felt burning against her skull. They lashed the dancing man's ankle with a desultory gesture, then pushed him to the ground without effort as they advanced on her. The man crawled and broke into a run, mounting the stairs behind Kenrig under a hail of spoiled food from the lounging creatures.

Kenrig's falchion was in her hand without hesitation. The creature crossed the distance between them in a few easy paces, whip raised high overhead to deliver a savage blow. She raised her sword through drilled instinct, cursing the stiff responses of her cold muscles. The creature tensed, ready to bring the whip down.

'Who comes uninvited?' a voice called out from beyond the dead pyre.

The creature stopped, poised to strike. It hovered its arm overhead for a moment longer, then slowly lowered the whip and withdrew toward the stone wall.

Kenrig was determined to maintain her guard, but found her sword arm was already hanging limp at her side. She ought to have been alarmed yet she felt a strange calm as someone entered the pit from a passage in the opposite wall.

The figure was tall and slender, but lacked the obviously alien proportions of the other seven. A hooded gown of silver gossamer disguised their movements so that it seemed they didn't move at all. They crossed to an alcove and sat in the throne-like hollow.

They reclined half in shadow, but delicate silver cords traced the lines of their hood, illuminating the ethereal face beneath. Their face was almost human, but the androgynous beauty of it bore an immortal symmetry. Kenrig found her gaze drawn uncontrollably toward eyes of frosted grey that nearly drove her to her knees again with the weight of sorrow held behind them.

She was so transfixed that she scarcely noticed the giant that followed close behind. He was taller than Kenrig by a full head and was stripped to the waist to reveal a frame of astonishing strength. His skin was fragmented like the bark of an ancient tree, ashen-grey with a recessed pattern of darker wood that made him seem as if he was clad with scales.

A lattice of slender branches wove a crowned helm around a face set in an animalistic snarl. When he spoke his face cracked and fused to create the movements of speech.

'This woman has drawn a blade in your master's presence,' he roared, jabbing a hand toward Kenrig. 'Kill her.'

The seven gangly creatures howled with sudden alarm, any trace of lethargy gone in an instant. Kenrig felt an answering thrill of terror beneath the muffling calm that held her sword arm still. She forced her eyes toward the creatures as they leapt to their feet in chittering motion, burning eyes darting toward her. She tried to grip her falchion tight and raise it into a guard, but her arm was dead to her commands.

'No, Holdainn, we will speak with her.'

At the sound of the calming voice her eyes were pulled to the slender figure now leaning from the recess.

The giant, Holdainn, turned to them, trembling with suppressed rage. 'But Ogda, she is uninvited.'

Ogda peered up into the giant's face, seeming slight beside him. Their pale eyes narrowed slightly and Kenrig was reminded of clouds drifting across the edges of the moon. To her surprise, the giant was cowed and his enormous body slumped in defeat.

He rounded on the seven creatures who leaned close, twisting their attention back and forth across the pit. In an instant his fury returned and he threw an arm toward the lurking creatures.

'Away, *sluagh*! Away, scavenging dogs! Find amusement elsewhere!'

Kenrig felt a surge of rage as if the giant's anger were her own, so fierce it stifled her next breath. The sluagh reacted without hesitation, bounding away to inflict fresh torments on the imprisoned villagers.

The numbing voice of Ogda spoke as if whispering directly into her ear. 'Approach, stranger. We three would speak with you.'

Kenrig hadn't witnessed the arrival of the final member of the trio now arrayed ahead of her. They were slight, no larger than a child and they skipped across the dusty stone with bare feet. Like the chastened creatures they wore tattered clothes sewn with ornaments. A flensing knife streaked with rust and a blood-stained garter, shrivelled hearts and blackened finger bones, corroded coins looped on strings alongside glass bottles, chicken feet and ragwort blossoms. None of it had any obvious value, but the objects were worn like the gaudiest jewellery.

Kenrig felt rather than saw the eyes that watched her. The child's face lacked any features, but she knew they were staring so intently she could feel her thoughts being subjected to their scrutiny. She was disgusted to see their face morph into the crude semblance of human features, as though an unseen sculptor pressed thumbs to their flesh. Slowly, the crude shapes became smoother and more detailed, settling into an exact replica of Lissi's face as Kenrig remembered it, though the pallor was unlike any living child.

Kenrig had been gripping her falchion tight enough that her fingers ached as she loosened them. She slid the sword slowly into its scabbard, warily approaching the trio lined up against the opposite wall. Holdainn the giant bared his sharp teeth in a hideous snarl as she approached and seemed to strain against some invisible force to reach her. In the alcove Ogda's expression remained unreadable while the child borrowing Lissi's face watched with unnerving curiosity.

Kenrig struggled to think clearly. Sorrow, rage and child-like wonder, none of it her own, warred for dominance in her mind as the trio watched her approach. Yet through the fog of conflicting emotions an understanding was beginning to form. Fragments of half-remembered stories heard on the road shuffling together with tales read in lonely nights of research. In the few paces it took her to cross the pit she rattled the names Ogda and Holdainn around in her mind, trying to gleam some advantage before she spoke to them.

The names were familiar to her. So too were the circumstances in which she now found herself, though not through any personal experience. She knew stories of the dead returned to a semblance of life in grand feasts, of spectres loosed from their proper place in the Otherworld to join their living relatives in celebration or torment. In all of these stories the dead were ushered from the Otherworld by the strange denizens of that place, chief among them the Unseelie, fey spirits that all the stories agreed were cruel beyond reason.

She had to swallow away the nervous croak in her voice. 'Hail, seelie wichts,' she said. 'Hail, good neighbours.'

She walked with her arms turned outward in greeting, hoping that she could do enough to garner the good will of the three entities before her. Her words were nothing more than flattery, a desperate attempt to avoid the ire of malevolent spirits.

I hope your dream had a good ending, Lissi.

4

The Good Neighbours

'You know us?' Ogda asked as Kenrig stopped a few paces from the trio.

'Your reputation precedes you,' Kenrig said, trying to keep her voice steady. 'Few would dare to forget you.'

'Then name us.'

Ogda leaned further into the recess, but their eyes didn't dim in the slightest. Kenrig shuddered despite the false warmth of the evening. Her heart was hammering in her chest, but her limbs felt bloodlessly cold. Two of their names had been spoken openly in her presence so she didn't doubt she was being tested, or that there would be consequences for failure.

Gloam Ogda, she thought, *the Crone.* Dozens of names passed through her mind, sifted from the remnants of old stories. *Mal Morbid. Wand-wedded and Stave-shaper. Lamith. Canny Glam. Tsara Loga. Carline. Wyrd-wife. Ma Rhigani. The Waesome Croon.*

She wasn't sure that any of those names belonged to the being before her so she used what she'd been told.

'You are Gloam Ogda,' she said. 'Lord and lady of the Seelie.'

Her lack of knowledge felt painfully exposed in that cold-eyed stare. She was gambling her life and those of the trapped villagers against folk tales. She'd never read or heard anything definite about the creatures or world confronting her, and she thought it was a matter of when, not if, her ignorance would doom them.

The only thing the confusion of stories in her mind agreed on was an absolute need to flatter such creatures. Though she believed that they were the Unseelie, to call them by that name, which spoke of evil and misfortune, seemed insulting. She scanned the unmoving face of Ogda, searching for some sign that she'd either addressed them correctly or made a fatal misstep.

Moments passed and their expression didn't shift even slightly. Unsure what else to do, Kenrig tore her eyes from Ogda's intense scrutiny and regarded the giant beside them. Seeing her attention move to him, the giant's face cracked into a snarl. He continued to strain against whatever invisible power held him back, leaning forward to bare his teeth.

She hesitated to name him, feeling like she was about to try and compliment a leashed bear. *Holdainn was what Ogda had called him.* She knew his name well enough. *Holdainn the Flesher who tortures his prey. Holdainn the Murderer who kills in cold blood. Holdainn the Mangler who tramples those that run.*

'You are Holdainn,' she said to him. 'Holdainn the Hunter who kills with clean strikes. Holdainn the Champion who wins with honour. Holdainn the Warrior who is merciful in victory.'

She needn't have worried that her compliments wouldn't reach the giant through his fury. His snarl broke into a wide grin and he settled back on his heels, seeming to grow even larger as he puffed his chest.

He looked to the others beside him and his face seemed to fall as he saw that their attention wasn't on him, but was still focused on Kenrig. His snarl returned as he considered her again. *That was short-lived.*

She broke eye contact with him and turned to the final member of the trio. It was then that she appreciated how she was being tested. The child, if child was the right word for a creature accompanying a host of dead spirits, was unknown to her. She'd been given no clues to their name and other than the unnerving parody of Lissi's face she didn't recognise any aspect of them.

Her eyes darted to Ogda's face and saw their neutral mask broken by a faint smile.

There had been no terms given when she was told to name the Unseelie, but she didn't doubt there was some stake involved that hadn't been revealed yet. She didn't think something as simple as introductions could ever be a trivial matter for a coven of immortal spirits.

The child seemed to have lost interest in her. Their unsettling attention was now directed at their own feet as they hopped from one to the other in a slow circle. They gripped a tiny bell between thumb and forefinger, ringing it as they stopped to stand on one leg. It produced a clear note that was audible through the din of human music, starting as a faint vibration that grew to a high peal strong enough to set Kenrig's ears ringing in turn.

The bell had only been sounded once and rested limp in the grip of the dancing child, but the ringing radiated from it in waves, increasing in strength until it was deafening. Kenrig felt tears form at the corners of her eyes and wanted to clamp her hands over her ears to hold back the noise, yet the attention of the Unseelie was still on her and she didn't want to show weakness. Her fingernails dug into the flesh of her palms as she fought to keep her eyes from clamping shut.

The child held the clapper in place and the sound stopped, followed shortly by the ringing of her own ears. They replaced the bell on a belt of ornaments and continued hopping as they rummaged through their collection of objects. Eventually they settled on a short reed pipe, pausing to balance so they could sound it in turn.

The music of the pipe didn't bring her pain, but it's sound was as all-consuming as the bell's had been, washing out the noises of the feast all around her. She started to lose the battle to keep her eyes open as a sudden drowsiness followed in the wake of the pipe's endless note. The child was watching her again, blowing into the pipe without a pause for breath.

Her eyes finally closed and she didn't notice the child replace the pipe with a pair of scallop shells. They used the shells to tap out a steady beat and in her drowsy state she couldn't resist the urge to drum her foot in time to the rhythm. She forced her eyes open and through blurred vision saw the shimmering strata of magic in the music, rippling through the overlapping magic that composed the world around them.

The child played and grew bored of more instruments in turn, casting a sequence of magic that broke against Kenrig's will, wearing down her resistance and sapping her concentration. A drum no bigger than a hand seized control of her heart's rhythm, forcing it to contract in time with the drum's own beating. A clay rattle wrenched the bones of her hands, straining to twist the joints out of alignment. A wooden ocarina forced her to take the first halting steps of a dance, and she collapsed to her knees in her effort to fight the control.

She gasped as the magic was withdrawn and pressed her hands to the dirt, no longer concerned about looking weak to the Unseelie.

'It seems our reputation has not preceded us as much as you claimed,' Ogda said, without the trace of a smile. 'You repeated the names you were given, no more. My daughter's name remains unspoken.'

Kenrig looked up at the Unseelie lord, unable to stand. 'If I could have a moment to think, I-'

'Enough!' Holdainn roared over her. 'She has insulted my sister. Father, I demand the right to kill her.'

Ogda leaned into the light. 'My son is right to ask this of me,' they said. 'And I see no reason not to grant his request. Your interruption of our feast provided some brief amusement, but it's time I put an end to it. Holdainn, you have my leave.'

Their hand rose and Holdainn lurched forward, suddenly freed from his invisible leash. He walked toward her, but his giant stride crossed the distance between them in a couple of steps. His hands were spread wide beside him as the bark covering his fingers stretched into claws.

'Wait,' she said, stumbling to her feet. 'I'll trade my name for your daughter's. A name for a name.'

The giant jerked to a stop inches from reaching her as if he'd been caught at the end of invisible chains. He roared, poised to tear her to pieces with his newly clawed hands, and she couldn't help but flinch as his enormous shadow fell across her. Ogda lowered their hand.

Holdainn fought against the force dragging him backward and she thought he might succeed as he managed to take a step toward her before being dragged by his wrists and ankles. His shuddering backward steps were almost comical, but the spittle flying from his mouth left her in no doubt that he was moments from killing her.

Ogda turned to their daughter and the child nodded eagerly.

'Very well,' they said, looking back to Kenrig. 'Speak.'

Kenrig briefly considered giving a false name, but she didn't think the Unseelie would be so easily deceived. They didn't know her name, otherwise her bargain wouldn't have interested them, but she couldn't risk a complete lie when her position was so precarious. The name she'd adopted years ago came easily to her lips.

'Kenrig,' she said. 'Kenrig Ebermann.'

The child stepped forward at Ogda's prompting and curtseyed. 'Saully,' she said. 'Saully-Menyie.'

Saully-Menyie straightened and hopped back to stand beside Ogda's throne. The lord of the Unseelie folded their hands in their lap and smiled, wider than before, leaving Kenrig to wonder if she'd come out the worst from that exchange.

'Why do you permit this, father?' Holdainn said.

During the trade of names the giant had composed himself and no longer wrestled with his invisible restraints.

'She has interrupted our feast,' he continued, never taking his eyes off of Kenrig. 'She must be punished and I tire of waiting. Why shouldn't I kill her? I can make her death slow if it pleases you, but let me begin now.'

Ogda didn't reply to their son and instead looked to Kenrig for the answer to his question.

Kenrig met his stare. 'Your patience does you credit.'

The murderous intent didn't leave his black eyes, but

she saw the change in his posture as she spoke the compliment.

She glanced between them, not wanting her gaze to settle on any of them fully for too long. The power behind their eyes terrified her, and she worried that her ability to resist any new compulsions was fading rapidly.

'I want to offer you a bargain,' she said. 'A real one. More than just the exchanging of names.'

Ogda held up their hand, cutting off Holdainn's next words. 'And the terms of this bargain would be what?'

'Set me a series of challenges. One from each of you. If I complete the three challenges you release the people trapped here. If I fail, then I join the feast and I am your guest here for as long as it pleases you to keep me.'

Ogda's face had returned to its neutral mask, but the child Saully-Menyie was nearly jumping with excitement and rocked back and forth between their heels and the balls of their feet.

Holdainn was the first to speak. 'This is absurd.'

He looked to his father and sister. 'Why would we bargain the lives we have trapped here against the prospect of adding one more?'

Kenrig addressed Ogda. 'Because you've grown tired of the amusement they can provide. The villagers of Karstend are exhausted and their waning enthusiasm doesn't do credit to the revels you provide them.'

She indicated the direction of the seven creatures who'd fled from the pit. 'Your own followers were sitting idly, no longer showing proper enjoyment of the festivities.'

She looked to Saully-Menyie next, hoping to capitalise on the child's obvious excitement. 'Challenge me. Set me tests for your entertainment.'

The child turned to Ogda. 'Oh mother, please say yes. *Please.*'

The Unseelie lord silenced Saully-Menyie with a gesture. 'Three challenges. One from each of us. Should you win, you may leave and quit this place for good. I will also release the people held here. *For one week.*'

Kenrig tried not to let her disappointment show. She'd been ambitious to ask for the villagers to be released indefinitely, but she would be bargaining one week of freedom for them against her own imprisonment and torture. If she walked out of that place with the villagers, would one week be enough time to understand how the Unseelie had arrived there? Could she send them away, or would she buy the villagers a brief reprieve only so they could be tormented anew?

'Should you lose,' Ogda continued. 'You remain here as our guest. Forever.'

Kenrig glanced between the members of the trio. She'd heard that the Unseelie weren't just honour-bound to fulfil bargains, but were entirely incapable of breaking them once an agreement was made. At least that's what some stories claimed.

Her chances of escaping the Unseelie's world alone were slim, much less with the villagers in tow. The bargain she was making felt like her best chance to end the nightmarish feast, at least for a short while, but there was no shaking the sense that some trap was being laid out for her. Ogda had agreed to the terms more readily than she'd expected, and she couldn't help but remember that the fey bargains struck in stories only ever ended one way.

'Agreed,' she said.

5

First Blood

Kenrig had barely agreed to the bargain before Holdainn was moving again. She took an involuntary step backwards, but he didn't move toward her. Instead he returned to the opening in the pit wall the Unseelie had entered from. He whistled and knelt before it.

With all the bizarre things she'd witnessed that night, the sight of an old wolfhound hobbling into the pit was so seemingly mundane that for a moment she thought she'd imagined it. The dog was unusually large in keeping with Holdainn himself, standing as tall at the shoulder as some horses, but otherwise seemed strangely ordinary.

Its coat was matted and discoloured, grimy with dirt and frayed with bald patches. The pale sheen of cataracts shone in its eyes, but it found its way to the kneeling giant with slow certainty, walking on legs that were arthritically-rigid.

It brought its head to rest against Holdainn's upraised knee and the giant, who moments ago had been almost foaming at the mouth like a beast himself, gently cupped the dog's neck. He brought his mouth down to kiss the wolfhound on its brow and whispered into its ear as he ran his hands across its neck and shoulders.

Kenrig found the giant's absurd gentleness with the wolfhound so out of character that she was almost too mesmerised to see the knife appear in his hand. The knife's ragged blade was curved like a talon and he pressed the edge to the side of the dog's throat. His other hand continued to stroke the wolfhound's neck and it blindly gazed up into its master's face, betraying no trace of fear or understanding.

Its body stiffened as the knife was dragged across its neck. Even in the act of killing the dog Holdainn continued to be gentle, moving the knife cleanly and quickly, and opening a wide wound that ended the wolfhound's life in moments. Blood ran thick down his arms, flowing into the cracks between the bark scales.

He wiped the knife's blade on the hem of his trousers and replaced the weapon in a sheath at his belt. The claws that had grown in his effort to kill Kenrig hadn't withdrawn, and he used them to pull at the wound in the wolfhound's throat, widening it further. Her disgust grew as he plunged his right arm into the wound up to the shoulder.

The muscles in his back tensed as he pulled at something. She expected to see him withdraw a handful of viscera and couldn't have predicted that he'd pull a sword from the wolfhound's body, drawing it as smoothly as if from a scabbard. The wolfhound seemed to deflate as the sword was removed, collapsing as though he'd drawn out its muscles.

The sword was a hideous weapon, an ancient blade of notched iron set into a hilt of antler bone that was nearly half the blade's length and still bore its sharp tines. To a mortal warrior it would have taken two hands to wield, but the giant held it out in front of him with a casual one-handed grip. He admired the weapon, raising it higher as he stood, and though his arm glistened with gore the sword's blade was clean.

He turned back toward her and held the sword briefly in two hands, hefting the blade in what she thought was a vertical salute.

'My challenge,' he declared. 'Is a duel to first blood.'

With that he charged, moving with no more restraints to hold back his astonishing speed. Her falchion was barely in her hand before he swept his sword in a horizontal arc that would have neatly decapitated her. She pushed her falchion upward, pressing her free hand to the flat of the blade for the strength needed to deflect Holdainn's strike over her head.

The giant turned with the momentum of his strike, angling himself side on to her. He struck with his elbow, catching her high in the chest and pushing her staggering backwards. She retreated, stepping back until she recovered her balance.

The giant followed, lunging forward and thrusting his sword straight out in front of him. She held her falchion awkwardly high, her arms numb and sluggish from the impact of his first strike, and couldn't bring it down in time to meet his next attack. The point of his sword hit directly over her heart, stopped only by her armour. Leather split under the blow in a narrow gash, but his sword came away clean and the duel continued.

Holdainn had claimed that the duel was to first blood, but he clearly intended to end it with a killing strike.

Kenrig had faced creatures far stronger than herself before, but none of them had fought with a blade or the martial prowess of an immortal warrior. Against mindless beasts and undead monsters her weapons and training had been one of her few advantages. Against Holdainn the advantage was his.

She was unable to do much more than back away or circle around him, using the flat side of her falchion to turn his strikes away. His reach was long enough that he controlled the distance of the duel, while his strength meant that moving inside his reach wasn't to her advantage either.

She whirled the falchion with the motion of her wrists, cutting at the inside of his sword arm when it extended past her, but couldn't part his scaled skin to draw blood.

Holdainn fought with perfect technique, yet beneath his precise skill there was a rage so powerful that she could feel a portion of it as if it were her own. Muscle memory carried her through the duel and her defence was instinctive. There was no time for her to think and their shared rage drove her into reckless counterattacks.

Holdainn's superiority brought out the best of her own abilities purely to keep him from killing her, but her defence faltered against his tireless assault. She couldn't see any way that she could win and her frustration at the inevitable defeat was fuel to the giant's infectious fury. She struck at him when she ought to retreat, leaving herself out of position and scrambling to defend herself when she regained control.

It was a moment of unconscious rage that ended the duel.

She'd been lucky that the loose dirt and uneven rise and fall of the pit floor hadn't turned on her sooner. She moved where she was able to, never finding enough of a reprieve to be concerned where her feet landed. Her boots skidded and caught, bringing her a hair's breadth from a fatal misstep, but she'd always managed to recover and save herself by the narrowest margin.

Goaded by rage she lunged at Holdainn, seeing a wide opening when a strike at her legs brought his head level with hers. Anger threw all of her weight forward into the attack, leaving her with nothing to regain her balance as he twisted his head out of the blade's path and shoved her with an open palm. Her first step backward met the charred frame of the collapsed pyre and caught in the tangle of wood.

She fell across the cremated remains of the priest and rolled away, gagging at the smell of ashen flesh. Holdainn pursued her relentlessly, kicking aside the remnants of the pyre as she pushed herself across the ground. She regained her feet and raised her falchion a moment too late.

Holdainn lifted his sword high overhead and brought it down in a blow that would have cut her in half from collar to hip without a final, desperate defence. She knocked the strike off its intended course with the falchion as she pulled her left shoulder back as far as she could. The point of his sword missed the killing strike, but carved through the leather pauldron at her shoulder, slicing into the muscle underneath.

He flicked the sword round in a tight circle and brought the blade in a cut that stopped a fraction short of her neck. She closed her eyes as she felt the faint chill of the blade's edge against her skin, not daring to breathe though her lungs burned. She expected every moment that passed to be her last, but Holdainn's sword didn't move and only her own trembling brought the edge any closer to cutting her.

She opened her eyes to the looming mass of him. Motionless, he was as massive and steady as the trunk of a tree. His black eyes didn't blink as he stared down with undisguised hatred. His chest didn't swell or contract with the rhythm of breath while she panted with exhaustion. His arm was fully extended, but the enormous sword held straight out before him didn't even shake in his grip.

The spreading warmth of blood saturating the clothes at her shoulder reminded her that she'd lost the duel, but she felt that to survive a duel against an opponent like him was a victory in itself.

She glanced past him to see that Ogda was standing before the recessed throne, their left hand raised in the gesture that had saved her. If they hadn't intervened, or had hesitated even briefly, she would already be dead.

As she considered the fact of her loss though, she wondered if death would have been preferable. She'd failed the first challenge and doomed herself to suffer alongside the villagers. She'd bargained with creatures no mortal understood and realised how desperate she'd been to suggest the bargain. Through some madness of self-preservation she had denied herself a quick death at Holdainn's hands twice over, guaranteeing that the remainder of her life would be spent in the torture of the Unseelie.

Holdainn finally lowered his sword and when he spoke his words bore a savage glee. 'I claim first blood. You've failed. Our bargain binds you here forever.'

He leaned down, bringing his face close enough that she was surprised when she didn't feel any warmth from his proximity. In the wide cracks of his face, where his eyes and mouth split the bark, she saw his flesh clearly. It was dark, a bloodless grey.

'Your death will not be easy,' he continued. 'And it will not come quickly.'

He straightened and turned his back to her. She hadn't noticed the sluagh return during the duel, but without the giant blocking her line of sight she saw them gathered above the pit, brawling over a pair of bronze shackles. *Those are for me*, she thought with renewed fear. *They're fighting for the honour of binding me.*

Weapons flashed and the shackles were traded back and forth through the shrieking melee. They hacked at each other without Holdainn's supernatural grace, whirling hooked knives and broad cleavers, or lashing out with short whips and barbed flails. They knocked each other down with fists and feet, and bludgeoned those that fell.

A pair of them gripped either end of the shackles, pulling the chain taut and spinning around each other to the howling cheers of the others. They stabbed and sliced with their knives across the chain, carving deep gashes into their flesh. One of them fell away during a violent turn and rolled, knocking another to the ground.

The victor of the bout held the shackles high before their fellows turned on them, chopping at their exposed torso. The brutalised sluagh hunched over the shackles and tried to push their way free as dozens of blows cut into the meat of their back. *All without drawing blood*, she realised. For all the hideous injuries they inflicted on each other, they hadn't drawn a single drop of blood.

She looked back at Holdainn who stood with his back to her, cleaning her blood from the point of his sword with a rag. Somehow her falchion had remained in her hand and a last desperate hope occurred to her. *If this doesn't work, maybe he'll kill me quickly.*

She charged across the pit, gripping the falchion with both hands. She didn't yell as she ran and if Ogda or Saully-Menyie saw her move they didn't warn Holdainn. He was preoccupied with the cleaning of his blade, polishing every last drop of blood from the metal, and it wasn't until the falchion cut deep into his muscle that he noticed her approach.

She planted her feet, exhaling as she swung the falchion with a power she couldn't have mustered in the duel, not while she'd been hard-pressed just to survive. The wide point of the blade bit deep into his shoulder and she dragged it down in a line toward his opposite hip. Scaled skin and muscle were peeled open, but as she retreated she saw no trace of blood in the injury.

All at once the noisy squabble of the sluagh fell silent.

Holdainn wheeled and the fury she saw then was unlike anything she'd seen from him before. It was the cold violence of a man who'd been insulted, of a warrior who'd won a duel only to be attacked while his back was turned.

'You don't bleed,' she said, by way of explanation. 'If you don't bleed, I couldn't have won your challenge.'

The giant didn't seem interested in the truth of his deceit. From the hatred he levelled at her she knew she wouldn't survive another bout with him. *At least make it quick.*

'She's right, Holdainn,' Ogda said, speaking for the first time since the duel began. 'You tried to cheat her. The challenge was unfair and must for honour's sake be considered complete.'

Holdainn didn't look as though he would abide by the decision, but he didn't make any further move towards her. He glared, seemingly held back only by his own restraint rather than any conjured force. When he finally turned away, Kenrig's disbelief at surviving curtailed her relief.

Ogda was watching her over the line of their son's shoulder, and she would swear that she saw a trace of something like anger move in their emotionless face. Kenrig had gambled on the Unseelie honouring the terms of a bargain, but with the almost imperceptible shift in Ogda's expression she had doubts.

If she hadn't revealed Holdainn's deception, would Ogda have intervened, or would they have allowed their son to kill her?

6

Her Left Eye

With the threat of death temporarily suspended, Kenrig could fully appreciate the wound in her shoulder. It wasn't nearly as deep as it might have been, and the bleeding had slowed to a steady trickle, but the gash ran from her shoulder to her bicep and the sudden rush of pain was dizzying. She pushed her hand under the split pauldron and clutched the muscle around the wound, unable to do more while challenges remained.

She followed in the giant's wake, coming to stand before the trio, keeping a healthy distance from him. The giant paid her no mind and stopped beside the remains of his wolfhound. He knelt over its body, placing his sword alongside it and drawing the knife he'd used to kill it.

He turned the knife to the grisly work of sawing the wolfhound open from the wound in its neck to its back legs. She gagged at the smell of rapidly putrefying flesh that emerged from its open belly, but watched Holdainn work with the same grim fascination as she had when he'd drawn the blade from its throat. He opened the wolfhound's belly wide enough to replace the sword inside its body.

When the sword had been drawn it had collapsed as though its body had been hollowed out. As Holdainn replaced the weapon the wolfhound took on something of its old shape, partially butchered as it was. The giant reached into a pouch at his belt and drew out a long hook tied to a thick cord of what looked like gut string. He began to close the gap in the wolfhound's belly with ragged stitches, sewing from its back legs to its throat, and then set to work closing the fatal wound dividing its neck.

The stitches were hurried and widely-spaced, leaving gaps along the length of both injuries, but when the final stitch was in place and Holdainn had knotted the cord the gaps began to close. The wolfhound's skin bridged the gaps, opposite sides of the wounds pressing together until there was nothing but two ridged scars to show that the wounds had ever existed. Then even the scars faded, melting into the smooth skin around them as the stitches shrivelled to nothing.

The wolfhound twitched and stirred, rolling from where it lay on its side to bring its feet underneath it. Hair regrew to cover its injuries, then continued to fill in the bald patches where its mangy skin had been exposed. Dirt and discolouration faded from its coat, and the blindness of cataracts gave way to golden irises. It leapt to its feet, springing high enough to press its front paws against Holdainn's chest.

The giant fussed over it, stooping so that it could lick at his craggy face. She couldn't reconcile the tender affection he displayed toward the wolfhound with the violence he showed to his enemies, or the brutal murder and resurrection of the dog carried out by his own hands, the same hands which worried its flanks with genuine affection.

He whistled and the wolfhound dropped back down to the ground, padding around to turn and lope off through the pit's entrance.

Kenrig tore her attention back to Ogda and Saully-Menyie where they'd remained by the throne. Ogda was seated again, one hand outstretched to rest on their daughter's shoulder. Holdainn joined them, looming over the throne but seeming diminished beside the seated lord.

'You did not succeed in your first challenge,' Ogda declared. 'But my son dishonoured himself through deceit, and so I must consider the challenge forfeited in your favour.'

They lifted their free hand and raised their forefinger. 'I will permit this once. You succeeded only by revealing my son's deception, but my daughter and I will not attempt to deceive you. You will complete our challenges truly, or consider your bargain failed.'

Kenrig struggled to believe that there would be no deception in the remaining challenges, but didn't voice that opinion. She simply inclined her head in agreement, the weight of the Unseelie lord's declaration holding her tongue.

They squeezed their daughter's shoulder then gently

pushed the child forward. The girl chewed her borrowed lips and looked down at her feet with an awkwardness that belied the cruel power she'd held over Kenrig through her charmed instruments. The look of serious concentration in her pallid face was a sickeningly perfect imitation of the look Lissi wore in Kenrig's memory.

Kenrig didn't know much about the third member of the Unseelie. The name Saully-Menyie had been a revelation to her, and she hadn't been given an opportunity to consider it. She thought about the name as she watched the child, struggling to fix anything in her mind that might provide some insight. Against Ogda and Holdainn she'd felt dangerously ignorant, but she had at least understood their names and could fit them into the stories she'd heard.

Nothing about the Unseelie had been straightforward, even Holdainn's ready violence had given way to an unusual affection, but Saully-Menyie was a true mystery to her. Ogda and Holdainn, whether known by different names or not, were definite presences in the stories she knew and were accompanied by a host of figures, as unrelated from each other as it was possible to be, and she couldn't match the strange child to any of them.

The child had possessed no face of her own when Kenrig had first seen her, instead shaping a face seemingly from Kenrig's memories. Kenrig wondered whether Lissi's face had been chosen to fit Saully-Menyie's child-like form or whether there had been any intention behind the transformation, and Lissi's face had simply been mimicked from Kenrig's recent memory. Was she tied to the form of a child, or could she take other forms?

Whatever the case, Kenrig knew nothing certain about Saully-Menyie and the supposed innocence of the creature worried her. The child returned her scrutiny and she felt an answering resentment as she remembered their brief battle of wills. Saully-Menyie's instruments had tried to strip away her control and to her there was nothing more terrifying than the surrendering of power to another.

Holdainn's challenge had sought to kill her in the most violent way possible. A handspan further and his last strike would have ended her life. His onslaught had terrified her, but she'd at least been in charge of her own strength and abilities.

The giant's blade was a more obvious threat, something easily understood that would kill or wound, but perhaps that was why it scared her less than the child's insidious music. She had lost control already to the magic of the illusory realm, and witnessed the torture inflicted on the trapped villagers. A quick death at the end of a sword seemed like a mercy by comparison and she had nearly goaded Holdainn into killing her when she'd believed the first challenge had been failed.

The child said nothing, instead studying her with unashamed curiosity and once again she could feel her thoughts being scrutinised. She tried not to let her uneasiness at the intrusion show and let her mind fill with undisguised contempt. There was no defence for her thoughts that she knew of, no way of resisting that occurred to her except to keep her mind rooted to the present.

Memories drifted randomly to the fore, unbidden by her but coaxed out all the same. There was no clear pattern to the memories that were selected and they passed through her awareness in a patchwork sequence that gave no clue to Saully-Menyie's purpose in searching them. Each memory lingered only for a few moments before she stamped them down, taking small satisfaction in doing something against the intrusion, even if it was ultimately futile.

Saully-Menyie fidgeted with the objects she'd collected, running them through her fingers without any obvious order. Kenrig was dimly aware of the action, enough to be distracted by it, and wondered whether her memories were being added to another unseen collection.

'Enough,' she hissed. 'Give me your challenge and stay out of my head.'

As Saully-Menyie's intrusion ended she felt a force contracting against her skull. It was gone the next moment, leaving a fleeting dizziness.

Saully-Menyie returned to her outward shyness, averting her eyes from Kenrig's face and kicking at the ground with the curled toes of one foot. Instead of responding to Kenrig directly she looked over her shoulder to her seated mother. It was only at Ogda's encouraging nod that she brought her attention back to Kenrig who could only guess whether the shyness was genuine.

Kenrig could hardly believe that an immortal entity who crossed the veil from the Otherworld to torture villages and steal memories, even one in the form of a child, could feel embarrassment. Genuine or not, it was with a timid reluctance that Saully-Menyie finally offered a challenge.

'Bring me that,' she said, pointing.

Kenrig followed the line of her finger to the bruised clouds of the distant sky. Since she'd arrived in the world of the feast the sky hadn't changed. The false sun's position was constant, fixed just above the western horizon where it lingered enough to fill the air with balmy warmth. Close to the horizon the clouds were a bright band of gold darkening to a sparse blue veil at the leading edge of a night that would never arrive.

Despite the apparent summer evening the moon was visible through a break in the clouds, surrounded by a ring of silver-limned vapour that circled continuously, neither contracting or expanding, nor drifting in the breeze that carried the other clouds. The moon was half-hidden by a curved shadow, as it was in the real world outside of the Unseelie feast, but its light in the illusory world was brighter, pale and blinding even in the false evening sky.

Kenrig pointed in turn. 'Bring you *that?* The moon?'

Saully-Menyie nodded, shyness forgotten for a moment. 'Yes. I want the Left-eye of your Mother.'

Kenrig narrowed her eyes against the moon's light. *I want the Left-eye of your Mother.* She rolled the words around in her mind trying to get a feel for their meaning. The followers of the Hieratic scriptures believed that the sun and moon were the right and left eyes of the Mother, the waking eye and the sleeping eye, each of them a gateway. Her Right-eye was gateway to a world of infinite light and was the source of both life and the raw elements that composed the Hieratic script. The mystics of the temple in Far Sostris risked blindness to draw those elements from the sun and shape them into the script's characters.

Her Left-eye was the dark mirror. It was gateway to the Otherworld through which the spirits of the dead travelled from the earth to their eternal rest. A veil of shadow existed to prevent spirits and worse things besides from crossing in the other direction, at least when the moon wasn't full. As the Goddess slept through the hours of darkness she did so fitfully and woke gradually to watch over her creations with her Left-eye, unwittingly lifting the veil as she opened it fully.

Although Kenrig superficially worked with the Hieratic temples she didn't share all of their followers' beliefs. She couldn't deny there was some truth to the superstitions surrounding the sun and moon. She had witnessed for herself the creation of Hieratic script, watching as a temple mystic inscribed blank parchment using nothing but sunlight.

Her work required her to walk in the darkest corners of the Marches, her paths lit only by the moon. Its pale gaze brought out the creatures she hunted from their hiding places, emboldening half-dead beasts and lending temporary substance to immaterial spectres. She'd have retired already if not for the full moon's dark influence.

Considering all of that didn't bring her closer to understanding what Saully-Menyie was asking of her. With moonlight flashing around her vision she looked at the child who was now sat cross-legged on the ground, rocking gently.

I want the Left-eye of your Mother. What did she mean by that? If the stories of the Otherworld were true then the Unseelie had passed through the gap in the moon's veil only days earlier. Was the challenge some cryptic suggestion to send the Unseelie back through the veil? Because if she knew how to do that she'd have done it already.

Saully-Menyie didn't seem to know she was being watched and began to hum a song. *Lissi's song from the crossroads*, Kenrig realised. The Unseelie child had been inside her mind, so was the challenge set in the belief that she was capable of achieving it? She tried to recall which memories Saully-Menyie had witnessed, but there were too many to call to mind.

She had to assume the challenge was possible. Ogda had claimed there would be no more deception and if they'd told the truth then she should be able to complete it. If only she knew what she was meant to do.

Bring me that, Saully-Menyie had said. Bring her to it or bring it to her? She looked up again and could almost swear the moon appeared closer there than it was in the outside world. Not quite large enough to simply pluck from the sky, but as her hand rose unconsciously to trace its outline it felt closer as well, as though some barrier between her and it had been lifted.

She ran her forefinger over the line of circling clouds, some unconscious instinct keeping her hand from straying over the moon's image, fearing that to do so in that place would be dangerous, though she didn't understand how exactly. She wanted to close her hand around it and pull it down to the earth, if it were only so easy.

She imagined herself pinching it between her thumb and forefinger and plucking a piece of it from the sky, hoping that a sliver of it would be enough to satisfy Saully-Menyie's challenge. *Maybe it would be.*

The child was a collector of trinkets, of odd ornaments that spoke to her powerful curiosity. Perhaps there was a way Kenrig could provide her with an object that would fulfil her request.

'Saully-Menyie,' she said. 'Do you have a mirror?'

The child stopped swaying and began to sift through her ornaments. 'A few,' she said. 'Like this?'

She held up a jagged shard of mirrored glass that was spotted with rust or dried blood at its sharpest point. 'This is just a piece of one,' she said, frowning. 'But a woman used it to kill her husband. After she found him with another woman.'

The mirror shard was gone in the next moment, replaced by a silver spoon. She admired her reflection in the back of it before pressing it to her tongue.

'It still tastes like poison,' she said with a grimace.

She rotated through dozens of objects, holding up anything that could carry a reflection and relaying their grim histories. A pendant used to choke a liar. A makeup box holding the tongue of an ancient singer. The broken blade of a knife that had blinded a prophet. A belt buckle from a captain drowned by mutiny. Coins once stained with the blood of the king whose image they bore.

Finally she settled on a true mirror, a little thing no bigger than her hand. 'This mirror stilled a mad man's heart with his own image.'

Kenrig had no real wish to hold any of the grisly ornaments, but held out her hand as she took a step toward Saully-Menyie.

'May I borrow that mirror?' she said.

The child brought the mirror to her shoulder, hiding it behind her clasped hands.

'Why?' she said.

Kenrig knelt down as if she were addressing a real, human child. 'I promise I'll give it back,' she said. 'I only need it for a little while and I guarantee it will be more interesting when I'm finished.'

When Saully-Menyie continued to withhold the mirror, she added, 'If I don't return it, you can send your big brother after me.'

Saully-Menyie lunged forward and pressed the mirror into Kenrig's hands. 'That sounds like fun,' she said, grinning. 'Now I don't know if I want you to return it.'

Kenrig stood and walked to Father Keld's funeral pyre. She squatted beside the priest's remains in the gap created by the violence of the duel.

'I'm sorry,' she whispered.

She removed Keld's pendant, carefully so that she didn't disturb his body. Taking the pendant felt like enough of a desecration.

The golden pendant was stained with ash from the pyre and sticky where it had lain against Keld's charred flesh. She cleaned it as best she could against the leg of her trousers. Her hand was grimy with ash and she left grey fingerprints across the gold, but the metal was clean enough that she could see traces of the script flickering across its surface.

She briefly wondered why the pendant hadn't protected Keld against the Unseelie, but abandoned the thought. Her own pendant was beyond her reach so the answer wouldn't help her. If she escaped then she could study the problem at her leisure.

She studied the mirror instead. Its glass was marred with scratches, but held a clear image. A frame of silver mottled with grey corrosion held the glass, bordering it with a pattern of leaves picked out in delicate filigree. She turned it over, pleased to see that the back was smooth and lacking any kind of adornment.

She knelt a few paces from the pyre, knowing that the magic she was about to attempt would leave her reeling, and she didn't want to fall. With the utmost care she laid the mirror face down on the ground and held the pendant over it, waiting until it had stopped quivering at the end of its chain.

She breathed deeply, then unfocused her eyes before she had a chance to hesitate. The last time she'd opened her senses to the magic around her she'd been subjected to the puppeteering power of the Unseelie. She was afraid to expose herself to that power again, but restricted her attention to the pendant and the mirror, letting the overlapping layers of magic that composed the illusion blur to an indistinct haze.

She looked past the skull of the carrion bird at the centre of the pendant which was inscribed with mundane script and searched the stained gold that housed it. Without the training of a mystic she couldn't create Hieratic script of her own, and even if she could she wasn't sure it would be possible inside the feast. She would need to take the script from the pendant and hope the characters she needed were inlaid into the metal.

The pendant doubled in her vision, splitting into the circular frame of ordinary metal and the near-transparent image of it overlaid above. She drew the image further from the physical pendant, coaxing the inlaid script from the metal to the empty air where she could freely search it.

The characters of the script drifted more quickly the further she pulled them from the metal, and she had to fight not to intentionally follow individual characters so that she didn't look at them directly. She let them move freely at the edges of her sight, noting them only in passing. She had to wait for specific characters to pass, often more than once when she wasn't sure that she had read them correctly. Sometimes the characters she needed weren't present and she worked carefully to collect suitable replacements, cobbling together the meanings of individual characters with a combination of others.

It took a long time to gather all of the characters she needed but she didn't dare to shift her attention to anything other than the pendant and the loose cluster of script she'd plucked from its surface. Slowly she let the pendant's double image snap back into place and lowered it to the ground. She picked up the mirror, holding it just below the assembled characters.

The characters shuddered in the air, fixed in place by nothing more than her own will. Air couldn't retain the script for long and the characters strained against her control, seeking the metal where they were originally bound. Despite that she had to work carefully to preserve their order as she directed them one at a time onto the mirror's back.

Sweat rolled down her face, stinging her eyes as she gasped with the effort of gripping the elusive script. Characters slipped free and floated down toward the pendant on the ground as she tried to hold them in order in both the air and against the silver surface. She worked as fast as she dared, risking mistakes to capture the retreating characters so that she wouldn't need to draw them out of the pendant again.

If she had to split her focus to draw those few characters out once more she wouldn't be able to hold those already in place on the mirror, and the process would need to be started from the very beginning.

When the last character was finally in place she stamped the script she'd created into the silver and wearily relinquished her grip on the magic. She tried to steel herself against the sudden shift in perspective, but she reeled and only stayed upright by virtue of being on her knees already. The magical strata of the illusion merged together again and the ordinary edges of the world resolved themselves, dizzyingly steady and solid.

She gripped the mirror in both hands against her chest, not wanting to drop it as her whole body shook. She took small comfort in the warmth of the characters freshly pressed into the silver, knowing that at least the script had bonded well, even if the spell didn't work.

She stayed on her knees, not trusting herself to stand for the next part of the magic. Her hands shook more violently as she lifted the mirror in front of her, angling its face toward the sky. The moon's image flitted around in the small mirror's surface, rolling with the pitch of her hands.

She braced her elbows against her knees, steadying her hands enough that she she caught the moon at the mirror's centre. The reflected clouds framed the bright oval of the half-moon, overlapping the silver filigree bordering the glass. She spoke quickly to empower the spell inlaid into the silver, rattling off a series of words that once spoken she had little memory of uttering. The Hieratic words were all known to her, but she would struggle to recall the order of them from that one instant.

There was no clear indication that the spell had worked. The moon and its circlet of clouds were reflected as they had been before, but there was no wobble to the image through the shaking of her hands. Experimentally, she tilted the mirror back towards her and when the mirror continued to reflect the moon above rather than her own image she allowed herself a relieved sigh.

She held out the mirror to Saully-Menyie as she struggled to her feet and the child grabbed it before she was able to stand. Saully-Menyie viewed the mirror with suspicion, testing it not by the quality of the permanent reflection in its surface, but by some other measures that were known only to her. She gauged the weight of it in her hands and sniffed along the filigree frame. She ran the tip of her tongue across the textureless inlay of the script on its back and flexed the metal between both hands.

It was only after she'd inspected the mirror through those strange means that she observed the reflected moon. She marvelled at the illusion, her face split in an open-mouthed grin as she twisted the mirror around. Her fingers followed the spiralling clouds which continued to circle the moon in flawless imitation of the sky above.

Saully-Menyie rushed to her mother's side and lifted the mirror to their face. Ogda scanned it briefly and inclined their head as their daughter whispered excitedly.

'It seems I must congratulate you,' they said, raising their head to look at Kenrig. 'My daughter is smitten with your gift, and has urged me to consider her challenge complete.'

Kenrig looked at Saully-Menyie, but the child was sat by the throne, absorbed in the mirror's reflection, so she inclined her head to Ogda instead.

'Thank you,' she said, not knowing what else to say.

Ogda gave another of their faint smiles. 'Thank me when *my* challenge is complete.'

7

The Gift of Names

'Perhaps you would prefer a reprieve?' Ogda asked, still smiling. 'A chance to regather your strength before we begin again?'

Everything in Kenrig begged her to accept. She swayed on her feet and the sweat of exertion clung as a cold film across her skin.

She shook her head. 'No, I'm fine to continue.'

She didn't believe that she would have found any kind of reprieve in that place had she accepted. It wasn't in the interest of the Unseelie to allow her to rest and risk her being recovered for the final challenge.

She'd witnessed the exhaustion of the villagers caught in the Unseelie feast. They were only being offered a temporary reprieve because of her bargain and she suspected the Unseelie had offered it so that the villagers were more energetic during future torment. She would rather take her chances, exhausted as she was, than linger a moment longer than she had to in the feast.

Ogda waved their hand. 'As you wish.'

They reclined half into the shadow of the throne, their outline traced with silver thread like the moonlit clouds above. Their eyes brightened in the darkness of their face, twinned by a white rime of sorrow.

Kenrig felt despair chilling her toward hopelessness as she gazed into those eyes, but she found it impossible to look away. Beneath the shining veil of ice she saw endless shadow in those eyes, an infinite well of cold darkness into which she could empty herself of feeling. Those eyes promised a comforting numbness, a balm against all future pain, if she would simply surrender her hope willingly into those limitless depths.

She was tired. Too tired for another challenge. She'd done well to survive against Holdainn's blade. Her resolution of Saully-Menyie's impossible request had been inspired. She'd impressed the Unseelie with her skill and her wits, but it was time for her to accept reality. She was mortal and desperately trying to succeed in a bargain with immortals.

It would be easier to accept defeat before daring the third challenge. Why even attempt it when failure was the inevitable outcome? She would only delay her fate for a sliver of a chance, a chance to escape and provide the trapped villagers with a fleeting pause from their imprisonment. Better to remain in the feast and let the villagers persist in the vague comfort of ignorance than let them awaken and consider the horror of their circumstances.

The clatter of metal to her left broke her from the binds of Ogda's stare. She snapped her eyes away, looking to the source of the noise before she could be drawn back in by that paralysing despair.

One of the sluagh, the largest of the seven, had jumped down to the pit. They held the brass shackles toward her and it was the clanking of the heavy chain that had caught her attention. The sluagh's inhuman flesh was ravaged by bloodless injuries, but they had clearly won the honour of binding her.

She feared in that moment that she had uttered some words of surrender as she'd been lost in Ogda's gaze, abandoning the bargain without any memory of doing so. The sluagh advanced on her quickly, though its alien body twitched with alarming spasms. Had the Unseelie hoped she would be too absorbed in Ogda's sorrowful gaze that she wouldn't notice herself being shackled? Had she given them leave to bind her or had Ogda attempted to trick her?

She tried her luck on the latter. 'You gave your word there would be no further deceit,' she said, looking above Ogda's eyes. 'You can't bind me until our bargain is done.'

The sluagh stopped at some unseen command, its sudden stop setting the shackle chain swinging against its chest with a dull thud. It was close enough that she wanted to turn her attention to it, in case she had to defend herself, but she kept her gaze levelled high over Ogda's throne.

She was relieved that she hadn't betrayed herself unconsciously, but her relief quickly gave way to anger at the treachery. It wasn't surprising that the Unseelie lord had attempted to trick her, she would have been surprised if they hadn't, but it felt good to stoke her anger and let the heat of it drive warmth into her blood.

'Your challenge,' she said, almost growling the words.

Holdainn attempted to step toward her at the threat in her voice, but he was restrained once more. Ogda inclined their head in faint acknowledgement.

'Of course,' they said.

Their eyes lifted toward hers, but she was prepared and shut her eyes. She imagined the Unseelie lord giving another faint smile at the gesture, or perhaps showing a dim flicker of annoyance. After a silent moment they spoke again.

'My challenge is simple,' they said, and Kenrig could feel the menace in the words. 'All I ask is that you name my sluagh.'

She turned her head toward the sluagh with the shackles and opened her eyes. The sluagh was stood where it had stopped, though its chittering spasms prevented it from standing still.

'All of them?' she asked.

'All of them.'

It didn't take much for her to imagine the Unseelie lord's face settle into a dim gloat. She'd shown weakness in her failure to name Saully-Menyie, weakness that they clearly intended to exploit.

By some cue the other sluagh jumped to the floor of the pit. They paced in the same convulsive way, easily covering the distance on their gangly limbs as they shuddered and twitched. They arranged themselves into a loose semi-circle beside the one holding the shackles.

She backed off a step so that she could keep them all in her eye line and stop herself from being surrounded. They loomed over her, but lacked Holdainn's sheer size. Their bodies were elongated beyond all human proportion and if they had been human she'd have thought that the painful bending and bowing of their joints would be the product of childhood illness.

They seemed to be unable to settle their attention on anything for long, watching her through the dark hollows of their masks for the briefest moments before their heads twisted sharply to observe something else, though she struggled to find whatever had caught their interest. It was only when she studied one of them for long enough that they returned her study and stared in turn. Even then their eyes didn't settle, their gaze following the sporadic movements of their heads.

She studied each of them, scanning their line for some clue to their names. She'd heard them speak and laugh so she assumed they could answer questions, but doubted they'd simply part with their names willingly. The Unseelie seemed to place importance on names and she regretted giving her own to secure their bargain.

The sluagh holding the shackles was taller even than its companions and had apparently fared the best from their battle. With them arranged so closely around her she was able to observe their differences clearly. While they all wore a disturbing collection of trinkets, the tall sluagh was the only one to wear anything resembling armour.

Its arms were sheathed in loops of finger bones woven together with what looked like braided hair and around its waist it wore a belt of rawhide hung with notched ribs. The metal of its mask was stitched together from scraps, looted pieces of metal held together by leather cords looped through crude holes. She saw a bronze nosepiece shaped like an arrowhead and the dented curves of cheeks guards, a corroded iron visor and a sheared brow plate, all of it held together by dozens of jagged armour fragments.

Those observations didn't bring her closer to understanding the creature's name. She understood a little of the sluagh, enough to know that they supposedly rode at the vanguard of the mythical Wild Hunt, stealing away dead spirits and living captives from west-facing windows. She'd seen the western windows of the houses in the village left wide open so she guessed that portion of their legend was at least true.

She'd never encountered anything close to individual names for them. She hadn't even known how many they were meant to number before she'd seen them for herself, since the accounts of their scale varied from a single individual to an entire host large enough to obscure the sky.

Was Ogda's challenge truly as straightforward as determining the names of the sluagh, or was there some obscure solution she wasn't seeing?

All I ask is that you name my sluagh. The Unseelie lord hadn't asked her to give them the names of the sluagh. They hadn't specifically asked that she determine the names. *Name my sluagh.* Was there room in the challenge for her to provide the sluagh with names of her own choosing?

'I name you Crow-feeder,' she said to the sluagh with the shackles.

Its attention was fixed on her, but it gave no sign that it acknowledged her words. She hurried on, trying not to let herself reconsider her plan.

'You've claimed many trophies,' she said, looking up into its patchwork mask. 'The bones of your enemies armour you, make you strong against their blows. Their bones are marked by the gorging of carrion birds and so I name you Crow-feeder, for you have made a feast of all who opposed you. Your prowess in battle is clear for all to see.'

Flattery can't make my situation any worse, she thought. She hoped that vanity would make the sluagh accept the name she'd offered. Her plan relied on the sluagh adopting the names she gave so that Ogda would consider the challenge complete. Among the Karlan clans it was believed that offering a creature a kenning as its name gave a measure of control over it. Assuming the creature accepted the name.

Something in Crow-feeder's manner changed and she realised that the noise rattling from its mask was a low purr of enjoyment. The spasms and twitches that moved its body grew more violent and it almost skipped from one foot to the other.

'I have killed hundreds of foes,' it declared, and she winced at the grating shriek of its voice.

'My name is Crow-feeder,' it said.

'Crow-feeder! Crow-feeder! Crow-feeder!'

The other sluagh chanted the name and the ringing cacophony of their combined voices set her teeth clenching. Her hands twitched toward her ears to cover them, but she held them at her sides.

Her jaw cracked when the sluagh fell silent as one and she relaxed her grating teeth. Crow-feeder held the brass shackles overhead like a prize as they wheeled and skipped from the sluagh's line. The gap it left in the line was swiftly filled as the remaining six pressed closer together.

'Name me next!'

'No, name me! Name me!'

'I want a name!'

They jostled each other to stand directly before her and she recoiled, but the line held and they didn't move closer toward her. When one of them gained the centre of the line it hissed and flailed until the others retreated.

It lowered its attention toward her and she paled under its scrutiny, though she didn't think she could tear her eyes away from it. She was transfixed by its mask which was crudely hammered into the leering face of some kind of predator. A pattern of scales were carved into its surface, the grooves shining with the black gleam of fresh blood.

The mask was open at the mouth and it bared its teeth at her through grey, quivering lips. Its teeth appeared to have been sharpened with a file and a pointed tongue flitted behind them, as restless as its other muscles.

Strips of skin hung from its scalp in place of hair, more circling its waist to form a ragged kilt. A bandoleer not unlike her own was draped around its chest and in the pockets and loops of the leather band were the tools necessary for the flaying of skin. Paring knives and shears of a dozen sizes, barbed hooks and rusted scalpels protruded from the bandoleer, encrusted with old blood.

'Courage-taker,' she gasped. 'I name you Courage-taker. No man, woman or child could look upon you without fear. Far will your enemies flee before you.'

It turned and lunged at the other sluagh. 'Courage-taker!' it bellowed.

The others mumbled its name in chorus and parted to let it pass, slinking back together after it had passed from the line.

Another of the sluagh found its way to stand before

her and she was certain it did so only by being less conspicuous than the others. It had slipped unnoticed to the centre of the line while the others brawled for the same position.

It was the most heavily clothed of the sluagh. Scraps of black cloth sewn together with rough stitching formed a rumpled mantle that ended with a short cape. Plundered trousers of dark wool stopped at the knees of its extraordinarily long legs, making it seem even taller though it stood with what seemed like a nervous hunch.

Its mask was shaped from black metal feathers welded into a pair of wings that curved from a long, dagger-like blade extending down to its chin. She tried to search the jagged holes of the mask for its eyes, but couldn't meet the line of its gaze. Whenever she moved her eyes to meet its gaze it had already shifted its head an instant ahead of her own movements.

Its arrival at the centre of the line had gone unnoticed by the other sluagh who continued to squabble over the position it already occupied.

'I name you Shade-lurker,' she said. 'Silent as a shadow and unseen by your enemies. No foe will have warning of your approach.'

It whispered the name and walked from the line without chorus.

The fourth sluagh skipped into place, dancing around the others. A skirt of mismatched feathers was its only clothing other than a beaked mask of silver as tarnished as Saully-Menyie's mirror. The mask was fringed with more of the motley feathers and a few of them came loose as it slipped around the grasping hands of the other sluagh.

'I name you Wind-stepper,' she said. 'Your grace and speed are unmatched. No quarry will ever outpace you.'

If she hadn't already named Crow-feeder she'd have said the fifth sluagh was the most threatening warrior among them. It had something approaching a coating of muscle over its long limbs and at its waist it wore a pair of hooked knives. Around its chest was a grim latticework of shrivelled veins and arteries which were woven up into a patchy cowl surrounding an expressionless copper face.

'I name you Thread-cutter,' she said. 'Your blades are sharp enough to shear the lines of fate. No enemy can escape your judgement of their life's span.'

Its name was chorused only by the two nameless others that remained. The rest had left the pit after receiving their names and Thread-cutter followed them, clearing the wall with an easy leap.

Kenrig headed off the bout between the nameless sluagh by nominating one of them to approach. She thought that they would come to blows anyway as they eyed each other warily, but she was surprised that they respected her decision and stepped apart.

The sluagh she'd chosen held her gaze with alarming steadiness. Spasms moved its body, but its head remained entirely static. Its round iron mask was scored with the image of a screeching owl and two hollows had been beaten into the metal over the sluagh's eyes. A narrow hole had been bored into each of the hollows to reveal the unblinking pupils under the mask. The skulls of birds hung around its neck, their empty sockets painted with staring eyes.

'I name you Lidless-watcher,' she said. 'No enemy will escape your sight. All the world is yours to observe. Nothing will remain hidden to you.'

Lidless-watcher backed away from her, holding her gaze until it arrived at the wall of the pit and turned away to climb.

The final sluagh didn't come any closer and stood like a grim sentinel. Of the seven its mask was the only one not fashioned from metal. Instead it wore a portion of a human skull as a face plate beneath a black funeral shroud. In place of ornaments its body was adorned with shining scars under cracked charcoal.

She was transfixed by the emaciated line of its jaw and couldn't help imagining it's tight-lipped mouth opening to announce her death.

'I name you Grave-hailer,' she said. 'To see you is to face death. No enemy will hear your coming and live to tell of it.'

Grave-hailer simply inclined its head and left with all the wild cheer its new name implied.

She turned to face Ogda with forced steadiness. Her time in that place had exhausted her and she was standing through whatever stubborn will she had left. She didn't feel any great relief at finishing the third challenge and feared that the Unseelie would find some way to triumph despite her efforts, but she'd also transcended hopeless despair and outright terror to feel a kind of dazed calm.

Whatever relief she did feel faded at the sight of Ogda's face divided by a wide grin. The smile was tight, almost lifeless, but the impossible curve of it chilled her.

'You impress me,' they said, their mouth hardly shifting from the grin. 'I'm forced to admire your solution to my challenge. I freely admit to underestimating your wits.'

She held her breath, certain she was being mocked. She'd expected Ogda to be angry or at least disappointed to lose the bargain, but it was foolish trying to understand the alien Unseelie. Holdainn's face bore the expected fury and Saully-Menyie glanced around, as seemingly confused as Kenrig, but Ogda looked gleeful.

'You completed our challenges,' they continued. 'And fulfilled your part in our bargain, so I must fulfil mine.'

They opened their arms wide. 'You are free to leave. The villagers of Karstend may leave for one week as agreed.'

They paused for a long moment and not knowing what else to do, Kenrig took a step toward one of the passages leading from the pit. Ogda's upraised finger stopped her after a single step.

'The child, however, will remain here,' they said.

'Child?' she asked. 'What child?'

She'd seen children among the feast, which of them did she mean? She didn't have time to question the Unseelie lord further as the piercing holler of the sluagh shattered any illusion she had that the bargain was concluded.

They leapt and tumbled back into the pit, pursuing Wind-stepper who lazily outpaced the others despite the bundle it carried. Its burden kicked and threw back her head to scream.

Lissi.

8

The Apprentice

Dandall watched Kenrig disappear through the barrier as she stooped to fit through the narrow opening she'd carved into it. The material of the barrier seemed no more substantial than the cloth of a curtain, yet behind it the entire summit was hidden.

The opening remained for a long while. A sliver of light spilled from the opening like through a crack in a tavern door, bright and inviting against the cold night. He could feel the heat of the other side from his hiding place beside the path and unconsciously he leaned closer to it. He heard the music of pipes and drums, voices raised in toasts and the clashing of cups. Shadows danced past the corners of the opening and he wondered what Kenrig had found on the other side.

It sounded like there was a celebration and he was tempted to peek through the opening. Kenrig had asked him to stay behind and he'd obliged her, but as he considered her reasons for going on alone he felt less inclined to obey. *Taking you might be a liability.*

'Liability,' he hissed.

He remembered the first time he'd met Kenrig and their battle against the creature she'd called an elemental. That bloated thing still haunted him when he slept. The ancient corpse of a long-dead man, given inhuman strength and made almost as impossible to harm as the water it lurked in. They'd killed it together and she had later admitted that she couldn't have beaten it without him.

He was angry when he thought about that. She'd needed his help then, but now that he was older she refused to take him more seriously. She didn't trust him and he didn't fully trust her in return. He'd sought her out to learn to hunt monsters as she did, yet he saw her making the same mistake that had killed his dad five years ago.

He heard the creak of the dagger's leather grip before he felt the pain in his palm where he squeezed it. The metal blade was hardly visible in the darkness, but he could feel its presence in a way he still didn't understand. He knew there were symbols moving under its surface. He'd caught glimpses of them out of the corner of his eyes whenever his attention had wandered, but even when he couldn't see them he could sense them tracing the blade's surface in the same way he could feel air brushing his skin.

The moment she'd left he'd hated her for making him stay behind, but as he looked down at the dagger he realised that she wasn't wrong to think of him as a liability. He'd stolen those daggers from her once. He hadn't been thinking clearly, how could he? He'd been eleven and he'd watched his father drown under the hands of an undead creature. Kenrig had saved him then and she'd saved him again when he'd stolen her daggers and tried to kill the creature on his own.

He wasn't angry that she'd called him a liability, not truly, because as much as he hated to admit it she was right, he was a liability to her. He wanted her to be wrong. He wanted to hate her for letting his dad die, for changing his life and making it impossible for him to ever see the world in the same way again, but he couldn't. He was often angry with her and he took out his frustrations at both of them by sulking and arguing, but he didn't hate her. He needed her help and he hoped that one day she would need his.

In the time that he'd wrestled with his indecision the opening in the barrier had woven itself back together, jealously taking back its warm light. The dagger in his hand could cut another opening, that was why he had it, but he wasn't sure he trusted himself to use it. If dawn arrived without her then he supposed he would cut the barrier, but he didn't trust his judgement to use it sooner.

He couldn't know what happened across the barrier. He'd heard the sounds of celebration, but what was truly on the other side? What kind of enemy did Kenrig face and how many were they? The girl had called them Eerie-folk, but what did that mean? Courage demanded that he stop hesitating and use the dagger. Fear reminded him that he was a liability.

He replaced the dagger in his belt and stepped out onto the path. The rain had cleared, leaving clumps of stars in its place, but his clothes were still damp and he paced to stay warm. He walked a short way back down the hill to where the steep slope dropped toward the western horizon.

Before he'd joined Kenrig he'd never left the North March and before he'd set off on his journey to find her he had never left the Bann, that corner of the North March the remnants of his people called home. It was cold and wet, *consistently miserable* as his dad had called it, but it was also beautiful. There were mountains tall enough to pierce the clouds, bordering lochs and rivers that emptied into the open sea, bearing forests into the sky where they were still too wild for humans to leave their marks.

As he looked down on the Middle March, that expanse of fields which spread like random squares of cloth to every horizon, he felt homesick. He wondered how the Marchers that called that place home didn't go mad staring every day over land that stretched flat and empty out of sight. The hill that he stood on was a bizarre exception in the landscape, a steep climb but hardly worthy of being called a hill to his mind.

He didn't consider it an ugly place. It was a land of a vast and open sky that covered everything like the domes of the mystic cities described in the Scriptures. Under rain and grey skies, with the land below and black clouds above both flat to the horizon, it was a bleak place. For hours on end he could barely bring himself to look out from his hood as they'd travelled and he had come to believe that the days were beginning to reflect his own gloomy temper back at him. But when the clouds parted and the land and sky became almost indistinguishable beneath the setting sun, bright with all the colours of fire, he would grudgingly admit that there was beauty in the Middle March.

Thoughts of home always brought with them doubts about his decision to leave. After the elemental was dead and its body had burned to ash, Kenrig had taken him home, back to Ushga and into the care of his grandmother.

Once she'd recovered from her injuries she'd helped him to find his dad's body in the forest and stayed for the funeral, saying the rites from the Scriptures in the absence of anyone else to speak them. He had resented her saying those words when he'd blamed her for Tanach's death. When she was gone he hated himself for missing her.

Life in the years that followed was familiar to him. On the surface it was the life he'd always led, working with the men and the other boys. They farmed mussels. Caught fish and crabs. Cut back the forest when it encroached on the shore and used the wood to build new homes on the loch. They hunted sometimes. Traded with Marchers when they had anything to spare. It was everything he'd been raised to do and it had become unbearable.

His father's memory was in the work, every moment of it. Everything he knew, all the skills he'd learned and the ones he'd only ever watched, they were his dad's legacy. He felt the ghost of guidance in his actions, the aching memory of pressure from strong hands directing his own. He would close his eyes and will his memories to become real, to let him feel that encouragement again. He wanted a hand on his shoulder when he'd done well and arms to carry him when he was hurt.

He wanted to hear the man's voice again. Laughing, praising, scolding, it didn't matter. It echoed in the words the other men had for their own sons, almost lived again in accents that were so achingly close he could almost believe they were the same voice. He repeated words from memory, spoke them aloud when he was alone until they grew dull in the act of remembering, replaced by his own pained recitation.

Four years he endured his grief there, until he couldn't bear it anymore. He wasn't sure when exactly the idea had come to him that he should search for Kenrig. He'd thought of her less with every year that had separated them, though he couldn't have forgotten her completely, not when she was so tied up in the events of his father's death. When he had thought of her it had been in the darkness before dawn, when nightmares had disturbed him from sleep.

In his nightmares he was powerless. He didn't always dream of the elemental, sometimes his nightmares came in the form of other creatures or other more abstract fears that had no form at all, but he'd dreamt of it often enough. Sometimes he'd watched it from a distance, helpless to stop it from killing. Sometimes he'd been the one in its grip, choking as his lungs filled with putrid water. Always he'd woken gasping and shaking, the power to breathe and move returned to him with the end of the nightmares.

He dwelled on the dreams, feeling frail in the wake of his helpless terror, and lived out his days tired and distracted. His work suffered, but no one admonished him, not even his granny, the way he wanted them to. They looked at him with a pity that made him feel even weaker.

It was only when he remembered Kenrig that he didn't feel so weak. When he remembered fighting beside her. She'd had weapons that could hurt the undead elemental, those he'd stolen from her and the ones she'd given him even after his ungrateful betrayal. Ordinary iron nails and salt, given the power to hurt monsters by her knowledge of the Hierat, the language he still couldn't understand, even with her instruction.

She had made it possible to fight and destroy that monster and he wanted to feel strong like that again. Once the thought was in his head there was no way for him to get it out. It burrowed deep into his mind, grew from his fear and his grief until they were small enough that he felt as though he might heal one day. They were still there, making themselves known whenever he had an idle moment to think, but he'd begun to feel strong enough to bear them.

After that he knew he couldn't stay in Ushga. The decision to leave was a fresh agony, to know what he needed and understand that it meant leaving his home. He harboured his thoughts in secret for so long that guilt almost stopped him from admitting them. He wondered if he might learn to be happy in Ushga again, if he might forget the need to leave.

He had doubts, about his ability to survive in the world outside his home and about being able to find a lone woman on the road. Was she still alive? Still in the North March or in any of the Marches? There were days that his doubts felt insurmountable, when he felt like a fool for ever considering following Kenrig, but in time the urge to leave became impossible to ignore.

It was like the pain of an injury or an itch felt at the cusp of sleep. His granny coaxed the thoughts from him before he'd summoned the courage to confess them. In a way she understood his thoughts better than he did himself. He wanted her to be angry with him. He wanted her to lament his decision and beg him to stay, or scold him as a fool and forbid him to leave.

He didn't want the sad smile that broke his heart, nor

the kind words of encouragement. He didn't want the feast in his honour or the village's approval. He didn't want new clothes and provisions or the gift of Kelpie, their youngest horse. He needed those things, yet they burdened him with guilt.

He'd had to leave without a final goodbye, in the hours before dawn, or he didn't believe he'd have been strong enough to do it. Three days took him further than he'd travelled before. Every night he lay awake telling himself he would turn around and give up, but every morning when dawn came he'd continued westward until one day he found himself on a road he didn't recognise.

The Marcher villages multiplied beyond the Bann's borders. Those closest to the border were welcoming of Cadogan and spoke his mother tongue, but further west his tartan cloak was enough reason for him to be chased away in some places. Villages became towns enclosed by palisades and drystone walls which barred their gates and set curfews after the sun set. Those he avoided entirely, preferring to hunt and forage or go hungry than risk being trapped for the night among Marchers.

He gained leads from fellow travellers. Rarely he met other Cadogan, those of his people who'd quit the meagre lands left to them by the Marchers to find work among their conquerors. Most of the travellers were Marchers, traders and cattle drovers on their way to distant markets, but he met Karlans too. Their musical language resembled that of the Marchers enough that he could make himself understood, though they scarcely had kind words for a lone Cadogan.

For the first time he met traders, soldiers and missionaries from Lanzaro, Mubrakh and Gaphrati, the kingdoms closest to the holy land of Sostris. They wore warm clothes bartered from Marchers and bundled themselves so warmly against the cold western climate that he could hardly see the rich, dark tones of their skin.

The stories they told of their homelands were the most fascinating to him. Tales of blue seas and golden sands that passed beyond the limit of sight. Mountains higher even than the ones he knew in the Bann, where men mined for ice more valuable than gold. Endless orchards of bright fruit ripening under the watch of burnished citadels.

His queries were often met with scorn. Where could he find a woman? A giant woman, armed, armoured and speaking the Scriptures like a priest? He was laughed at and spat on. Hit with rocks and threatened with drawn blades. Chased by men, dogs and even mounted guards who he escaped by virtue of knowing how to navigate amidst dense forest.

He spoke to anyone who would listen and with enough questions he found a trail. There were stories, gossip and first-hand tales of a woman who hunted beasts and lifted curses. She wandered in the strangest of places and went where no one else dared. Took coin from any who could pay, but helped those that couldn't without concern.

Some of the stories seemed absurd in the telling and he could hardly credit the rude and arrogant woman he remembered with half of the deeds people ascribed to her. The stories led him across the length of the North March, west through villages spared from curses, monsters and even common plagues by her intervention. He saw from afar the castle of Lutoran rising from the earth like a white mountain, a home fit for giants or the Mother herself, not a mortal king in his capital.

His search had been difficult. He'd gone without a warm bed, without reliable meals and without friends, yet he'd enjoyed himself. He'd had a purpose and he almost hadn't wanted the search to end, but eventually he'd found her again.

A chill wind climbed up the Dullie Fell's slope and pulled him from his memories. He returned to stand in the shelter of the field of boulders. He untied his sling from where it was looped around his belt. He had no shortage of ammunition where he stood and he slung loose stones against the boulders further down the hill to keep his mind from thoughts of the past.

The stones fractured against the boulders or chipped shards from their hard edges. He emptied his thoughts into the movement of his arm and felt his frustrations ease with every stone that cracked. He set himself the challenge of skipping the stones over the boulders, aiming to send them over the sheer slope. He chose pale stones from among those at his feet, those that caught the moonlight as they skittered and clacked across the field of boulders.

A scream stopped him mid-swing, the stone swinging down in its pouch to strike against his hip. He squatted down behind a boulder, wincing at the bloom of pain.

'Are you daft?' a voice shouted. 'Flinging stones about.'

The girl, he thought.

'Lissi?' he shouted back.

He stood and hobbled into the path. The girl leaned out from the cover of a boulder.

'You won't throw more stones?'

He glanced down at the ends of the sling still gripped between his fingers.

'You promise you aren't a pucky or a bogle?'

She nodded. 'I promise.'

He tipped the stone from the sling's pouch and replaced the cord around his belt. The girl stepped out from the boulder and finished the rest of the climb. With the moon behind him he could clearly see the crimson flush in her face and the sweat beaded across her forehead.

'You're meant to be asleep,' he said.

She huffed, clearly exhausted and he was amazed she'd made the climb on such short legs. He offered her his waterskin and she clutched it in both hands as she gulped water until she nearly choked.

'I was,' she said. 'But I had another dream.'

'And?'

'*And* I want to tell her about it.'

He looked behind him to the summit where the barrier still stood, whole and unblemished, the darkness stark against the night sky by the absence of stars. He turned back to her and shook his head.

'You can tell her when she gets back,' he said. 'She said to keep you from sneaking about.'

He didn't think her face could have grown any redder. 'I'm not sneaking though, am I? Don't be stupid.'

After all he'd done to reach Kenrig, to apprentice himself to her, his role was to deal with a stubborn child?

'I don't care what your dream was,' he said. 'You'll wait here.'

She leaned to look past him. 'Why are you out here? Did you get left?'

He tried not to let his temper show, but somehow she'd cut to the heart of his uncertainty.

'I'm keeping watch,' he said. 'Someone has to stay here, if something goes wrong.'

He felt a surge of fresh anger at Kenrig's decision to leave him out there, waiting in the frigidly cold night on an exposed hilltop. He was angry at the girl for highlighting the obvious slight in the decision and hated himself that he felt the need to justify that same decision to her.

'Uh huh,' she said. 'Can I go in now?'

He held his hands palms out towards her. 'You're not going through.'

He didn't expect her to throw his waterskin back at him and foolishly he caught it with both hands. She slipped past him while he was distracted and ran for the barrier. For someone with such short legs she was quick and with a lead on him he wasn't sure he could catch her.

'Wait!' he shouted. 'You can't go through.'

He was a handspan from reaching her when she contacted the barrier. He expected to see her crash against it and fall backward at his feet, but she passed through effortlessly like a swimmer leaping into dark water. He tried to follow and his outstretched hand crumpled against the black curtain an instant before his body crashed to a sudden stop.

He tipped backward, gasping as he felt the shock of blunt pain across his chest and shoulders. He was stunned, his chest too tight to draw in a breath. The barrier was solid above him, without even a ripple or a tear to indicate where Lissi had crossed it.

He crept his hand to the dagger and wondered if now was the time to use it.

9

Cruel Bargain

Kenrig had her falchion drawn in an instant. Lissi's cries lent her a speed she couldn't have mustered alone and she moved to intercept the brawling train of the sluagh.

Dandall, she thought. *Why didn't you stop her?*

Wind-stepper's speed and eerie grace mocked the efforts of the other sluagh. They lunged and grabbed at it, their hands coming away empty or holding feathers plucked from its skirts. It led them in a circuit of the pit, effortlessly clutching Lissi to its chest even as she wriggled and thrashed.

Kenrig tensed to dash forward, but Holdainn strode from his place at Ogda's side, murderous intent plain in the cracks of his face. He had no weapon other than the short claws capping his fingers, but she didn't rate her chances of surviving another bout. The giant looked entirely recovered after their duel and though the surprise of Lissi's arrival had given her a surge of strength she knew it couldn't match Holdainn's deathless vitality.

Ogda spoke and their voice cut through the sluagh's screeching.

'Let her try, Holdainn,' they said. 'I want to watch what she does.'

The giant obeyed and rooted himself where he stood. Kenrig watched the sluagh and turned to follow Wind-stepper at the lead.

'Attempt to take the child,' Ogda said, more loudly. 'Take her from the sluagh's clutches. Outpace them to the threshold if you can. How will you cross into your world if I do not permit it?'

Her falchion felt heavier with every moment she hesitated. Ogda's words paralysed her. They gave voice to her own unspoken doubts.

'You were equal to our challenges,' they said. 'Show us how you will escape with the girl. Show us how you, tired and mortal as you are, intend to flee the sluagh. How will you escape my hunters when you freely gave up your name?'

She understood then the trap set for her. In giving up her name she had given up her chance of escape.

She turned too slowly to follow the sluagh. Her legs felt like she'd danced in the feast for days on end. The wound at her shoulder re-opened as her falchion shook in her grip, a fresh trickle of blood weeping across her numb arm.

Ogda stood and the sluagh came to an abrupt stop as their path was blocked by the Unseelie lord. The sluagh backed away with their heads bowed, but at a gesture from Ogda, Wind-stepper shuffled forward. Lissi continued to fight, but its grip was unbreakable, until Ogda lifted the girl from its arms with a single hand.

The Unseelie lord held Lissi by the collar of her dress at the limit of their arm. Lissi swung her legs and arms in an effort to escape, but Ogda had a strength which defied their delicate frame and their arm was impossibly steady.

'Try to take the child from here,' they said. 'And I will trap you and the villagers here in her place. She entered after our bargain was struck. She is not covered by its terms.'

Ogda lowered their arm and dropped Lissi to the ground. The girl landed hard and seemed too stunned to move. Then she lifted her face and her tear-filled eyes met Kenrig's.

Kenrig dropped to one knee and lowered her falchion as Lissi ran into the embrace of her numb left arm. Her fingers were pierced with prickles of pain as blood rushed into the arm, but Lissi was reassuringly ordinary in that strange place. The girl cried against her chest as Kenrig adapted to the Unseelie's latest cruelty.

'How?' she whispered. 'How is she here?'

Even away from the recessed throne Ogda was half-obscured by shadow. A shroud of darkness had clung to them as they left their throne. It extended from the seat of the throne and stretched to coil around the lower half of their body.

'She is a member of the village,' they said. 'She was invited.'

Kenrig looked down at Lissi. 'I told you to stay at home.'

The girl pushed away and Kenrig let her go. 'I'm sorry,' Lissi said.

She wiped tears on the back of her sleeves and looked down at her feet. Kenrig noticed the absence of the pendant around the girl's neck.

'Do you still have my pendant?' she said.

Without looking up the girl reached for a pouch hanging from a rope clumsily tied around her waist. She scowled as she touched the black iron chain and held it away from her as though it were about to come alive in her hand.

'I brung it with me,' she said.

'I asked you to wear it.'

She looked up at Kenrig without losing her scowl. 'I did,' she said. 'But it itches something awful.'

She held up the pendant and Kenrig took it from her. Kenrig didn't fail to note the relief on the girl's face. She understood the feeling well enough.

Lissi's relief was short-lived as Kenrig draped the pendant chain around her neck. 'I told you to wear it.'

The thought of abandoning the girl in the Unseelie's feast was unbearable to her, but she had to prepare for that terrible eventuality. She gripped Lissi's shoulder.

'It's important that you don't remove it again,' she said. 'Do you understand?'

When Lissi opened her mouth to object, Kenrig

interrupted her. 'No matter what you feel. No matter what anyone here says, you don't remove it. Tell me you understand.'

Lissi nodded glumly. 'I understand.'

Kenrig felt little comfort at the girl's agreement. She remembered the pendant worn by the priest Keld and how it had failed to protect him. She couldn't leave Lissi without understanding how the Unseelie had avoided Keld's protection.

She didn't believe the Unseelie would answer any kind of direct question so she decided to exploit their vanity.

'You must have been clever to trap the villagers here,' she said. 'Karstend was protected. Those protections aren't easily overcome.'

She addressed her words to Ogda, but hoped that their children listened as well. Holdainn hadn't stopped glowering since their duel had ended so she was certain she had his attention at least. Saully-Menyie held the enchanted mirror at her side and seemed more interested in the girl whose face she had borrowed.

'Indeed,' was all Ogda said in reply.

She turned to the giant. 'And to take the village bloodlessly as well. You must have been cunning to avoid a battle, though I'd have thought you wouldn't shy away from a chance to prove your mettle.'

She wasn't sure that Holdainn's face was capable of softening, but his obvious hatred of her lessened slightly.

He crossed his arms and glanced at Ogda for a brief moment.

'Had it been my decision,' he said. 'I'd have allowed the village a chance to rally and led the sluagh in a slaughter of their defenders. The survivors would have been driven to our feast in chains. But their wall was-'

Ogda stopped him speaking with a wave, but Kenrig could guess at what he would have said.

'Their wall was warded wasn't it?' she said. 'Protected by Keld's mysticism. Or through some kind of charms.'

The Unseelie met her words with silence, but even in their immortal faces she could read the truth.

'Keld invited you into the village, didn't he?' she asked.

She received no answer, but Saully-Menyie shook as though she were about to burst without Ogda's restraint holding her together. Kenrig focused the next question on her.

'Why would Keld willingly invite you into the village? I mean no offence, but you don't have the look of ordinary travellers.'

'We tricked him, of course! We were disguised!'

Saully-Menyie blurted her answer before she could think better of it. She was grinning from Lissi's borrowed face before she noticed Ogda's attention and lowered her head.

So Keld invited them over Karstend's threshold and unknowingly removed the village's protection. The thought didn't bring her any joy, but she felt more certain that her own pendant would protect Lissi. As long as the girl didn't surrender its protection.

She looked down at Lissi again. The girl was staring into her own eyes reflected back at her by Saully-Menyie's imitation. Kenrig turned Lissi's head back to look at her instead.

She pulled the waterskin from her belt and handed it to Lissi. 'Don't accept anything from them,' she said. 'Don't eat or drink anything they offer you.'

Lissi accepted the waterskin and held it in both of her shaking hands. Kenrig wanted to reach out and clench Lissi's hands in her own, but she was shaking just as much.

'Look at me,' she said with forced confidence. 'The people here aren't friends. They'll try to trick you, so do your best to ignore them. Don't answer their questions and don't tell them about yourself. Keep your name secret. Okay?'

Lissi met Kenrig's eyes, but her own eyes were almost vacant with fear. Despite that she managed a small nod in answer.

Kenrig drew one of the daggers from her bandoleer and held it out to Lissi hilt first. 'Use this if any of them tries to touch you.'

The daggers had been effective at cutting through the Unseelie magic between the real world and the world of the feast. She hoped that meant it would prove effective against the Unseelie or the sluagh, enough to discourage them at least. She hadn't found an opening to test them against Holdainn so hope was all she had to go on.

Lissi didn't take the offered dagger so Kenrig tucked the blade through the girl's rope belt.

'I had another dream,' the girl whispered.

Kenrig tilted her ear closer. 'What about?'

'The boy.'

'Dandall?'

Lissi nodded. 'He betrayed you.'

Kenrig's neck stiffened. 'Betrayed me? How? When?'

'Don't know.'

'What did you see, exactly?'

'I saw-'

Lissi's eyes dulled. She tensed suddenly all at once and would have fallen if Kenrig hadn't steadied her. When she spoke it was with the voice of true prophecy.

'A feast will come, of carrion all, where murder rests 'neath funeral pall. A thread to unravel, a thread to weave. A pattern to wind, a pattern to cleave. Traitor to one and hero to none. The fate of the kingdoms unjustly won.'

Her prophecy delivered, the girl sagged and woke from her vision with a start.

'It's time you leave,' Ogda announced. 'The girl will stay here, as a guarantee of your cooperation in returning the other villagers to my feast.'

Ogda's hands were open at their sides as though they might push Kenrig away with a gesture.

Kenrig ignored them to speak with Lissi. 'I have to leave-'

The girl's vacant eyes brightened with fear. 'No, don't leave,' Lissi said, her voice slurred after her prophecy. 'Please don't leave me.'

Kenrig gripped the girl's shoulders. 'I'm not leaving you here, not forever.'

She swallowed as she felt her voice about to break with emotion. 'I need you to be brave for a little while. I promise I'll come back for you.'

'Do not interfere,' Ogda warned. 'You are being permitted to leave, but we have your name. Be on your way now or I will unleash my sluagh against you.'

Kenrig reached for her falchion where it lay on the ground. Her hand tightened around the grip and as she looked down at the strange girl of the crossroads she wasn't certain that she wouldn't try to carve a path for both of them to escape, hopeless odds or not.

'Swear she won't be harmed,' she said to Ogda.

Ogda smiled. 'I swear she won't be harmed. For one week.'

Kenrig leaned down and whispered so that only Lissi could hear her. 'I'm coming back for you. And I'm sending these creatures back to the Otherworld where they belong, kicking and screaming if I have to.'

She might have said more, but with a wave of Ogda's hands the world darkened around her and she was freed from the feast.

10

The Celebrants

Kenrig had no memory of leaving the world of the feast. Only an instant of darkness, then she and the villagers had come to in the frigid air of true night, as if they'd all woken from the same nightmare. She'd collapsed soon after.

The descent down the hill passed by in flashes of feverish awareness. She was borne along between two men at the rear of a grim procession of exhausted villagers. Few words passed along the ragged column and when she was conscious she heard only the pained gasps of her bearers and the shuffle of feet against the rocky slope.

When she woke properly she was lying on her side tangled in her own cloak. She rolled to free herself and narrowly avoided falling from the table where she'd been placed. She had to throw her hand against the bench beneath to stop the fall and the stinging in her palm cleared any grogginess from her mind.

'Are you alright?'

The man that had asked the question sat opposite her

at the bench of another table. A cluster of candles sat by his elbow and provided just enough light to see him by.

He was short, but broad-shouldered and looked strong despite his apparent age. The candlelight beside him deepened the wrinkles creasing the dark bronze skin of his face and shone gold in his sparse grey hair. His tunic and trousers were of fine green linen stained and torn by the events of the Unseelie feast.

'Fine,' she grumbled. 'How long have I been asleep?'

'Couldn't have been more than a couple of hours,' he said. 'Sleep of the dead though. The horns of the Wild Hunt wouldn't have woken you.'

She righted herself and swung her feet down to rest against the bench. She winced at the sequence of pains cascading through her body.

'And where are we?' she asked.

'The village hall,' the man said.

He glanced right and she followed his gaze, but the hall was in complete darkness beyond their small area of candlelight. She couldn't remember seeing Dandall in her patchwork of memories following the feast.

'I was travelling with a young man,' she said. 'Cadogan, around sixteen.'

'Dandall?' he said with a shrug. 'Eh, he was around. Helping some of the older folk off the hill. I can have a look for him?'

She waved away the offer. If she'd spoken to the boy then and there she wouldn't have had kind words for him.

She'd tasked him with preventing Lissi from passing the barrier and now she was trapped with the Unseelie, alone with only a pendant and a dagger to protect her. Yet if he hadn't let the girl slip past him, she wouldn't have received Lissi's warning. *He betrayed you.*

She wished she could question Lissi about the dream. She believed that the girl's dreams provided accurate prophecies, she had seen for herself some of the events they'd predicted, but without knowing the specific details she couldn't know what to expect. Her old mentor Garnham possessed a similar gift, but his own dreams always bore with them uncertainty that was easily warped by interpretation. What Lissi interpreted as a betrayal might be explained some other way.

Until she'd had time to think she wouldn't be ready to face Dandall.

She flexed her shoulders to dispel some of the ache in her neck and felt the tightness of bandages across her left arm.

'We had to remove some of your armour to stitch and bind your wound,' the man said.

He reached for a dark bundle on the bench beside him and passed it to her.

'It was my wife that treated your wound,' he continued. 'But she left me to watch you.'

Her leather breastplate was offered to her like a bowl and it contained her left pauldron and the drawn falchion. She accepted the bundle, but when she didn't see the bandoleer of daggers she stared into the man's oak-brown eyes.

'Ah, of course,' he said.

She hadn't noticed the bandoleer resting in the dark pool of his lap. He picked it up and slid a loose dagger back into its sheath.

'If I hadn't lived through the past few days,' he said. 'I'd have thought those blades were the strangest things I'd ever seen.'

He held the bandoleer out, but didn't pass it across as he had her other belongings. When she pulled it from his hands she had to fight his sudden grip. He almost looked embarrassed as he let go of the weapons.

'Who are you?' she asked as she checked the three remaining daggers.

The man cleared his throat and shifted on the bench. 'Daglan,' he said. 'I'm the smith,' he added, as though to explain his interest in the daggers.

Daglan, she thought, trying to place the name.

'Kenrig,' she said by way of introduction. 'Lissi mentioned you. You were looking after her, right?'

Daglan had sat slumped over with absolute exhaustion, but when she spoke Lissi's name he sat a little straighter.

'You've seen her?' he said. 'When we came down from the fell I searched the village for her. She wasn't in the village when those...*things* took us, so I thought maybe she'd hidden herself.'

Kenrig felt herself softening at the sight of Daglan's

concern. She'd known Lissi for less than a day and yet the thought of her trapped with the Unseelie made her sick with worry. She steeled herself to explain something of the night's events.

Daglan was a patient listener though she could see the desperate energy coursing under his skin. He kept his eyes on her and listened without interruption, but she knew he wanted to move around, if only to do something. She knew because she felt the same need.

'She was always wandering off or finding places to hide,' he said once her story was finished. 'It isn't strange for us to lose her for a while, but I knew something was wrong this time.'

Tears at the corners of his eyes caught the candlelight and he marshalled himself with a breath.

'I used to scold her for disappearing,' he said. 'But she'd always just smile and say she never got lost. Sure enough she always found her way back, no matter how long she was gone. Her dreams...they unnerve other folk. But I always took comfort knowing she'd seen where she needed to go.'

He shook his head, then fixed Kenrig with a hopeless stare. 'Now though, if those things have her...she won't find her way back, will she?'

'I'll return for her,' Kenrig said. 'I'm going to banish the Unseelie and bring her home.'

Saying the words aloud helped her to believe them and she shared a slight smile with Daglan.

'And how do you intend to do that?'

She turned her head at the sound of the unfamiliar voice and saw another man approaching with a small lantern in hand. The man was tall, but as thin as a scarecrow, a comparison made easier by the ragged black gown that hung from him and the limp blond hair drooping to his shoulders.

His lantern travelled over the sleeping forms of the other villagers who were lined up along the walls of the village hall, asleep on whatever rough bedding they had gathered to soften the hall's tables and floor. Some of them stirred at the man's passage, but most slept on undisturbed.

The new man stopped at the edge of their candlelight and held his lantern high. Once he was close she could see that although he wasn't old his face was heavily pock-marked and lined with traces of illness. In the lantern light his skin had the pallid colour of wax.

'How do you intend to banish those creatures?' he asked.

He didn't whisper in deference to the sleepers behind him, but his voice emerged as a low wheeze.

She hadn't had a chance to sit and consider a course of action. Her time in the feast hadn't given her an opportunity to think further ahead than solving one problem before she was confronted with another, and since leaving she had slept away the intervening time.

Though something had bothered her since Saully-

Menyie's challenge when she'd observed the moon to capture its image. In both worlds the sky held a gibbous moon and during the challenge she hadn't been able to consider the implications of that, but without imminent danger to occupy her she could finally think.

'The next full moon won't be for another week,' she said to no one in particular.

'What?' the new man asked.

She was looking at the bandoleer across her knees while she thought. 'Spirits as powerful as the Unseelie shouldn't be able to appear outside of a full moon. Not fully-formed anyway.'

'What is this nonsense?'

'Unseelie?' Daglan asked. 'Like fairy-folk?'

She glanced up at the smith. 'More or less.'

No matter what she told the smith he always took time to consider what she said before speaking in turn, a trait not shared by the third member of their conversation.

'Are you unhinged, woman? Fairy-folk? You expect us to believe fairy-folk are living at the top of our hill?'

'Leave it alone, Lymann,' Daglan said, before she had a chance to say something worse. 'I wager we have her to thank for our freedom. And if it wasn't fairy-folk, then how do you explain what happened to us?'

The corners of Lymann's mouth moved as though the man were silently practicing what he intended to say. After a few moments his mouth stopped moving and settled into a grimace.

'How much do you remember about the feast?' she asked Daglan.

'Feast?' Lymann said. 'Is that what we're calling it?'

She ignored him and focused on the smith.

'Not much,' he said. 'I mean, I can remember what happened to us in there, but...there are a lot of bits and pieces that don't make sense to me. I don't think I want them to make sense.'

Kenrig could understand why ignorance was preferable to the truth of what had happened. She wouldn't burden any of the villagers with her own observations. Instead, she relayed the entire story from the moment she met Lissi at the crossroads, through to the end of the challenges.

Once again Daglan listened quietly, seeming to carefully consider her words. Lymann on the other hand questioned everything she said. Throughout her story he remained standing though the effort clearly tired him. His hand trembled as it held the lantern and his breath came out in an open-mouthed pant. She wondered why anyone who'd survived the ordeals of the Unseelie would choose to stand and whether he did so only to loom over her.

Whatever the reason she grew tired of craning her neck to look up at him and so she continued to address Daglan.

'The Unseelie released us, but not Lissi?' he asked. 'Why?'

'She snuck into the feast after I made the bargain.

So the Unseelie claimed she wasn't a part of it.'

'But why would they let us leave, and keep one girl? That doesn't seem like a fair exchange.'

Kenrig hated having to break so much bad news.

'A week?' Lymann hissed. 'Your bargain only gave us a week?'

Disgruntled voices called for quiet down the hall and Lymann leaned in closer to whisper.

'One week, and then what? We return to that, that-'

His throat bobbed up and down as he swallowed, and she felt a momentary pang of pity at the fear in the man's eyes. She didn't like the man, but could at least sympathise with the torment he'd experienced.

'I'm afraid so,' she said. 'But I intend to banish the Unseelie before then.'

Lymann straightened again. 'I am Karstend's reeve,' he said. 'The laws and safety of this village are my responsibility. Any discussion concerning the banishment of these *Unseelie* from the Fell is also my responsibility.'

'It's a hereditary position, I assume?' she asked, and saw Daglan fight to keep a smile from his face.

'What?' Lymann asked.

'It doesn't matter.'

She met his eyes which wobbled at the attention. 'Do you have a plan to banish the Unseelie or shall I tell you mine?'

Lymann's nostrils flared. 'I won't be talked down to in my own home-'

'I think,' said a new voice. 'We've all suffered an ordeal and could use some sleep.'

A woman appeared at Lymann's side and next to him she radiated good health. Although her eyes were shadowed with fatigue, her cheeks glowed pink where she'd scrubbed away the dirt of the previous days. She wore a clean dress of brown wool and her own blond hair was neatly tied into a bun.

Lymann's anger stilled as she took the lantern from his shaking hand and gently pulled his arm down to rest at his side. His exhaustion and ill-health were amplified and he sagged so suddenly that Kenrig thought he would drop to his knees. He opened his mouth as if to make some protest, but closed it after a moment and allowed himself to be led away.

Kenrig regretted some of what she'd said as she watched the reeve shuffling through the hall. The man clearly bore the signs of chronic illness and yet he had survived days of torment. The woman led him between the sleeping villagers and then turned him left towards some other chamber.

She returned and took a seat beside Daglan. She set the lantern on the floor between the benches, then folded her hands in her lap. Her eyes reflected the orange light of the lantern as she studied Kenrig.

'Ida,' she said.

'Kenrig.'

Ida coughed. 'I won't make excuses for my husband.'

'You don't have to,' Kenrig said. 'You were right, you've all suffered.'

'Not just us, I think.'

Kenrig shifted, feeling a little awkward. 'My ordeal was short-lived by comparison.'

Ida's eyes wandered over Kenrig's armour and weapons before settling on the wound in her shoulder.

'Perhaps,' she said. 'But I think you suffered in entirely different ways. I heard something of what you told Daglan and my husband, about how you were tested by those monsters. You have my thanks for your efforts.'

Kenrig rubbed at the back of her neck. 'Don't thank me yet,' she said. 'I've only bought you a week of freedom.'

Ida looked down as she considered the point and Kenrig noted the obvious deference with which Daglan regarded the reeve's wife, deference that hadn't been apparent towards the reeve himself.

'You were about to explain a plan?' Ida asked.

'It's not much of one,' Kenrig said with a shrug. 'But based on what I know, it could work.'

When neither Ida or Daglan asked any questions she continued. 'As I said before, powerful spirits rarely appear in a physical form if there isn't a full moon. If they were human spirits *returning* to the earth from the Otherworld into a host body it wouldn't matter, but the Unseelie were likely born *inside* the Otherworld. Normally, they shouldn't be able to cross the veil to get here.'

'Normally?' Ida asked. 'But it's not impossible?'

Kenrig looked up into the hall's dark rafters as she gathered her thoughts. How had her own mentor, explained everything to her?

'There are *events*,' she said. 'Incidents that can change the balance between life and death. When an imbalance happens it can give rise to new creatures or bring out those that already exist. Some are spirits like the Unseelie that may never have been truly alive. Others are the spirits and flesh of humans and animals given new life.'

She looked down to see Ida and Daglan exchange a look of shared horror.

'In the...feast,' Daglan said. 'We saw people that we'd lost. Family, friends...were they truly with us?'

'I'm not sure, but it's possible.'

'The things some of them did-'

Ida placed a hand on Daglan's shoulder. 'Best not to dwell on it, eh?'

He nodded. 'What sort of incidents are we talking?'

'Battles, massacres, plagues,' Kenrig said. 'Large-scale slaughter of animals. Anything that causes a significant number of deaths.'

At their wide-eyed expressions she quickly added, 'But it's not just death that creates the imbalance. When human populations expand rapidly or powerful magic is attempted, that can also create imbalance.'

She glanced between them. 'Did Father Keld ever use mysticism?'

'He did,' Ida confirmed. 'When he was blessing homes or protecting the palisade.'

'Mysticism, and all other forms of magic, depend on the same imbalance. But when it's used by a small number of mystics there usually isn't a problem. The process of creating Hieratic script from sunlight is so gradual that the changes it creates in the balance are indistinct.'

She gestured broadly with her hands. 'But if a large number of mystics gather together to script a single spell, or if too many individuals use mysticism at the same time, the effects are more *dramatic*. The temples strictly control the use of magic to prevent that.'

'But Keld never did all that much,' Daglan said. 'And there haven't been any battles or anything around here for a while now. Nothing big anyway.'

Kenrig frowned. 'And this village isn't nearly large enough for the population to be a problem,' she said. 'It might not have been anything as large as a battle or a massacre. There are other, stranger incidents that might have drawn the Unseelie here. Anything unusual happen recently?'

Ida and Daglan shared another look.

'Apart from the arrival of fairy-folk?' Ida said.

She ran her hands over her legs, smoothing the creases of her dress. 'There were some young men that went missing not long before this all started,' she said. 'Four of them. Not from the village, but some of the farms.'

Daglan leaned forward. 'Aye, just young lads,' he said. 'We were going to organise a search for them, but we didn't get the chance.'

'Do you know where they were going?' Kenrig said. 'And why?'

Daglan scratched at the rough stubble on his chin. 'Thurlay, he's a lad about their age, said that a group of them had planned to visit Orveng. It's an old Karlan fort in the hills.'

'This land belonged to a Karlan kingdom,' Ida said. 'About twenty years ago. They kept to their old faith and lost a war against their neighbours who'd converted to the Hierat.'

'Heathens, Keld called them,' Daglan said. 'He tried to get us all riled up about it one day, said it was wrong that the Karlan holy places were still standing, but none of us paid him much mind. Why give up a few days's work to ransack an old fort?'

He shrugged. 'Maybe those lads took him seriously. Or maybe they're just wanting to loot the place.'

'Can you think of anything else unusual about the fort?' Kenrig asked.

Ida finished fidgeting with her dress. 'Well, there is a story about the siege that ended the war. The fort was meant to be proof against siege for weeks but, according to the story, the defenders surrendered as soon as the army arrived at their gates. They didn't even defend themselves as they were robbed and beaten.'

Kenrig leaned back against the table. 'The timing of those boys disappearing makes me think it's worth investigating. I don't have much else to work with.'

'If this has something to do with the Unseelie, what will you do?' Ida said.

'If their appearance is connected to this fort somehow then there may be an object or an individual important to their presence. Maybe even the entire fort, but I won't know until I search it. Destroying the fort or an object might be enough to send them away.'

She looked between them. 'An individual would be more complicated.'

'Why won't they disappear on their own?' Daglan asked. 'If an imbalance brought them here, wouldn't they leave when the imbalance is over?'

'Sometimes, but once a creature is established it can feed to sustain its presence.' She cleared her throat. 'I suspect the Unseelie were feeding on your energy somehow.'

Daglan paled and shuddered, but Ida sat steadily and met Kenrig's eyes. Only the shaking of her hands in her lap betrayed her.

'We hardly know you,' she said. 'And yet we are in your debt. For a reprieve if nothing else. We can't ask you to help us further.'

'You aren't asking,' Kenrig said. 'I'm volunteering.'

'Who are you to offer your help to strangers?'

She grimaced. 'I'm someone who follows the sound of singing.'

11

Sanctuary

Karstend's chapel had been converted from the lower floor of one of the tall houses built onto the hill. The front doorway had been widened to accommodate a larger door and led directly into the confines of the small chapel. Benches were placed into every foot of available space through the centre of the room and against the walls.

The only light would have been provided by lanterns mounted to the walls and candles lining the blocky altar at the rear of the chapel, but none were lit and Kenrig left the door open to let in the brilliant sunlight of morning.

After her conversation with Ida and Daglan she'd managed a few more hours of sleep. She'd woken to the dawn light seeping in through the hall's western windows which hadn't been shuttered, and after imagining the sluagh stealing in through the openings any further sleep was impossible.

She'd exited through those windows rather than walking among the sleepers. She was hesitant to wake any of them given all they'd suffered and if she was being honest she didn't crave company.

The rain clouds that had followed her since she'd crossed the border were burned away by the low Autumn sun to reveal a beautiful morning that didn't suit their grim circumstances. She'd unhitched Stoic from the market stall and walked with him in the shadow of the hill so that she could stretch out her mounting aches. They circled the hill as she studied the summit for any sign of the feast or its inhabitants, but she'd walked a complete circuit of it without catching sight of the barrier.

Afterwards she'd searched for the village's chapel and, having no one to guide her, simply searched the tall houses on the hill until she'd found it. None of the villagers had returned home to bar their doors so she'd had free rein to wander as she pleased, though it hadn't taken her long to find the chapel.

Dandall sat on a bench against the wall. His head was bowed as if in prayer, but his eyes were open and she could see that they were red from lack of sleep. Deep shadows lined his eyes and his skin was pale and drawn.

He glanced up as she entered the chapel and just as quickly looked away. 'I'm sorry,' he said.

His voice was quiet enough that she barely heard him, even in the cramped space. He looked so defeated that any of the angry words she'd imagined herself saying, the reprimands she'd rehearsed before she'd risen, vanished without passing her lips. There was nothing she could say worse than whatever he might have told himself.

She sidled between the benches to the altar and positioned herself to one side of it so her shadow didn't block out the light from the door. The altar was a single large block of finely cut stone polished to a smooth sheen. A bowl of rough pink quartz rested on a square of black linen between two rows of candle stubs. Behind the altar was a ladder leading to the upper floor where Keld must have lived, which left a gap just large enough for someone to stand behind the altar.

'Did you hear me?' Dandall said.

She didn't look up from the altar. 'I heard you.'

Keld's copy of the Scriptures were relatively plain, but neatly crafted. Precisely cut squares of parchment were bound together between two boards of varnished cedar, and she was pleased to see the dazzling characters of true Hieratic script burnished across its pages rather than a painted imitation.

Dandall was watching her when she looked up from the Scriptures, not fully meeting her eyes. 'I tried to stop her,' he said. 'I'm sorry.'

'It doesn't matter now,' she said. 'If you feel bad about it you'll do something to fix it.'

His hands wrung the hem of his cloak. 'What happened? Behind the barrier?'

She closed her eyes as she wearily considered the

events of the feast. She had no wish to relive them again, but if Dandall was going to help her he needed to understand them.

'The Unseelie are real?' he said, once she'd relayed her story. 'My granny used to threaten to give me to them if I didn't behave. She said they'd come with their Wild Hunt and wheech me to the Otherworld before my time.'

'They're real enough.'

'What does *that* mean?'

The text of the Scriptures swirled at the edge of her vision and she idly traced the edges of a page with her fingers.

'The Unseelie are spirits,' she said. 'At least from what I'd read. Now I've seen them with my own eyes. They're powerful, able to take physical form with the right circumstances.'

Dandall looked at her intently, his shame evidently forgotten in the moment. 'What kind of circumstances?'

'That is what we're going to investigate.'

She closed the Scriptures and tucked the book beneath her arm. 'First though, we're going to make sure the village is safe.'

Dandall frowned and made no move to rise. 'Lissi...she wanted to tell you something, about a *dream*. That's why she went after you.'

Her eyes darted away from his, just for a moment. 'She didn't mention anything about a dream.'

She brought the Scriptures to the village hall while Dandall and Daglan searched for the hall's missing charms. The villagers had woken in her absence and though they were as hollow-eyed and languid as lost souls, Ida had managed to cajole them to a semblance of activity.

She directed some of them to return home so that they could bathe and change out of the rags that had been their best clothes. Others reorganised the hall and cleared away the previous night's bedding to arrange the tables into a long line down the hall's centre.

Food was brought out from a cold store beneath the hall and assembled under Ida's direction into something that bore an unfortunate resemblance to a feast. Kenrig couldn't remember when she'd last eaten anything larger than an apple and her stomach whined at the sight of smoked sausages, blue cheese and thick slices of salty bacon. She helped herself to all of it, perhaps a little greedily.

Few among the villagers shared her appetite, for which she couldn't blame them. For days they had been forced to consume the vile sustenance of the Unseelie, and she wasn't surprised to see that a number of them had grown sick from consuming it. She chose to sit on the slope of the hill under the sun, feeling too awkward to eat in the taut silence that filled the hall.

When she'd finished eating the sigh that escaped her mouth was one of pure contentment. Her enjoyment of the food was soured slightly by a familiar guilt, the sense that rarely let her enjoy moments of peace when she felt she ought to be moving and doing something. Even so, the life she'd led meant she would never take being warm, well fed and clear-headed for granted, and she allowed herself a few minutes in the unfamiliar light of a sunny day to do nothing more than breathe.

Eventually, her guilt won out and she climbed reluctantly to her feet. She returned to the hall and drew Ida outside so they could talk privately.

'I have a way to protect the hall,' she said. 'But I need you to keep everyone inside it until I get back.'

Ida considered her words for a moment. 'I can do that, but I'll need to know more about this protection. People will have questions.'

Kenrig held the Scriptures between them. 'I can use mysticism to ward the building, the way a priest would. If you can get someone to replace the threshold charms, I can create a barrier outside. The Unseelie have some sort of claim to you, so I don't know if it will work, but it might keep them out when your week is done.'

Ida looked down at the Scriptures and Kenrig thought she saw fear in the older woman's face, but when their eyes met again Ida's gaze was steady.

'I don't see that we have any choice but to trust you,' Ida said. 'Though once again we'll be in your debt, knowing so little about you.' She shook her head and smiled. 'You're clearly knowledgable about *spirits* and *mysticism*, but you don't seem like any priest I've ever met. Are you part of a temple?'

'No,' Kenrig said. 'I was, in a way at least, but not anymore. My mentor was a priest, now disgraced.'

She was surprised to hear Ida chuckle, the sound seeming out of place with the woman's dour expression.

'We had a priest of our own who wasn't disgraced,' Ida said. 'And he brought those spirits to our doors. I don't suppose it means much.'

Ida entered the hall and from the clamour that followed Kenrig guessed she was explaining the plan to the villagers. Dandall and Daglan returned soon after, bearing between them shield-like discs of inscribed copper and iron. In the morning light the smith looked drawn, like he'd been beaten out of a too small piece of metal.

'Daglan, I need a favour,' she said as they set the charms down.

The smith knelt beside the charms, frowning as he studied the broken mounts on each disc. 'Something easy I hope,' he said.

'I just need as many iron filings as you can spare.'

He looked up at her with a smile. 'Is that all? You can have every last scrap of iron I own if it will change anything.'

With Dandall's help she carried buckets and barrels of iron filings from the smithy to the hall. They passed villagers carrying their own burdens of food, water and belongings into the hall in preparation for the week ahead. Their own preparations were viewed with suspicion as they emptied the iron filings into a circle broad enough to surround the hall.

She waited until the villagers were settled inside before she completed the circle. Daglan arrived with the repaired charms soon after and eyed the wide border of iron uncertainly.

'I almost don't want to cross it,' he said. 'Knowing I might never leave it.'

He hesitated, then took an exaggerated step across the border.

She sent Dandall to ready their horses and opened the Scriptures. She shifted her focus to draw out the characters inlaid into the parchment. In the bright day the sunlight script was almost invisible at the corners of her vision, and she had to fight not to blink away tears as she scanned the dazzling pages. Her efforts were slowed by the blinding light, but unlike her trick with the mirror for Saully-Menyie, she had performed the spell before and knew which pages she could draw from.

The mystics of Sostris strictly regimented their spellcraft into Doctrines, rigid guidelines that directed mystics in the creation of curated spells. Mastery of Doctrines was the work of a lifetime and few mystics were able to learn them all. She had spent three years learning just one of them.

The Doctrine of Sanctuary was tenuous in her

memory, the Hieratic characters as elusive in her mind as they were drifting freely in the air over the surface of the parchment. To consciously remember the Doctrine and fix it firmly in her mind could send the characters scattering from her memory as surely as staring at their physical counterparts would push those from her sight.

Her ability to repeat the Doctrine was the result of intense practice so that she could recall it without thinking, in the same way that her muscles recalled her martial training without conscious effort. She had to step around the circle of iron to inlay the characters across the entire barrier, but the movement of her legs helped to keep her from focusing too closely on the spell in her memory.

The characters drifted in sequence down to the iron filings and buried themselves down into the metal. The ephemeral script burned red-hot through the iron and melted the filings together into searing emblems that held the characters against the earth.

When she was finished the loose circle of filings began to break apart as the wind frayed its edges, but beneath it she had composed a new border from hundreds of characters set directly into the rock and soil. The metal characters cooled to the regular dull grey of iron, but in the periphery of her vision she could see the sluggish blur of movement at their edges.

When the hour of work was done she let her focus return and crossed the iron script to lean against the hall's front wall. Ordinary reality settled into place with an overwhelming surge of sensation. The outlines of her hands resolved themselves from the neat lines of the wooden panels they pressed against, moments before her stomach churned and the pain of her wound reasserted itself. In the exhausted delirium that followed she didn't notice someone arrive at her side.

'Are you well?' they asked.

She couldn't gather her wits enough to recognise the voice. Bile gathered at the back of her throat and she tried to wave away their concern rather than risk speaking and lose her breakfast.

'Can I help you to sit down, or bring you some water?'

'I'm fine,' she gasped. 'A moment. Please.'

She hated the thought of appearing weak in front of anyone from the village. Her plan required them to trust that she could do as she said she would and that they should sacrifice all comfort, pressing themselves together into one room on what might be their last week free from torment. If she was one of them, and could see herself panting and barely able to stand, she would have had doubts.

As if voicing her thoughts, her audience spoke again. 'Are you sure you're fit to travel?'

She forced herself to stand straight though it cost her to do it. Her left hand found purchase on the coarse grain of the wall and she crawled it upward to drag herself upright. She gripped her belt with the other hand to hide its shaking. There was no disguising the sweat beaded across her forehead, but she managed to look into Lymann's eyes though she had to squint against a gathering headache.

'I'll be recovered,' she said. 'Soon enough.'

The reeve himself seemed remarkably recovered after a night of rest. The scars of some old illness pitted his cheeks and dark bags lined his eyes, but there was a trace of pink in his cheeks. He wore a fresh gown of undyed wool and though it hung off of him he was able to stand straight without visible effort.

'At least allow me to send someone with you,' he said.

She shook her head and immediately regretted the movement. 'No. When the week is up, if any of you are caught outside, you'd be easy pickings for the Unseelie. You're safest here. And I have my apprentice.'

'Forgive me, but you're asking us to trust you while we do nothing to help ourselves.'

'I'm not asking you to do nothing. You and your wife least of all. You're going to be trapped in there. Maybe for a week, maybe for longer. It won't be easy and it isn't nothing.'

She stared up into the reeve's eyes until he averted his gaze. 'They'll need leadership.'

He nodded at the implication. She didn't think he could have failed to notice her mention of Ida, who had organised the village in his absence.

'I actually came out here to apologise,' he said.

He met her eyes sheepishly. 'Although I seem to be doing a terrible job of it. I ought to be thanking you, instead of casting doubt against you.'

She watched the anxious bobbing of his throat for a moment before speaking. 'You all survived an ordeal, and hope never to return to it. You've nothing to apologise for.'

'I don't deserve your understanding, but I am grateful.'

She pointed to the circle of iron script. 'If you'd like to show your gratitude, then keep everyone behind that line. If I return, I'd like our efforts to mean something.'

He nodded. 'I will. You have my word.'

12

The Debated Lands

Kenrig was surprised by how much she enjoyed being on the road again. Her enjoyment had little to do with her physical state which hadn't improved since she'd left the hall. The swaying motion of Stoic underneath her threatened the delicate balance of the breakfast in her stomach, and riding west toward the setting sun pushed slivers of white-hot pain into her aching skull.

Dandall led the way while she rode hunched over, eyes fixed on the coarse red hair of Stoic's mane. Despite her discomfort she was glad to be moving. The air outside of the village felt lighter, less burdened by a sense of doom. Their path led them away from the shadow of the Dullie Fell, through sunlit fields and along deserted tracks that stitched the landscape together into a patchwork of autumn colour.

Without Lissi's guidance they used up the rest of the day returning to the crossroads. They set camp beneath the apple tree and tied the horses away from the road so they couldn't gorge themselves on fallen apples. The evening was warm and dry and they didn't bother to erect a tent. They nestled between the roots of the tree on opposite sides of the trunk, bundled in their cloaks.

Fatigue brought dreamless sleep and she woke to find that she'd slept undisturbed through a rain shower. She rose stiff and cold, but without the previous day's frailty. Dandall shrugged when she saw his attempt at a fire and they ate a cold breakfast.

Wind lashed grey clouds across the morning sky and the new day settled into an irregular rhythm of rain broken up by brief patches of clear sky. The land was flat toward the western horizon, empty of any shelter except for sparse avenues of stooped trees and rows of wild hedges. Their view of the distant hills was obscured only by the curtain of grey clouds hanging below the sky.

Their progress was slow, or so it seemed to her when the only landmarks were unremarkable fields and abandoned cottages. They picked their way along dozens of branching paths, never able to simply travel west, but having to ride north or south at times to avoid riding through fields overgrown with crops that had begun to rot unharvested.

A day's ride beyond the bounds of Karstend the land turned toward ruin. The fields were choked by sodden mats of burned crops and water flooded from their borders. Dirt tracks became stagnant streams littered with debris and fences bowed outward into their path under the weight of fallen trees. Whatever homes still stood had been hollowed out by fire or dragged down by the elements. She didn't want to breathe in that blighted land in the fear that the musty stink would settle into her lungs.

The first body floated at the centre of a track, face turned down into the claggy water, hair spread in a filthy mat around its head. Grey flesh darkened by decay protruded from a tear in its ragged clothes, withered around the broken shaft of an arrow.

Crows and rooks had lain noisy claim to the contested farmland, gathering in such numbers that their passage darkened the sky. They scavenged the rich pickings of the abandoned fields in mock of bowing scarecrows. The birds sustained themselves on seeds and worms unearthed by the weather and the passing conflicts, but refused to supplement their diet with the foul carrion of that corpse and all the others that followed.

There were only a few bodies at first, abandoned out in the open or half-hidden by a land that had continued to grow around them. The further they travelled the more of them they saw.

Armoured men left to rust on farms that had become battlefields. Families slaughtered together on the move as they'd fled violence. Households burned down to bones huddled together in their final moments. Whole villages piled high in mass graves.

Some had been picked clean by carrion birds or wild dogs. Others had putrefied before they'd been scavenged and were food fit only for maggots. She recognised them by the clothes they'd worn and the objects they'd carried.

Marchers lay armoured in padded coats of once-bright cloth, unified only by the bizarre assortment of colours they'd worn and the weapons they'd brought into battle. Some of them hardly seemed dressed for battle at all, killed in whatever they'd worn to work their farms and armed with nothing more than tools. Others had carried shields and axes in imitation of their Karlan ancestors.

Their Karlan cousins had been stripped of their wealth by looters, left the small dignity of bearing their arms and armour only when those items were too damaged to be worth stealing. Unlike the Marchers the Karlan men and women had dressed for the sole purpose of war and some still carried sundered blades or wore scraps of corroded mail. They continued to wear the talismans of their old faith only when those talismans were carved from bone rather than forged from silver and gold.

Some bodies were wrapped in mantles and cloaks of faded tartan, but the Cadogan dead were few and scattered wide. The dead warriors were testament to the continued pride of the Cadogan, but the Marches' original inhabitants had lost their wars long ago. Like the Karlans they had been robbed of their most valuable possessions, their necks and arms bare of the rings that ought to decorate them.

Dandall had gradually fallen behind as the day dragged on and she turned in her saddle to watch him. His eyes were hidden beneath his cloak, but she could see the grim set of his mouth. He stared at the Cadogan dead and she could only guess at the thoughts he guarded.

He hadn't spoken much as they'd travelled together, but she'd rarely needed him to confide in her to know the workings of his mind. He was young and normally wore his emotions plainly. She could usually read the language written in the movements of his face and the set of his shoulders, even if he wouldn't voice his thoughts aloud, but as she watched him then he suddenly seemed a mystery to her.

He betrayed you. What had Lissi seen? Why had the girl believed that Dandall would betray her? Did all of Lissi's dreams predict future events? How far into the future was she able to see? *A traitor to one.* Was she the *one* the prophecy referred to?

She wished that she could pose those questions to Lissi, but more than that she wished she could consult her old mentor.

Where are you, Garnham? It had been Garnham's dreams that had set her journey in motion and she trusted the power that prophecy held, but it wasn't infallible. Garnham's gift had been astonishingly powerful and one day it had been fatally flawed. Prophetic dreams were open to interpretation and so they were open to mistakes. Garnham had only been able to attach his own meanings to the dreams he saw. He had made mistakes, innocent until they had become deadly.

She knew that there was more to Lissi's dream than she could understand, but even knowing that she couldn't guard her mind against doubt. Dandall frustrated her. He was stubborn and grumpy, qualities she hated in herself if she were being honest. He was quiet when he ought to speak and spoke when she'd rather he didn't argue. He had rarely, if ever, heeded her instructions. She had tasked him with keeping Lissi from passing the Unseelie's barrier and he had failed.

Even considering all of that she didn't believe he had ever given her a reason not to trust that he was sincere in his desire to learn from her. It wasn't him that worried her, it was the uncertainty of the prophecy. A betrayal could mean anything, especially alongside the rest of the prophecy, and until she knew what it might mean she could do nothing but worry.

Dandall had attached himself to her cause and for all that he annoyed her, he was worthy of the benefit of her patience. Still, she couldn't rid herself of doubts once they'd wormed their way into her thoughts.

They stopped only briefly to let the horses rest for a few minutes at a time. Starved dogs prowled among the battlefields and after a few hours it became obvious the dogs followed their trail. The emaciated beasts snuck closer whenever they stopped, silent and patient except when their ranks erupted with violent skirmishes.

The land was so saturated with death that she wasn't surprised the Unseelie had been drawn to it, yet she was left with a sense that something else had brought them down on Karstend. There were no signs of recent battle. All of the corpses they'd passed were long dead and the farms had been abandoned longer still. If the death of anyone in those battlefields had attracted the Unseelie, they'd have appeared soon after one of the larger battles.

They didn't stop when night fell. There was no shelter to be found that they were willing to occupy and no rest to be had while they travelled blind through the restless noise of darkness.

They travelled without lanterns until they'd left the fields behind, afraid that they would make targets of themselves to anything desperate enough to attack them, and relied on brief tracts of moonlight to illuminate their path. They navigated west through the dim outlines of distant landmarks and arrived at the edge of a forest some time after midnight.

Amongst the cover of trees she allowed them to light lanterns, accepting that the risk of the horses stumbling and falling was greater than an ambush. They shone their lanterns behind them and watched as the light was reflected back by distant eyes, then turned to enter the forest.

The noise of the fields was silenced by the press of trees and the mat of pine needles covering the path muffled the rhythmic step of their horses, until the only sounds came from the horses' huffing breaths and the jangle of their harnesses. Without human interference the forest had begun to reclaim the path and loomed so close that branches scratched at her legs and caught in Stoic's coat.

She had to huddle over the lantern to keep it from being whipped out of her hand and enjoyed the faint warmth that leaked from its iron shell. The looming pines leaned in close to the small flame, as though they craved the light that was ordinarily denied to them during the night. Ahead of her the shadows stretched out of sight, driven reluctantly before the lantern's flickering radius.

She heard the flow of a stream in that soundless place long before she saw it. The stream's dark currents reflected her own lantern back at her and she was surprised at how badly she'd misjudged its depth as she drove Stoic across it. The forest cleared a little around a bend in the stream and they emerged from the water into a patch of moonlight.

The forest yielded more than enough material to build a fire and she gratefully took the chance to prepare a hot meal while their boots dried. Ida had provided them with food and they cooked sausages skewered on a stick over the flames. They scorched the sausages one at a time and ate each one as soon as it was ready. Her fingers and mouth were burned by the time the meal was done, but the blissful feeling of a warm belly was a balm against the death and darkness of the day's journey.

With her hunger satisfied she gathered pine branches

together into a rudimentary bed and spread her blanket over the top of it. Dandall stared into the heart of the flames long after they'd eaten.

'I know you don't always like to speak,' she said. 'But sometimes it helps.'

His jaw worked as though he chewed on the suggestion. 'I knew that the Cadogan here fought for whatever land they could,' he said. 'But I didn't expect-'

Sparks scattered as he drove a branch into the fire. 'There were so many. So many Karlans and Marchers, but so few of us. Those Cadogan that died were warriors, like we all used to be, but how many of them can there be? Where do they have to go when everything is being taken from them?'

She joined her hands across her stomach and faced up toward the sky. 'Outside of the North and East Marches there are too many kingdoms for any real peace. There were no marriage alliances here between my people and yours. No reading of Banns to return Cadogan land, however insulting that might be. Here the Cadogan either fight to survive or they live among their enemies.'

'Do you help them as well?'

'Who?'

'The Cadogan. Do you help the Cadogan that live here the same way you help Marchers?'

She took a breath before she answered. It was a dangerous question he'd asked.

'I try,' she said. 'Some accept my help. Others don't.'

'What happens to them if they don't accept your help?'

She shrugged. 'I help them anyway, the difference is that they don't know I've done anything until I'm gone.'

Their eyes met over the fire. Dandall's eyes shone black behind the flames.

'Why help someone who doesn't want your help?' he said.

'Because some people are too proud for their own good. That doesn't mean they don't deserve help.'

'And if the people you help go on to kill someone, what then? What if you help a Marcher and that Marcher steals Cadogan land? What if you help a Karlan and that Karlan takes a Cadogan as their slave?'

'You and I don't have the benefit of seeing the future in our dreams. We can't know what someone will do with the gift of a longer life. We can't choose not to intervene based on what someone might do in the future. It's not our responsibility what happens after we help.'

She closed her eyes briefly. She didn't remember sleeping, but when she opened them again she saw Dandall watching the fire as it burned down to embers.

'I'm not sure I can ignore it,' he said. 'I'm not sure I could forgive myself, for helping someone who might hurt my people.'

13

Twinned Souls

Kenrig dreamt of starving dogs nipping at her heels and woke to find her feet buried in stinging pine needles. Dandall's eyes were hollow from lack of sleep again but she made no comment and helped him to rise.

The sun shone unobstructed throughout the day, but its light failed to reach the forest floor and they wandered in the gloomy shade of towering pines. Another day was almost done when the path turned north to meet the hills at the border. They climbed the bare southern slopes of the hills and emerged high above the forest into a sky the same russet red as Stoic's own coat.

Their path narrowed and skirted sheer cliff as it ascended slowly but relentlessly into the barren heights above. They had to dismount and lead their horses along the narrowest sections so often that they didn't bother to ride any further and struggled upward on legs made stiff by the cold.

From the vantage of the hills she was able to appreciate the scale of the forest and the mountain valleys it gave way to along the western horizon. The wild landscape divided the Middle March almost in half and formed an effective barrier for the original Karlan territories that thrived in the West March beyond the mountains.

As the road climbed higher and turned north deeper into the hills there were signs of old construction half-buried under coarse grass. Flat stones, cracked and pitted with age, bulged upward from the pressure of grass growing beneath them, where they'd once paved the road. In places there were short sections of ravaged fencing, bent under the wind or dragged over the cliff by landslides. Sections of the road had collapsed into the ravine below, forcing them to skirt around the gaps, but they made good progress and came within view of Orveng before the sun had fully set.

The fort enclosed the summit of the hill inside two ringed walls, the outer a palisade of sharpened trunks from the forest below and the inner a drystone wall that had collapsed along its south side. Orveng was near-black under the bloody red light, but above the ragged line of the palisade she could see the tops of sloped roofs. At the summit inside the ruined stone wall, was the darker mass of a longhouse, its roof open to the sky.

The road met a narrow river before it reached the fort, the water only distinct from the red landscape surrounding it by its rippling shine. An arched stone bridge crossed where it became a waterfall at the end of a ravine. The bridge's mortar had cracked, but after some deliberation they managed to pull their reluctant horses across it.

On the other side the road forked, one branch north toward the fort and the other headed down the hill, west into a wooded valley. The fort was the more obvious target for their search, but pressed into the wet ground alongside the river there were traces of old footprints along the western path. They moved off the road to avoid disturbing the prints and lit their lanterns.

Dandall took Stoic's reins as she knelt to study the prints. 'The missing men?' he asked.

'Maybe,' she said. 'The tracks aren't that old.'

Several distinct prints overlapped to form the trail in the road. They were shallow, evenly spaced and unhurried all the way to the edge of the valley where they met a log stair that descended the hillside into the woods. At the edge of the stairs her boot caught on something in the grass and when she stooped to examine it she saw the wooden handle of a tool, snapped and discarded in a confusion of prints and shallow grooves that returned in the direction of the bridge. The prints in the second trail were driven deeper into the mud and spread erratically.

They left the horses to graze at the top of the stairs and followed the muddy tracks imprinted onto the logs. They found none that ascended until they were partway down, level with the trees. A single set of prints climbed from the woods, but abruptly turned into the hillside. She held her lantern high and saw the ruts and grooves dug deep into the slope where someone had climbed it rather than take the easier route up the stairs.

The base of the valley was littered with boulders so densely covered by moss and stark-white lichen that the stone underneath was barely visible. Stunted oak trees clung to the boulders, rooted into every gap and crack available to them. Their trunks grew at distorted angles so that they twisted together into an impenetrable lattice of branches heavy with dying leaves and tendrils of silver-grey moss.

Faded streamers had been hung from the branches of trees to mark a crooked path between the boulders. The branches hung so low that she had to push the streamers aside to progress through the narrow path and her efforts disturbed the tokens tied to the faded cloth. Polished stones, glass baubles and corroded coins were knotted into the streamers beside animal skulls and talismans of bone and wood carved with intricate spirals. The tokens rattled and clinked and their similarity to the ornaments worn by Saully-Menyie made her shiver.

The crunch of glass underfoot alerted her to tokens and streamers carelessly trampled into the mud. She knelt to examine a scrap of yellow cloth tied to a single brass bell, and noticed a straight edge where it had been deliberately cut from a branch. She examined a few more in turn and saw that all of the streamers that lay in the path had been vandalised in the same way.

'This place reminds me of the fairy trees we have in the Bann,' Dandall said, his voice a respectful whisper. 'We tie things to oak and ash trees to keep spirits happy. Or to ask for favours.'

'The idea here is similar,' she said. 'The bells and trinkets are meant to distract any spirits that might try to loot anything precious from graves or shrines.'

The path eventually steered them to the centre of the woods where they opened into a broad clearing. The tangled canopy parted enough that she could see the night sky hung low overhead, star-speckled blue except for a last trace of golden red. She knew she shouldn't be able to see the sky so clearly in that place, that there shouldn't be a gap in the canopy.

A mound of earth occupied the centre, its surface knotted with the enormous roots of an irminsoul, one of the sacred ash trees that dominated the Karlan faith, now felled on the other side of the clearing. Within the hollows between the roots lay the graves of generations of kings and queens, defiled and exposed to the elements.

She saw the gleam of bone within the unearthed graves and scattered across the mound where the bodies had been broken and discarded. Gold and silver jewellery, rings, necklaces and brooches, had been gathered in a loose pile at the base of the mound, abandoned before they'd been entirely looted.

They carefully ascended the mound using the roots of the felled tree which were each as thick as one of her legs. The dense knots of the roots provided effective footholds for the brief climb, but she couldn't help but feel she were a trespasser as her eyes met the empty sockets of the disturbed rulers. The broad stump that capped the mound had been brutalised by savage strikes, leaving it ragged with deep grooves. The blows that had finally felled the irminsoul had carved a clumsy wedge into the stump.

The irminsoul lay at a steep angle with its ravaged base supported against the mound. The black residue of ash near the base showed an attempt to burn the tree, but the true damage had been done by axes. The carvings of the Karlan gods had been mangled almost beyond recognition.

'I've never seen an irminsoul,' Dandall said. 'What do the carvings mean?'

'They're not common in the North March anymore,' she said. 'Most of them were uprooted and replaced by temples.'

She pointed along the length of the trunk which had been scraped clean of its bark, following the engraved knotwork serpents that coiled under and over each other to the tree's crown.

'These are two of the Karlan gods,' she said. 'Fimbul the Moon-eye, dragon of ice and sea, and Fulgur the Sun-scaled, the dragon of fire and earth. There are others, but these are the most important because it's their bodies which formed the world we stand on. The two are siblings, twins, that split from the first god at the start of time. Each of them contains only half of the original soul and they are driven to battle each other until the two halves are reunited into a single soul, both male and female in one body.'

She moved her finger to point at the tree's base where the serpents' tails twisted together. 'Their split wasn't complete, they stayed joined at the tips of their tails. As they fight over the ages their bodies and souls move closer together and merge. In the earliest days their battle brought flame from beneath the earth and sheared ice from the northern sea. Winds raged, seas rose and fell and their sundered scales became mountains dividing the land.

'As the two moved closer together their battle calmed enough that the world could support the lives of plants, animals and people. In the earliest days the world was a paradise, but Fulgur's heat will eventually be dimmed by the ice of Fimbul and a great winter will follow.'

She pointed to the serpents' eyes, the sun and the moon at the centre of their heads. 'The moon will cover the sun and the earth will become so cold that the blood of the last people will freeze in their veins. The serpents will be reunited, one body and one soul, and this world will end.'

She lowered her hand. 'Time will pass. The serpents will split apart again and a new world will form. The cycle will repeat over and over to the end of time.'

Dandall let out a breath. 'That's...actually quite beautiful. For such a cruel people.'

Kenrig's work took her across the March Kingdoms and with the spread of the Hierat she spent most of her life aiding the Marchers that emerged in its wake. She had trained under a temple mystic and carried temple relics, but she helped whoever she could and had been welcome among the Karlans as well. She was under no allusions that the Karlans were not simply suffering the same fate that they had inflicted on others themselves, but as she looked down at the ruined irminsoul, at the defaced carvings, she felt sorrow to see a holy place vandalised.

'They brought this on themselves,' Dandall said. 'They did this to my people. Broke our circles. Tore down our domes. Killed our old gods and made us weak.'

'True,' she said. 'They destroyed the holy places of others and now their holy places are destroyed in turn. It's been the way of things for a long time, but that doesn't mean we ought to continue that way. Taking revenge for damages done won't repair that damage, it will only create more pain. And pain empowers the things we'll face.'

The only grave that hadn't been disturbed by the vandals was that of the kingdom's original founder, safe from their axes beneath the irminsoul stump.

'The kingdom's founder would have led their clan from a parting stone to find a new land to settle,' she said, continuing her history lesson. 'Once their people were safe they would have willingly sacrificed themselves. Their body would be buried beneath an ash sapling carried from their homeland, and that sapling would grow into the irminsoul. Every king and queen that followed would be buried beneath its roots and in that way the irminsoul would prosper.'

She kept a reverent distance from the stump as she crossed the mound to the trunk of the irminsoul. Her lantern deepened the gouges hacked into the carved surface as she held it high overhead. Only the base of the tree was stained with ash, yet further up the trunk she saw a dark pattern spread across it. She picked her way down the roots on the other side of the mound and brought the light closer. Blood had dried against the trunk, a fatal amount spread in a wide vertical arc.

Bloody handprints had pressed against the carved serpents and worked their way along the trunk as if someone had leaned against it. A trail of blood led her down the roots to the base of the mound and it was there that she found the first of the missing men. He was young, not much older than a teenager, and had died with his hands pressed to the side of his ruined neck.

She pried the thin-fingered hands away from the wound. Whatever had caused the wound had not done so cleanly and she had to guess that it had been inflicted by an animal. The man's blood-crusted tunic had been ripped by several slashes that had also opened frayed gashes across his chest, but those wounds had bled little, perhaps inflicted after his death. Teeth and claws could have caused his wounds, but as she turned over his body she couldn't find any sign that he'd been fed upon.

'There's more,' Dandall said as he passed her. 'Two of them.'

The other men were as old as the first and had died only a short distance away at the tree line. One had fallen on his front clutching an axe and had only a faint splatter of blood on his clothes. When she lifted the hem of his tunic she saw the deflated right side of his chest where his ribs had been crushed. The third man had left a trail in the mud as he'd crawled. He'd made it further than the others, but died of blood loss through deep wounds in both thighs.

The third man's trousers were torn scraps. She and Dandall cut them away from his legs, revealing teeth marks around his calf. The marks were shallow, barely deep enough to puncture the skin, as though whatever killed him had abandoned the effort to eat him. Two grooves lay beside the man's leg where someone else might have knelt next to the body and when she scanned the ground she found more footprints leading around the outside of the mound.

The prints were only lightly imprinted on the ground, but they were unmistakably human.

'Whatever killed these men was trying to feed,' she said. 'But it was interrupted by a fourth man fleeing out of the woods.'

The men from Karstend had been confident in their vandalism, but had died soon after. Their killer had either ambushed them from somewhere else or had been unearthed by their grave robbing.

She scanned the mound, searching each of the graves in turn. Few remains had been left intact by the looters, but they had stopped short of digging up three of the graves, which lay in a rough line out of reach beneath the irminsoul. Those graves were untouched, still capped with the inscribed stones that identified their occupants. She followed the line of graves to a fourth at the mound's base, out of the irminsoul's shadow.

An iron shovel head was stuck into the ground beside the grave, its wooden handle snapped just above the socket. The grave was only partially uncovered, but entirely empty.

14

Bedside Story

They left the wood and returned to the fork in the road, following the branch north to the fort. Orveng's gates lay wide open and Kenrig was reminded uncomfortably of their arrival into Karstend. The twin wooden doors were drawn back and secured with ropes, as though the fort's inhabitants had prepared for company.

'Just like Karstend,' Dandall said, mirroring her thoughts. 'Is that important?'

'Perhaps, though I'm not sure how.'

The road crossed a grass-covered ditch over a narrow bridge and continued inside the fort, splitting to circle the summit between rows of homes. The outer palisade enclosed dozens of buildings, each one set into deep foundations so that they seemed short beneath their steeply angled roofs which extended almost to the ground. The roofs were tiled with wood or covered with turf and showed signs of neglect even in the relative darkness of their lanterns.

She hated the thought of leaving the horses tied up

with whatever had killed the missing men, but they couldn't risk the horses wandering off. They tied the horses to a hitching post that was going hollow with rot and she hoped that they might at least stand a chance of breaking free of the post.

'We'll search the houses first,' she said. 'Then the longhouse.'

She drew one of her daggers and Dandall did the same with the one she'd loaned him.

'That will take all night,' Dandall said. 'We've already spent two days coming here. I'll search the houses down here and you search the longhouse.'

'We shouldn't separate. Something killed those men and chances are good that it's still here.'

He met her eyes without blinking and gestured at the longhouse. 'I'm sure whatever it is, it will be living up there. You'll probably be in more danger than me.'

She shook her head. 'We have no way of knowing that. If it's not up there, I might be too far away to help you. We stay together.'

'I'll shout if I need help,' he said. 'And run for the horses if I have to.'

'No, we-'

His free hand slashed the air between them. 'Why can't you trust me just to search some houses?'

The outburst caught her off guard. 'It isn't about that. If we separate, we're vulnerable.'

He pointed at his chest. '*I'm* vulnerable you mean.

That's what you meant, isn't it? If we separate you can't protect me, because you think I need to be protected.'

She was too slow to form a response and he took her silence as confirmation. 'I knew it,' he said. 'You think I'm too weak to look out for myself.'

'You apprenticed yourself to me,' she said. 'Your safety is my responsibility.'

He turned his back to her. 'I spent months alone while I searched for you. I don't need you to protect me.'

She lifted her hand to touch his shoulder, but thought better of it. 'This isn't just about protecting you. We're safer together. I'm concerned for myself as well.'

He was quiet for a moment, then took a step away from her. 'If I never do anything alone, you'll never trust me again. I made a mistake and I need to prove myself before you take any other chances away from me.'

Why did you have to pick now to prove yourself? She was quiet for a time then reluctantly acquiesced.

'Fine,' she said. 'Search the houses.'

His shoulders relaxed as she gave him leave to do as he pleased.

'Shout if you're in danger and flee if you have to,' she said as he walked away. 'Don't draw attention to yourself.'

Assuming we haven't been noticed already with that outburst.

She held her hand against Stoic's nose as she watched Dandall walk away, finding resolve in the horse's warmth and steady breath. If he shared her fear he didn't show it.

'Watch him,' she said. 'Even proud people need help.'

Stoic only snorted in response.

'No sense waiting.'

The path to the longhouse was on the opposite side of the summit to the gate, presumably to force an attacker to circle the entire town before they could assault the inner wall. The drystone barrier was too high for her to reach the top and the gate set into a stone arch was barred when she pushed it. She skirted the wall around to its damaged southern side and climbed over the rubble. From her position atop the collapsed stone she could see that the damage to the wall aligned with the hole in the roof.

The longhouse was an enormous building, larger than the village hall in Karstend. It stood two storeys high, its hunched roof supported by thick wooden pillars crossing underneath it. The building's walls were coated white with cracked lime and its pillars and roof tiles were painted in patterns of red ochre and black charcoal.

The doors and windows were barred and shuttered, and she was reluctant to make a racket forcing them open. She backed away from the building and looked up at the hole in the roof. There was a light inside, weak and flickering, but constant.

She snuffed her lantern and set it on the ground by the wall, then waited until her eyes had adjusted before she climbed to the second storey. A wide, shallow lip ran around the edge of the roof, low enough that she was able to haul herself onto it by using one of the angled pillars to propel herself up. The motion wasn't graceful, but it was quiet, and she crawled to the edge of the hole before standing to peer inside.

She reeled at the sudden stench that emerged and threw her hand at the roof to catch hold of it as she staggered. Her eyes stung and she suppressed her instinct to gag at the overlapping smells of rot, mould and human filth. The air on the other side of roof was polluted with the overwhelming pressure of the smells that accompanied fresh killing, so thick it spread to the cold night air outside.

The hole was easily wide enough for her to enter the building, but she felt she had to push herself against some internal force to cross the threshold. The light she'd seen from outside was faint, produced by the stub of a candle that slowly oozed over the edge of a bedside table. A narrow bed dominated the room which was cramped beneath the slope of the roof. The torn remnants of soiled sheets had been scattered around the room as if by a strong wind, leaving the bed's occupant naked except for a thin blanket.

The body of an ancient man lay limp atop a pile of vile straw. His flesh was withered down to the bone of his tall frame, but not decayed. Rats scurried around his legs and nibbled at the exposed flesh, but the man had died not long before her arrival, though the cause of his death wasn't clear from where she stood.

She crept closer, straining her eyes in the candle's

fitful light. Encrusted sores were visible beneath his shoulders and only a few strands of grey hair clung to his paper-thin scalp. His fingernails had grown into long, brown talons, but they were blunt and ragged, and she doubted this man had been capable of murdering a group of young men even when he'd been alive. From the state of his body he'd been bed-bound for a long time before his death.

A cluster of other candles sat on the table and she whispered them to life. She was leaning close to examine the corpse when she heard a sigh of breath and had to clamp her mouth against a yelp of pain as her hand passed over a candle flame.

Her eyes hurried around the room, but she was alone in there except for the body. She leaned in close to it, unable to tell if the blanket over its chest truly rose and fell or whether that was a trick of the erratic candlelight. She held her own breath, relieved at the temporary lack of smell, and listened for another sign of breath.

The man didn't sigh but writhed in a fit of heaving coughs that racked his entire body. His muscles were too weak for him to rise and fall with the coughs and he lay choking like a man narrowly spared from drowning. Without thinking, she grabbed him just below his armpits, wincing at the feel of diseased skin, and pulled him up to rest his chest against the bed's single pillow. His coughing eased gradually, replaced by steady gasping breaths. His eyes fluttered open, blinded by cataracts.

'Gods,' she said. 'I thought you were dead.'

The man's voice was frail, barely audible, and she had to hold herself uncomfortably close to hear him. 'Death would be a mercy.'

He spoke in the peculiar Karlish that had evolved in the Marches and she had to focus to understand him.

'I live,' he said. 'Only as punishment.'

The effort of speaking set him coughing again. She held her waterskin to his cracked lips and held his head as he sipped feebly.

'I do not deserve your kindness,' he said.

'Who are you?' she said.

The man was silent for a while except for the wheeze of his breath. 'Ayvin. I was king here.'

'*Was?* You're the only one alive in this place, I doubt anyone would challenge you.'

'Not so. My brother, my elder, has returned. If he were ever truly gone.'

Understanding came quickly to her. 'He was buried beneath the irminsoul, wasn't he?'

The man, the prince, nodded slightly and when he spoke again his voice broke with emotion. 'I shamed myself. I killed him. With his own knife. And buried him in an unmarked grave.'

Movement at the corner of her eye signalled the return of the rats who'd been disturbed by Ayvin's coughing. They crawled around his legs, nibbling at his skin, until her swatting drove them away again.

Ayvin did not seem to have noticed the rats. 'I went mad with guilt,' he said. 'I found him. Returned him to Orveng, to bury with respect.'

The prince thrashed his head. 'Too late,' he moaned. 'Too late.'

She sat perched on the bed's frame as she placed a hand at the side of his head, shushing quietly until he was calm. Cloudy tears ran from his blind eyes and pity moved her to wipe them away with a scrap of cloth.

'My crime cursed us,' he said. 'I'm a coward. A traitor.'

'What happened?' she said. 'Between you and your brother?'

His eyes searched the darkness of the rafters, darting left and right as the bulb of his throat rose and fell.

'Our father wanted peace,' he said. 'With the Marchers. He entertained their priests here. Morgen hated him for it. They fought and our father died. He was a kin-killer, but his huscarls were loyal. He was king. And I was too scared to challenge him.'

She helped him to drink more water and the relief brought a toothless smile to his face. 'Morgen returned us to the old ways. We fought Marchers. Burned their holy places. Stole their food and made slaves of them.'

His mouth moved soundlessly and his eyes trembled, fixated on a point above him. The flesh of his neck was so wasted that she could see his feeble pulse quicken in the corded vessels underneath.

'I betrayed him,' he shouted.

She shushed and held his head again, but he wouldn't be calmed.

'The Marchers raised an army. I went to them. Bargained for my people. Begged for my own life. I offered to kill Morgen. I killed my brother for peace.'

He took in slow, shuddering breaths and strained against his own frailty. He made an attempt to rise, but she held him down without effort. He struggled against her, managing to bring one of his clawed hands to his chest to pry her hand away, but he tired quickly and shrank back into the straw.

'I cursed us,' he said. 'Kin-killer. The serpents saw my crime. They cursed my cowardice. I buried Morgen with our father. Too late. He lived again. Beneath the irminsoul.'

Ayvin's exposed hand gestured in a slight circle. 'We lived a half-life. While he slept we grew weak. Too weak to hunt. Too weak to farm. Our animals sickened. People sat down to meals and never rose. They lay down to sleep and never woke.'

His voice caught. 'I was strong while they died. Strong, but powerless. I didn't weaken until they were all gone. I lay down here, but did not die. I have not eaten, nor drank. I have not slept, since that day.'

'That was twenty years ago,' she said.

'An eternity to me. I thought myself mad, when I heard distant voices. But Morgen came for me soon after.

There was a crash and I felt clean air, for the first time, in a long time.'

With his tale concluded he seemed to breathe without trouble. 'I have kept you too long. I apologise. My brother will wake soon.'

He pressed his hand against hers. The touch of the withered hand chilled her, but she didn't pull away.

'Perhaps I lived,' he said. 'To tell you my story.'

The pressure of his hand was so faint it was almost imperceptible, but she felt the relaxation of his grip all the same. She laid the hand against his still chest and stood as she closed his eyes.

15

Charnel House

Instinct demanded that Kenrig leave before Ayvin's brother woke, but the only course she knew of banishing the Unseelie lay with the undead king. She found a brass candleholder knocked from the bedside table and fitted one of the candles into it. At the door to the bedchamber she drew one of the daggers from her bandoleer, then pushed her way into the corridor outside as quietly as she could.

The stench of death was far worse on the other side of the door. In the close confines of the narrow passage there wasn't even the relief of fresh air to lessen the stink. The air in the corridor was humid despite the chill and she could feel it cling to her skin like sweat.

Other chambers occupied the corridor and she checked each of them in turn. Some lay empty, while others held the remains of men and women dressed in once fine clothes. They'd died in their beds, granted a mercy denied to their doomed king for twenty years. The candle illuminated no further than a few feet ahead of her and she lingered in each chamber, reluctant to press forward.

The corridor ended at a thin pit of darkness that hid a steep stair running down along the building's west wall. The darkness of the stairway lingered under the weak candlelight as she leaned over the gap. The stench was strongest there and she pressed her nose and mouth into the crook of her elbow. She waited, breathing as little as possible, and moved when nothing emerged.

She paused at each stair, straining her ears to hear over the deafening beat of her heart as the wooden boards bent and groaned under her weight. The side of the stair opened into the chamber beyond, and though she couldn't see into the darkness she could sense the scale of it.

There was an appalling heat in the air, a lifeless warmth so heavy with moisture she had to work harder to draw in breath. She felt unsteady as she cleared the stairs. The full force of the stench staggered her, but she lifted the candle higher, using the pain in her shoulder to help her ignore it.

From the base of the stair she could see the bodies piled across the floor. They were stacked carelessly, scattered like the boulders of the wood that surrounded the irminsoul. The candlelight was too weak for her to distinguish individuals.

Clotted blood clung to her boots with every hesitant step forward. It had flooded so thickly across the floor that she couldn't see the wood beneath it. Humans and animals were thrown together into piles, men and women sprawled across the remains of pigs, deer and dogs. They'd been feasted on sporadically, only small amounts taken from each body before the rest was left to rot.

There were Karlans and Marchers among the piles. The Marchers were hard to distinguish, but the Karlans wore jewellery, gold arm rings and pendants, that identified clans separated by miles of wilderness. If Morgen had killed all of them alone then his hunting ground was vast.

She couldn't begin to count the bodies. There were too many of them piled together beyond the close edge of candlelight. She thought she understood then how the Unseelie had manifested. The undead king, Morgen, had slaughtered so many since his return, taken so many lives in a matter of weeks, that he'd upset the balance across the region. The longer he prolonged his unnatural existence with more deaths, the worse the problem would become.

What she didn't understand was why the Unseelie had appeared in Karstend, a village untouched by the king's indiscriminate violence. Why hadn't they appeared somewhere closer to Orveng, somewhere that he had visited? Had he depleted them entirely, leaving no one alive for the Unseelie to ensnare? Or was there some connection to the men from Karstend who had exhumed him?

She swept the candle slowly ahead of her, searching for movement in the darkness, but the flickering light only set the shadows of corpses writhing against the walls. The light was reflected back at her from the untouched eyes of the dead animals, dozens of metallic sparks gleaming like funerary coins. The king had only been active for a matter of weeks and she could hardly imagine the strength and speed required to kill and gather so many in such a short time.

The light settled on a Marcher, a man young enough to be one of the grave robbers. She squatted beside the body, bringing the candle close to study his features though she wouldn't know him from any other Marcher. His narrow features had tightened into a mask of extreme pain, sallow skin drawn taut against a fractured skull. She examined his fingernails looking for traces of soil, but found only dried blood beneath them.

A thud echoed from deeper in the hall and she stood, whirling so quickly the candle was almost snuffed by the rush of air. The light stretched as the flame shifted and she barely caught the rolling movement of a second body dislodged from its pile, closer than the first.

She backed toward the stairs. She'd descended into that charnel pit in search of Morgen, but had no desire to confront him there. In the darkness with no clear footing he had the advantage. She needed to understand what he'd become, but it wouldn't serve her to stay there and face him unprepared.

She kept her attention forward toward the fallen body, stepping backward and feeling her way to the stairs as her heels bumped up against the bodies lining her path. The darkness followed her, filling the space left empty by the retreating candle.

Reflex saved her as a hand shot from the shadow beside her, fingernails grown into ragged claws slashing a hair's breadth from her throat. She had an instant to glimpse a broad face mottled with purple bruises before another hand gripped her left arm over the bracer and the candle fell from her hand. Darkness surged around her, reducing her world down to the crushing pressure gripping her wrist.

She couldn't hear herself scream through the encompassing pain as her bones flexed beneath the unseen hand. She hunched down as she took a step back, trying to use her whole body to free herself. Her opponent followed and her wrist pressed against her as the distance between them collapsed. Her right arm was held across her chest and she felt the dagger twisting in her grip as her opponent's movement pushed him against the blade.

The grip on her wrist fell away. Morgen's scream gurgled from his throat as the pain of the mystic blade forced him back. Foetid breath, cold and metallic, cut through the vile stench in the air and she swung with the dagger. Her swing went wide, hitting nothing, but he retreated further.

Hieratic characters flared, pale and golden under the metal where Morgen's blood clung to the dagger. The blood smoked in contact with the characters writhing within it and the blade hummed, high and musical like a ringing glass as it twitched in her hand. In its fleeting glow she saw her path to the stairs and ran.

She clutched her left wrist to her stomach and used her elbow to help pull her upwards. Her right hand held the flickering dagger ahead of her to light her way. The acrid wisps of smoke from the burning blood stung her eyes, but lessened the stench of the slaughter below.

She leapt over the final stair, twisting so that she could bring her left shoulder around and stop her movement against the wall of the passage. The impact rammed the air from her lungs, but she sprinted without waiting for her breath to catch up. The passage felt narrower as she ran, shaking with the pounding of her boots against the wooden boards. Her cloak whipped back and forth, trying to coil around her legs and trip her.

She reached Ayvin's chamber and ran for the hole in the roof. Morgen's pursuit of her was silent and she had no warning before he collided with her back, launching her into the open air. The toe of her right boot caught on the edge of the opening and she swung hard into the lip of the roof. Momentum carried her into a roll and she fell, landing hard on her back to the ground below.

The dagger leapt out of her grip. It spun briefly in the air, catching the moon's light before it bounced out of sight over the ruined wall. The fingers of her right hand clenched at her side, but she couldn't raise her arm to reach for another dagger. She felt like someone stood on her chest, trapping the spent breath in her body.

She stared up at the sky, unable to do more than turn her head. The moon looked back at her from a mist of stars, its intangible surface drawing back to open the Otherworld's veil. She could sense the menace of the Unseelie in its gaze, further from her than in their illusory realm, but seeming no more distant than the reach of her hands. The thought that they might somehow be spectators to her in that moment gave her strength enough to crawl her hand to her chest.

She inched a dagger from its sheath as the king landed silently. His leap carried him in a high arc and he stopped a short distance from her, perhaps wary of the dagger in her hand. When she managed to turn onto her left elbow he stalked a couple of paces closer, animal ferocity replaced with predatory caution. He paused when she did, then took another step when she brought her knee under her hip.

In the moonlight she could see him more clearly. He was clothed in the ruin of funeral garb, trousers and a gown of white linen torn by claws and stained with dirt and dark patches of blood. In his broad body she could see a hint of the strength he might have had in life, but the muscles of his chest and arms seemed to hang slack from his wide skeleton. The bruising she'd seen in his large face spread across his entire body in thick blotches.

His mouth shone amongst the cracked gore slathered across his jaw and coarse white beard, his lips slick with fresh blood. He breathed as if he were panting, wide-mouthed as his chest heaved beneath sloped shoulders, but his breaths were slow, spaced further apart than her own. She couldn't see his eyes in the dark hollows that ringed them, but she felt him studying her as closely as she studied him.

They watched each other for a long time, neither of them willing to make the next move. She knew that as soon as she rose to her feet he would move in turn to cut off her escape. She needed a plan to get past him, but she was reluctant to try and break the peace they were locked into. While she waited the threat of violence was nothing more than a threat and as the seconds stretched between them it became harder to move knowing she'd make the threat a reality.

She started to assess her chances of killing him and quickly abandoned the thought. Her left arm was useless. The wound at her shoulder had reopened and her wrist had swollen so far she couldn't move her hand. She would escape and return for him once she'd had time to think and understand what he was. She needed to find Dandall and prepare.

The weakness in her limbs faded and she knew that she couldn't hesitate any longer. She shifted her weight to her left knee and brought her right foot around to stand. Morgen paced forward, keeping his distance.

She circled toward the collapsed wall. It was an obvious route for escape and she could feel intelligence lurking in the undead king. In the time it took her to move a few paces his loping stride had carried him to the wall's opening. He paced across the gap, never once removing his gaze from her. Her lantern lay unnoticed in his path.

As his foot came down beside the iron lantern she breathed her entire will into a single word, commanding the oil to burn all at once. The iron frame buckled outward, pushed by the sudden expansion of heat. Glass panels burst into fragments and flew out in all directions, borne along by the swelling flames. Dozens of shards scattered against Morgen's legs, some driven fast enough to embed themselves in his skin before the flames caught in the trailing scraps of his trousers.

His patience exploded in a howl of rage. He beat at the oily flames spreading across his legs, hammering glass shards deeper into the meat of his calves. She sheathed her dagger and charged for the wall, using the distraction to clear his reach. The fallen stones shifted under her feet, but she kept her balance enough to leap from the summit.

She collided with the sloped roof of a house on her way down. The old wooden beams collapsed beneath her, sending her tumbling through the roof in a shower of rotten tiles. She bounced against a table and rolled through the empty hearth, knocking stones loose from crumbling mortar. The stones rang against iron pots as she came to a stop, her arms braced around her tucked head.

She scrambled up, stumbling for the building's door. It yielded without effort and she emerged into a narrow animal pen. The king's howl ended and silence rushed back into the empty air. She ran across the street, making for the cover of the buildings on the other side.

Fear urged her to sprint for the gate, but she forced herself to creep through the shadows between the houses. She worried that the king retained enough of his old mind to target the horses, rather than waste time hunting her, but there was nothing she could do except make her way to the gate and hope Dandall had heard everything.

Stoic snorted as she broke from the cover of the buildings into the street a few paces from where she'd tied him. He pulled at his reins as she stepped toward him, rearing up to stomp the ground. His agitation spread to Kelpie and she tried to shush them both, fearing that they would bring Morgen down on them.

Too late she realised their terror was a warning.

16

Broken Blade

Dandall didn't wait for Kenrig to leave before he entered the first house. He was worried that if he turned around and looked at her she would reconsider letting him search alone. Or worse, that he would reconsider going.

He tried not to acknowledge that she was right. They were safer together, but he couldn't bear to do nothing more than stand beside her while he carried the weight of his mistake around. Lissi was trapped because of him. He had failed, but he wasn't going to stand idly and let Kenrig fix his mistake for him.

If he waited too long to work alone, she would never trust him again. He would never trust himself.

He felt ridiculous being afraid as he pushed open the front door of the house, though he couldn't help the tremble in his hand as he pressed the back of it to the wood. The sight of those dead men had unnerved him. They hadn't been much older than he was and whatever creature was loose in Orveng had killed four of them without effort.

Kenrig's dagger hummed in his trembling hand. Against the door its edges were outlined in the brassy light of his lantern, but deeper than that he felt the Hieratic characters in the metal. They were sluggish while he let them drift just outside his awareness, but when he tried to focus they scattered like fish disturbed by a stone, their shapes blurred by the movement of water.

His attempts to learn the magic that Kenrig taught had brought him nothing but frustration. Perceiving the characters of the Hierat made him sick enough that he couldn't eat for hours afterward. The words of the supposedly simple spells Kenrig employed were too tenuous, to the point that the act of remembering could drive them from his memory.

Yet for reasons he didn't understand he was able to feel the characters inside the dagger's blade, a small comfort against his fear. He sensed them clearly, a feat he'd only achieved with one other thing. The Unseelie's barrier.

Their magic hadn't been what he'd expected. Not created from the Hierat, but wild and natural in some strange way. He'd only been able to perceive it for a short time, seconds at most, before the nausea was overwhelming, but he'd seen the complex pattern under its surface.

He remembered wondering what it would be like to reach out and touch the pattern. What would happen if he just plucked one of the strands inside the weave. Would it begin to unravel, like he'd pulled at a loose thread?

He shook his head to clear the blade's characters

from his thoughts. With the dagger held ahead of him he pushed the door open.

The doorway was low and he had to duck to step through it. There was a short drop to the floor and he almost slipped as his foot met a woven mat. His lantern swung as he corrected his balance and for an awful moment he thought that the family seated around the far table moved at his entrance. He had an apology ready before he realised that the lantern had only set their shadows swaying against the opposite wall and that the people were long dead.

The deep foundation meant the house was warm despite the cold hearth at its centre, and he lingered for a while to get some heat back into his veins. Since they'd arrived in the Middle March he could hardly remember being entirely dry.

He shuffled around the underside of the roof to avoid the debris of the family's former life and bent to examine the bodies.

Two women sat at opposite ends of the table with five children between them, mostly of teenage years or slightly younger, though he found it hard to tell with Karlans because of their absurd height. Three of the children slumped backwards against the wall behind them, while the other two had collapsed forward against the table, arms crossed under their heads like they'd decided to nap. The women were sat almost upright in their chairs as if they had died suddenly in conversation.

The bodies were withered down to the bone, their grey flesh smelling of nothing worse than the musty building around them. Their clothes were moth-eaten, but otherwise unharmed and nowhere on their exposed flesh did he see any injuries or obvious traces of disease. The table before them was coated with a layer of dust, undisturbed even by animal tracks. Except where the two children had fallen forward and knocked over their bowls, the table was set for a meal, the bowls filled with the dried remains of untouched food.

Good, he thought. *Let them rot.*

As soon as the thought crossed his mind he knew it was unworthy. He wanted to hate them. Karlans were invaders. They were blue-eyed killers. As a boy he'd feared them. Then he'd hated them.

On the road he'd encountered a Karlan family travelling in a wagon. Their group had been small. Two men, one young and one old, a woman and three children. They hadn't been aware of him hidden in the cover of trees and without knowing why he'd begun to stalk them.

He'd followed them for two days. Watched them struggle with their wagon on narrow tracks. Stared through the shadow of the forest as they'd talked around their campfires, all of them comfortable enough to laugh in a stolen land. Their children played without any of the fear a Cadogan child needed to survive.

On the third day he'd wandered too close and the

young man chased him off with a bow. After that they took turns keeping watch at night and he continued on his way, wondering why he had followed them, unsure of what he would've done if they hadn't discovered him.

The dead Karlans sitting around the table didn't look like invaders. They just looked like people, sitting down to a meal that would end up being their last. He didn't hate them then, not truly. All he felt was a cold horror that anyone should die in such an unnatural way.

He left the house and found similar scenes in every building he searched. Entire households gathered around uneaten meals. Men, women and children slumped in seats in the midst of some activity, or stretched out on the ground, heads cushioned against their arms. Even the livestock had died in their pens, dropping down where they'd stood. Every human and animal in the fort was dead, and from what he could see they had died around the same time, as if they had agreed to die all at once.

Everywhere he walked he stepped over the remains of lives abandoned before their natural end.

'What happened here?' he said.

He winced at the loudness of his own voice. The people of the fort didn't look like they'd been killed by anything except time, but he was wary of whatever murdered the men in the woods. After he'd searched the first house he crept between the others, clinging to their shadows. He clutched his lantern to his chest and drew his cloak over his body to shield it a little from view.

He regretted his decision to separate from Kenrig and decided he'd seen enough to know that nothing lived in that fort but them and their horses. He'd circled around to the other side of the fort and when he looked up at the longhouse the undamaged side of the building loomed black against the sky. He had time to wonder whether he should follow Kenrig into the building before light burst on the other side, bright enough to carry above the roof for a brief moment.

The hot flash faded as quickly as it appeared and the heavy silence covering the fort was thrown off by a scream of rage.

The scream deepened to guttural snarling. He heard stones scatter and bounce an instant before a dull impact heralded the crack of splintering wood.

He opened his mouth to shout but his voice escaped him. Dimly he was aware that he was afraid, but it seemed to him that he was observing someone else's fear as it locked his muscles in place. He watched the fear spread in his body with a strange detachment, as though he stood outside a house and watched through a window as fire raged inside it.

Move, he begged himself. *Do something.*

He looked down at himself, hoping that if he saw his legs he might command them to move, but he might as well have commanded the ground to drag him forward.

Kenrig's dagger was still clutched in his right hand. It trembled against his leg, its edges blurred by the vibration of his clenched fingers. He stared at the blade, seeing the characters moving in its surface.

There was a pattern to their seemingly random movements, a sequence that they followed without fail again and again in the few moments that he watched them. When he'd watched them before they'd seemed to move of their own accord, but he saw then that they were guided by a web of golden light so delicate he imagined he could simply pluck its strands apart.

A bright mote fell from the blade like a spark struck from molten metal. It landed against the fabric of his trousers, just above his knee and for the briefest instant he saw the shape of a character in the burning light. He blinked away its afterimage and yelped as fire caught in the fabric.

Pain broke through his paralysis as the small flame burned down to his skin. His lantern fell from his left hand as he swatted at the flame. He winced at the sight of pink flesh through the hole in his trousers, but he'd moved and that was all that mattered.

The sounds of a struggle shifted and he ran for the gate, hoping his inaction wouldn't prove fatal. He stowed the dagger in his belt and untied his sling, readying it with a clay shot. If he could help it he didn't want to get close to something that had torn four men apart with ease.

Without his lantern he ran near-blind through the fort, unable to hear above his own ragged breath. The road to the gate was littered with the debris of abandoned lives, but he kept his feet even as he stumbled and tripped.

He saw the shadow of the horses first, rearing as they strained at their reins. Before them, stark in sullied white rags, what looked like a man held Kenrig over its head with impossible strength. Kenrig struggled in the man's grip, but there was no contest between them.

Dandall spun his sling and let the clay shot fly, pulling a second from the pouch on his belt before the first hit. The first shot struck the man's leg where thick trails of black blood stained the trousers. The second shot impacted low on the man's broad back, near to his spine.

His grip loosened and Kenrig dropped to the ground. Her knees buckled, but her attacker held her up in a bear hug. The man's body blocked her from sight and Dandall aimed higher. His next shot struck above the man's ear, tearing a chunk of flesh with it.

The man turned, spinning Kenrig around to stand in front of him like a shield. Jagged teeth flashed in a bloodied face and his eyes met the black gleam of a predatory gaze. A reek of carrion followed as the man roared and Dandall paused the reloading of his sling to cover his nose and mouth against the nauseating stench.

A metal edge flickered in the corner of his eyes. Kenrig slipped an arm free enough to bring a dagger against the inside of the man's wrist. She sawed the blade, too weakly to have made an impact with an ordinary weapon. The man's skin burned under the slightest touch and as his arms flew wide the wound in his wrist left a trail of smoke in the air.

Kenrig twisted as she fell and landed on her back. Dandall could hear her choked gasps. Her feet tried to find purchase on the ground to push herself away and he moved to help her.

His eyes watered against the man's foul stink, but his aim was good as he slung another shot, drawing blood above the man's eyes. The man's blood ran as black and slow as tar, but distracted him enough for Kenrig to put a few feet between them.

Dandall rushed forward, releasing another shot as he ran. To his surprise the man retreated, backing away with an arm curled across his face. Kenrig rolled to her side and Dandall squatted beside her to hook his arms under her shoulders.

'Run,' he said, as she regained her feet. 'We have to run.'

She nodded and staggered toward the gate, her breath emerging in a hollow wheeze. Dandall turned toward her attacker. The man had stopped retreating and held both arms open, clawed fingers splayed out beside him.

Slowly, Dandall pushed his sling through the loop of his belt and drew Kenrig's dagger. He brought it in front of him, holding both arms in a guard over his chest the way she'd shown him. As he looked into the cracked gore streaked over the man's mottled face he was amazed that his hands had stopped trembling.

He blinked and the man was on him. Air brushed his skin as claws missed his eyes by a finger's breadth. He reeled back in surprise and without skill he thrust the dagger forward, saving himself from another attack.

The man took a single step back to avoid the dagger's point, his arm still raised overhead to deliver a blow that would have crushed Dandall's skull. His eyes never left the blade and Dandall kept it between them, realising the man's fear of it was the only chance he had.

He took a step to the side, angling his back toward the horses and the man mirrored his movement. There was silence between them as they watched each other and Dandall could hear Kenrig working to untie the horses. He wanted to turn and run for Kelpie, but didn't dare remove his eyes from the man.

He barely saw the next attack coming. The man dropped his raised hand and struck upward, forcing Dandall to pull back his arm to protect himself. He caught the attack on his elbow and couldn't help but close his eyes as his arm was forced against his body and pain flared in his hip.

With the dagger out of his way, the man stepped in close and struck with his other hand. Claws glanced over his collarbone, parting the skin without effort.

The man's foul mass loomed over him and he gagged as the feel of blood soaking his shirt set his head spinning. He pressed the dagger against the man's chest, but his arm was numb from blocking the first blow and he couldn't feel whether he'd driven it hard enough.

He opened his eyes and saw the blade embedded just below the man's ribs. He'd pushed it in all the way to the hilt, but only a thin stream of viscous blood trickled from the wound and the flesh around it didn't burn. A moment passed between them as they each understood the blade was harmless.

Dandall threw himself backwards, still holding the dagger in front of himself as the man charged, bearing him to the ground.

The road beneath them was slick and they slipped apart, the man's speed carrying him clear over Dandall's head. Dandall dragged himself over into a crouch. He was only a short distance from the gate, but the man was hunched on all fours in the road, blocking his escape.

Kenrig had freed Stoic from the hitching post. The horse bucked under her the moment she was in the saddle. He reared high on his hind legs and as he dropped down she was thrown forward. Her head struck his neck and she lay limp against him, her arm caught in his harness. Dandall couldn't do anything as Stoic bolted, clearing the gate with Kenrig across his back.

The man was distracted by the fleeing horse and Dandall took his chance to run. Mud dragged at his boots and it only took two steps to know he was too slow. The man sprang like a wild dog, digging his hands into the mud to gain traction. He caught Dandall in a single leap and they crashed against the wall of a house.

Dandall felt the old boards of the wall buckling as the man drove him against it. The man gripped him by his collar and pressed him back, one arm enough to overpower him. The other arm was drawn back, fingers poised in a wedge at a level to punch through his throat. He grabbed the man's wrist with his free hand, knowing he couldn't hope to hold it for long.

In desperation he felt for the magic in the dagger, willing it to work. He found it faster than he ever had before, his desperation lending him the necessary focus. Inside the blade the Hieratic characters were sluggish, listlessly drifting along the frayed weave that dictated their pattern.

In his earlier fear he'd plucked one of the characters from the blade and in removing that single character he had rendered the blade's magic entirely useless.

He couldn't breathe against the pressure pinning his chest. His grip on the man's wrist seemed far too feeble and he closed his eyes, not wanting to see the attack that would kill him. Sparks burst behind his eyelids as blood rushed from his head and he remembered how his leg had burned when the character fell from the blade.

He'd imagined himself reaching out and gently plucking it free from the pattern it followed, but as he aimed the point of the dagger toward the man's face he wanted to free them all at once. He didn't picture himself pulling at them one by one, delicately freeing them from the pattern, he imagined them scattered from the pattern like dust motes blown by a breath.

New lights burst across his eyelids and he opened them to the sight of dozens of tiny embers catching against the man's skin. The outline of the characters burned briefly in each flaming mote, their edges blurring like ink running across wet paper. The man's skin sizzled as the embers grew into flames and the pressure left Dandall's chest so suddenly he almost fell.

The man's hands flew to his face and neck as he tried to stifle the rapidly growing flame. His palms came away smoking and scorched. Dandall skirted past him and sprinted before he could learn what damage the flames would do.

Kelpie strained against the rotten wood restraining her. The post creaked and bent under her efforts, bulging around the knotted loop of her reins. She'd drawn the reins so tightly against the wood that he couldn't work his shaking fingers in to untie them and the dagger was too fragile to saw through leather.

He stepped back from the post and threw his weight behind a kick. The post weakened under his heel as he kicked again and again, enough that Kelpie's efforts finally snapped it. Wood splinters flew out towards her and he lunged, managing to grab her reins before she could abandon him. He propelled himself from the ruined post and into her saddle.

He let her follow her instinct to flee and they ran from the fort, leaving the howls of rage to fade into the distance.

17

The Nature of the Enemy

Kelpie didn't acknowledge his commands until they were far from the fort where the road met the cliffs. His lantern lay abandoned somewhere in the fort and clouds blocked out all other light, so once Kelpie was calm enough he dismounted and led her as far as he dared down the first cliff. The road levelled off for a short distance and he drew Kelpie into a nook of overhanging rock to wait for dawn.

He didn't sleep much in the hours that passed and when he did sleep it was unintentional, sneaking up on him when his tired mind was distracted. Kelpie was skittish, perhaps taking her cues from his own fear, but she didn't startle and he hoped that meant they weren't being pursued.

He clutched Kenrig's dagger to his chest for comfort, though after he'd expelled all of its magic it wasn't much use to him. Maybe if he managed to drive it into the man's brain or heart it might be enough, but he had no idea what he'd faced in the fort. Only Kenrig would know what that man was.

Waiting for daylight to search for her was torture, but he had no hope of finding her in the dark. All he'd accomplish trying to navigate the cliffs in the dark would be a broken neck. He didn't know how badly she was injured, but she'd been breathing when he'd last seen her. He tried not to dwell on the thought of Stoic fleeing over the edge of the road, but he had nothing to occupy his mind except pain.

He could feel bruises spreading across his chest where he'd been pinned, no doubt as big as those that mottled his attacker's body, but he could breathe freely and didn't think anything was broken. His worst pain came from his collarbone and shoulder where the man's claws had scraped long gouges. He could feel his pulse pounding under the injured flesh and didn't want to acknowledge how close those claws had come to hitting something vital.

Without light he couldn't investigate the wounds except to probe their edges with his fingers, but he managed to peel his bloodied shirt from his body to clean them. Tears pricked his eyes by the time his shirt was off and flowed freely across his cheeks as he emptied his waterskin over the wounds.

Dawn was dull and grey when it arrived, but it was a relief to see it. He rubbed at his stinging eyes and stood with effort, his muscles stiff from the cold and his clothes wet from the damp air where they weren't caked with blood.

After looking at his wounds in the daylight he had no stomach for breakfast and set off with Kelpie immediately to avoid thinking about them. The grass covering the path was slick so he led Kelpie all the way down to the edge of the forest. He kept careful watch for tracks, but saw none other than those he and Kenrig had left the previous day.

The shadows dwelling in the forest hadn't been diminished by the arrival of dawn and he was struck by the enormity of finding a lone person in that wilderness.

'Okay, Kelpie,' he said. 'If she's in the forest she had to come down the cliffs.'

He scanned the line of trees stretching east and west for miles. 'So we should search along the cliffs, right?'

He climbed back into the saddle more gingerly than when he'd fled the fort. His arm pained him, but he wasn't sure if it was pain or revulsion at the wounds which made him hesitant to use it. Lacking any other plan he set off west through the forest, skirting its edge so that he could keep the line of the cliffs in sight.

He wanted to shout in the hope that Kenrig would hear him, but he was afraid to make too much noise in that place. The trees dampened all sound and even the birds refused to break that silence with their songs. He had no reason to believe he was safe from pursuit and kept his mouth shut.

The sun climbing higher into the sky brought mist from the cold shadows. He huddled into his cloak against the chill and kept his eyes down as he searched. His attention faltered after an hour of riding, his mind too exhausted to hold his focus, and in the end it was Kenrig who found him.

Her appearance on the path was sudden enough that he startled and had to wrestle Kelpie back under his control.

'You look as bad as I feel,' she said.

She leaned heavily against a tree, her face drawn and pale. She'd removed her armour and he could see her clothes were dark with sweat. Dandall dismounted and she took Kelpie's reins so that she could support herself against the mare's shoulder. Her breaths were laboured and their progress deeper into the forest was slow.

'Thought I'd retrace Stoic's steps,' she said. 'And hope to find you on his trail. The effort was more than I expected.'

She looked at the dense patch of blood clotted on his shirt. 'How bad is it?'

He raised his arm carefully. 'I'm scared to look at it again.'

Stoic's flight had eventually ended in a moss-covered space just large enough to be called a clearing. He looked up as they arrived then returned to grazing.

Kenrig sat Dandall down on a fallen tree. As she searched for a needle and thread he removed his cloak one-handed and eased his shirt over his head. He caught sight of his wounds and the swollen, pink flesh crusted brown and yellow that surrounded them. Suddenly he was glad he hadn't eaten.

Kenrig built a fire with dried pine needles as her kindling and emptied the last of their water into a dented pot. When the fire was large enough she set the pot on a stand above it to boil. She worked slowly and coughed whenever she hunched her back, but she refused his help.

Once the water had boiled she stood behind him to clean his neck with a cloth. She was tender, but he winced and gritted his teeth as the near scalding water ran into the wounds.

'They're shallow,' she said between heavy breaths. 'Look worse than they are. You were smart to clean them though. Who knows what filth those claws carried.'

'What is he?' Dandall asked. 'He can't have been *human*, right?'

'He was. Once, anyway. What he is now...I have some theories.'

As she slowly wiped the dried blood from around his wounds she relayed the story of the man, Morgen, and the betrayal that had led to his death. Dandall shuddered as water ran down his naked back.

'So was he ever truly dead?' he asked.

'I suspect he was. For a time at least, though he wouldn't have been truly dead if even a portion of his spirit remained with the body.'

She threw the bloodied cloth into the flames. Goosebumps pimpled his skin as he watched her place a hooked needle at the edge of the fire.

'Violent or traumatic deaths can sometimes leave a

spirit lingering with a body,' she said over her shoulder. 'Sometimes they move on without help and sometimes they become trapped in-between this world and the next, unable to either travel to the Otherworld or enter their body again.'

She watched the needle as it began to glow red hot. 'More rarely a spirit lingers inside its body. In those cases the body's connection to the Otherworld is strengthened in some way and that gives rise to creatures, usually humanoid but sometimes animals, able to exceed their body's previous abilities in a horrifyingly diverse number of ways. The nature of the individual in life and the nature of their death can tell us some of what we need to know to identify them.'

Dandall remembered Morgen's speed against which he may as well have been standing still. Across his bruised chest he could almost feel the crushing strength, so powerful he couldn't have opposed it if he had been even three times as strong.

'From what you told me, the king was a warrior,' he said. 'A powerful one.'

'Cruel and ambitious too. It's not much, but we also know how he died, what he's done since he returned and, to our mutual detriment, what's he's physically capable of. That's enough to speculate.'

Speculate? he thought. *You speculated about what killed my father and we nearly died putting it down.* He left his thoughts unvoiced. He was too tired to argue.

She picked up the glowing needle and dropped it into the empty pot to cool. 'He's fast enough to be an *erkling*,' she said. 'Though far too strong.'

She rose, producing a spool of cord from a pocket, and walked behind him once more, the needle poised in her good hand. 'Hold still. I mean it, I can barely sew a button.'

She didn't give him a chance to tense his muscles before she pushed the needle through the edge of the wound closest to his neck. For a few seconds he couldn't do anything more than screw his eyes closed and hiss through his teeth. Afterward he realised Kenrig had continued speaking.

'I've never heard of a male *baobhan sith* before, so maybe we can eliminate that. He could be a *lierg*. He was strong and had at least some intelligence left, but as far as I know they only kill for the challenge, never to feed themselves.'

He was grateful for the distraction her speculation provided. The needle she used to close his wounds felt like it was as wide as the claws that had opened his flesh in the first place.

'He definitely wasn't a *hulderkall*,' she continued. 'He'd have tried to seduce me into surrendering if he was.'

She must have sensed his bemusement. 'I'm not joking.'

While she slowly stitched his neck back together down to his collarbone she rattled off a bewildering list of creatures, every name introducing him to fresh strangeness. When they'd first met, Kenrig had never faced anything like the creatures she described, but it was clear to him how much she had learned in the years that followed. He supposed that was why he'd stuck around.

'A *haugr*?' she said, her needle pausing for a moment. 'He didn't rise for twenty years, not until his grave was disturbed. He's strong, fast, got a good appetite and he gathers all of his prey somewhere familiar...terrible conversationalist too. Fine, *haugr* is my best guess.'

'So you know how to kill him?' Dandall managed through gritted teeth.

The needle plunged under his skin again. 'Decapitation is always good. Decapitation, burn the body and bury the head, preferably at a crossroads. If you're ever in any doubt, that's always a good place to start.'

She finished stitching and wrapped his neck and shoulder with clean linen. 'There we are, now we've got two good arms between us.'

The day had dimmed around them and he shivered. He found a stream a short way into the forest and soaked some of the blood from his shirt, the effort made awkward with the use of only one hand. When he returned he hung it from a branch to dry before settling by the fire bundled into his cloak.

Kenrig sat against a tree, unable to suppress a groan as she struggled to the ground. She held her eyes closed long enough that he wondered if she'd fallen asleep.

'Thank you, Dandall,' she said.

Her voice was a sigh hardly loud enough to carry over the crackle of the fire. 'I haven't been a good mentor to you and I didn't trust you when I should've. You're young, and I used that as an excuse not to take you seriously.'

'I understand,' he said. 'I made mistakes. Bad ones.'

She opened her eyes and he saw the irises, pale enough to be almost grey, wavering. 'Mistakes aren't a problem exclusive to youth. If you learn something from them, that's what matters.'

He poked at the base of the fire with a stick to dispel some of the awkwardness he felt. Neither of them had spoken like that before.

'Do you think Lissi will be okay?'

'I hope so. As cruel as they are, the Unseelie have a strange honour. I believe they'll keep their word not to harm her.'

Dandall's jaw worked back and forth as though his next words were stuck between his teeth. 'I shouldn't have let her pass me. She shouldn't be in that place.'

Kenrig's eyes seemed piercing to him and he couldn't meet them. 'I shouldn't have judged you as harshly as I did. You shouldn't judge yourself harshly either. You want to make things right, don't you?'

He nodded. 'But I don't know how.'

'After tonight we have three days to try.'

The fire spat as he added more fuel. 'Why did they

give you a week? Why not give you less time and make it impossible to banish them?'

She rubbed a hand over her brow. 'I've asked myself the same questions.'

She looked up and he knew she was looking for the moon. He'd seen her staring at it as they'd travelled to Orveng.

'I can guess as to why they only gave me a week. They're powerful spirits, but that means they ordinarily can't stay here for long. A week might be as long as they can hold themselves here without drawing strength from the people of Karstend. The full moon comes not long after our deadline, if they can persist until then...I'm not sure we could force them to leave.'

She shrugged. 'As to why they gave me as long as a week, I'm less sure. Their reason for being here in this world is to find entertainments lacking in the Otherworld. When I challenged them I think they accepted out of boredom. Maybe they're gambling what time they believe they can spare against the prospect of more entertainment.'

Dandall followed her gaze to the darkening sky. 'Can they see us?'

'It wouldn't surprise me.'

He looked down again to see her eyes were closed as she leaned her back against the tree.

'If we kill Morgen,' he said. 'Will it really be enough? Are they actually here because of him?'

'I can't know it for sure, but we have nothing else.' She sighed. 'I can't believe the timing is coincidental. His power was great enough to drain the life of everyone in Orveng while he waited in his grave. When those boys from Karstend dug him up he started killing and claimed dozens of lives in a matter of weeks.'

She shook her head. 'I believe he's responsible for drawing the Unseelie here, but there were no victims for them in Orveng, or anywhere else nearby thanks to him, so they had to conjure their feast elsewhere. And Karstend was once part of the same kingdom. It isn't anymore, but those old borders still matter. If we can kill him before the full moon, I think we have a chance.'

'I hope you're right,' he said. 'We don't have enough time to try anything else.'

'Maybe desperation will inspire us,' she said before yawning. 'Right now I'm going to sleep. You can take the first watch, my eyes haven't uncrossed from sewing you back together.'

She drew her cloak around her body like a blanket and within moments she was snoring quietly.

'I suppose I have no say in the matter,' he muttered.

He doubted he could have slept anyway. The pain in his neck had settled from the raw, sharp agony of the open wounds to a tight ache. He was acutely aware of the pulse throbbing under his skin and how the stitched cord seemed to stretch with every beat.

He was painfully awake, and couldn't stop his mind

from wandering. His injury reminded him of the very real and physical danger posed by the undead king, but his thoughts dwelled instead on the spectres of the Unseelie.

He hadn't seen them, only listened as Kenrig relayed her experiences inside the unearthly feast. Some of what she'd described fit with the stories his grandmother had told, stories he'd dismissed as fantasy not so long ago, and some of it was stranger still. He'd thought he knew what life at Kenrig's side would entail, but he was realising how little he understood.

The presence of the Otherworld had often been an intangible comfort to him. He'd imagined his mother watching him from the other side of the moon's veil. He'd never known her, not that he could remember, and his image of her was pieced together from what little his father would tell him. In his imagination she'd only ever been half-real, her features beautiful but hard to discern, like looking at someone standing with the sun behind them.

He'd never known her, but he'd felt her absence keenly and it was through his belief in the Otherworld that he'd soothed the ache of that absence. When his father had died, he'd consoled himself with the thought that they were reunited, that his mother had waited patiently beyond the veil for her husband's spirit to join her in that place of souls.

He'd found it difficult to reconcile the comfort he felt from his belief in the Otherworld with the existence of cruel spectres within its borders. Through the dark canopy above he could see the first traces of the moon's lambent glow, but he found no comfort in seeing it then. He shuffled closer to the fire, immersing himself in its wavering aura until its heat was uncomfortable and he sweated under his cloak.

A howl disturbed his thoughts. The sound echoed strangely in the dense forest and he wondered if he might have imagined it. He looked up from the flames, his night vision ruined by the light. Stoic and Kelpie stood undisturbed and he stopped watching the darkness before his eyes had adjusted.

The second howl was unmistakable. It sounded closer than the first though he didn't trust his ears. He moved away from the fire and knelt with it at his back. His cloak slipped from his shoulders and his skin pimpled in the sudden chill. The irregular noise of the forest fell silent and he realised he was holding his breath.

He loaded his sling. He doubted a lone wolf or even a pack would approach their fire, but he was worried they'd attack the horses at the edge of the camp.

The next howl was cut short, strangled into a high whimper. A moment of stillness passed before the silence broke into a frenzy of barking. He couldn't tell how many wolves there were, but they were scattered through the forest. Their savage cries were silenced one by one and he followed the sweep of the pack's destruction in a wide arc.

The last wolf fought harder and elicited a scream of pain before it was killed in turn. He stiffened at the scream, hearing the human voice in its echo. *Morgen.*

He crept around the fire and knelt beside Kenrig. She woke slowly, her exhaustion clear in the dull glaze filming her eyes. Dimly, he remembered how she'd nearly gutted him with her falchion the last time he'd woken her by surprise.

She struggled upright with his help and together they listened as the final wolf died slowly, its suffering drawn out with pained whimpers. Bone snapped and flesh tore in the quiet that followed.

Kenrig stamped out their fire and in darkness they readied the horses, fleeing before the king's feast was done.

18

Hunting Ground

Kenrig felt like she'd been rolled down a cliff. Bruising closed around her ribs and spread across her back, making every breath seem too short. The movement of Stoic under her made her bones rattle like they'd been knocked loose.

She distracted herself from her pain with the dagger Dandall had returned to her.

'What do you mean 'broken'?' she asked.

He rode alongside her on the flooded track. Kelpie stepped quickly to keep pace with Stoic, her hooves kicking muddy droplets up onto their boots.

Dandall shrugged. 'I don't know. Broken. The magic is gone.'

It didn't take her long to confirm that what he said was true. Pain, fatigue and movement all combined to let her focus shift with ease. The blade's edges bled silver under the grey dawn blurred like ink run off a wet page, the deeper metal entirely blank.

'How did this happen?'

Dandall swatted a fly from his ear. The persistent creatures followed them everywhere they went in the clogged fields, but he seemed to be singularly affected by them.

'I'm not sure I can explain it,' he said, his brow creasing. 'Before I found you, when you were fighting Morgen at the gate, there was a moment when I was too scared to move. I could barely feel my own body, but the dagger...I sensed it. The way you taught me to.'

She didn't interrupt him with questions, though she had more than enough of them chasing each other through her head.

'It seemed so simple,' he said after a breath. 'So easy to just pull one of the characters out of the metal. It was like...pulling on a thread, or...tearing a pattern. And, I guess, that's what happened. One of them fell onto my leg and burned me.'

He pointed to the bandoleer across her chest, to the two remaining daggers not lost, given away or damaged.

'I saw you hurt him with one of them,' he said. 'So I thought I could too. But the dagger didn't work. Not the way it was meant to. I guessed I'd broken it when I took the character out. Then when he had me pinned I didn't know what else to do, so I pushed out all of the characters. They burned him and I ran.'

Kenrig turned the blade over, unsure what she was hoping to see. Removing a single character from a Hieratic object was difficult enough with practice, but removing them all, without training, would have been impossible if she'd considered it even a few minutes earlier.

'Is that normal?' Dandall asked. 'You could do that too, right?'

She stowed the dagger in the bandoleer, sliding it into the pouch furthest from the others.

'With enough time,' she said. 'And if no one was trying to kill me.' She shook her head. 'So no, it's not normal.'

Dandall was quiet for a time. 'What does it mean? How did I do that?'

'I'm not a mystic, but I do know that even a highly-trained mystic couldn't repeat what you did. Not that I know of, anyway. I'd have to ask my own mentor for a clear answer.'

Now would be a good time to appear, Garnham. She'd already wanted to ask her mentor about Dandall and his connection to Lissi's prophecy, but her new apprentice had surprised her yet again.

'You should get some sleep,' she suggested.

The boy looked half-dead. She felt awful enough after snatching a couple of hours sleep while he was on watch so she knew he felt even worse. He stared ahead, a distant look in his eyes, and simply nodded at her suggestion.

She took Kelpie's reins from him and led both horses as he slumped in his saddle, his hood covering his eyes against the brightening day. Eventually, his breathing softened and his head lolled against his chest.

Asleep in the saddle he looked so ordinary. His face was young enough to be almost hairless and although he was taller than when she'd first met him he was just as scrawny. He didn't look like the subject of prophecy, nor the possessor of an unusual power.

She breathed and pushed any thought of prophecy aside. She looked past Dandall as a turn in the track brought the forest in view again. The forest was a few hours distant, but nothing taller than a fencepost stood in the intervening miles.

Morgen hadn't followed them into the fields though his pursuit through the forest had been relentless. In the sheer darkness they'd been unable to ride at speed and he'd kept pace with them all night. They hadn't seen him behind the cover of the trees, but he'd made no secret of his presence. He'd charged after them without exhaustion, tearing through the trees beside their path and growling loud enough to frighten the horses.

They'd kept ahead of him enough to clear the tree line before dawn and rode until they were sure he hadn't followed them any further. Whether he was reluctant to leave the cover of the trees or didn't hunt during the day, they'd taken the chance to let the horses recover and keep a careful watch behind them.

The flooded fields provided Morgen with few places to hide, but it had taken a long time before she could relax.

Afterward Dandall had revealed the inert dagger to her, compounding her fear that the king was too powerful for them to kill before the week was up. Unconsciously, her hand fidgeted with the remaining daggers, to reassure her that they were still there and to focus her mind as she made plans with their dwindling time.

If he didn't pursue them beyond the forest they'd need to turn back and hunt him in turn. If he continued his pursuit, and she hoped that he would, then she intended to catch him in a trap.

At dusk they found shelter in a gutted cottage. The building's windows were too narrow to pass through and entrance was only possible through a single door. The roof was partially collapsed, but intact enough to keep them dry as rain broke in the night.

'I never knew how much two horses could stink,' Dandall said. 'You don't notice when you're outside.'

There wasn't room for Stoic and Kelpie beneath the remains of the roof and the two horses stood under the slow drizzle. The stench of wet horse hair helped to distract them from their desire for a warm meal. Kenrig wanted to be sure Morgen was following them, but didn't want a fire to give them away completely.

'With a little luck he'll be too distracted to sniff us out,' she said.

The cottage sat on a low rise that overlooked the fields draped across its western slope. The fields had been left fallow before they were abandoned and only weeds grew in the quagmire. Water cascaded in rivulets down to the paths below, reflecting the violet light of an approaching storm.

Kenrig stood in the shadow of a narrow window as she watched the crossroads between three paths. There she'd piled the last of their meat ration raised up on stones to keep it out of the shallow water. The meat was bait but not for Morgen.

'Now we know dogs were following us at least,' Dandall muttered.

Five dogs detached themselves from the shadow of a wall. In the strange brightness of the evening their bodies were clearly visible, distorted by starvation and scarred with disease. While the leader of the pack ate first, the other four fell into a violent quarrel, yapping, barking and whining as they disputed their hierarchy.

'That's right,' she said. 'Make plenty of noise.'

Dark clouds blossomed like bruises across the sky while they watched the dogs eat, slowly covering the evening light. The air pressed uncomfortably close and a few miles distant the first note of thunder growled low along the horizon.

Dandall's stomach whined in response. 'I hope the dogs are enjoying my dinner, at least.'

The dogs were reduced to dim shades in the early night, but she could see them startle at the sound of thunder before they continued eating.

They made short work of the meat and she worried they would slink off before Morgen showed, but her concern was quickly eased. Food in their stomachs only served to fuel their aggression.

Consumed by their own struggle they didn't notice Morgen stalking them. Veins of lightning burst in the clouds and in their brief flashes she saw the king, eyes gleaming with storm light. The dogs confronted him too late and the starving pack provided little sport.

'What now?' Dandall asked.

'Now,' she said. 'We need a trap.'

*

The villagers watched from the shelter of the hall's windows to see what had become of their saviours. Only Ida, Lymann and Daglan braved the rain to meet Kenrig and Dandall at the edge of the mystic barrier. They left the hall wrapped in heavy cloaks, carrying lanterns against the early morning gloom.

Rain sizzled and steamed against the inlaid metal, a good sign that the barrier still held. The trio approached the barrier warily and stopped well short of it.

'Sorry to wake you,' Kenrig said.

'You didn't,' Ida said. 'Few of us have found peace in sleep of late.'

The three of them had regained some of the colour and strength they'd lost to the Unseelie feast, but their eyes sat dark and hollow. They slumped under the rain as if even the weight of the water was too much to bear.

'Please tell us you brought good news,' Lymann said. 'Can we leave this prison?'

'Some,' Kenrig said. 'Though I wouldn't expect to enjoy it. I have bad news as well.'

Lymann closed his eyes and breathed as if bracing himself. 'We've had little enough hope since you left. We had doubts you would even return, so for you to stand here and deliver any news is welcome, at the very least.'

'We hoped to return sooner and with a happier story,' she said. 'But our trip to Orveng was more complicated than I expected.'

'Our missing lads aren't with you,' Daglan said, looking past her. 'Can we assume they're dead?'

She nodded. 'And the creature that killed them is the root of your current problems.'

She didn't want to burden them with a long tale under the elements and relayed the story of the journey and subsequent flight from Orveng as quickly as she could. They looked tired enough to lie down and give up like the Karlans of the fort, but they listened patiently. Their faces were stoic and the new horrors she revealed to them only seemed to harden their expressions.

'And killing this creature, this king, will drive out the Unseelie?' Ida asked.

'If we can kill him,' Kenrig said. 'And keep you out of the Unseelie's hands. Then the powers that brought them here, and keep them here, should both fade.'

'*Should?*' Lymann asked. 'We need better than *should.*'

Kenrig met his gaze. 'I'd love to offer you certainty, but I can't. There are no easy answers when the Otherworld is involved.'

'There isn't time left for doubt,' he said.

She regarded each of them in turn. 'I can't guarantee you that what we try will succeed, but you're right that there isn't time left for doubt. Doing nothing will have the same outcome as failure, but personally I'd rather run the risk of failure and take a chance of success than do nothing.'

Ida looked down at her feet. 'Hope has been in short supply,' she said. 'We've found it difficult to *do nothing* as you say. We've had no sign of either of you for five days. And some of us...'

Ida swept her hand to the eastern end of the hall. In the cover of an empty wood store six graves had been dug. Scrapped wooden boards marked the head of each mound. One of the graves was too small for an adult.

'Some of us didn't recover from that nightmare,' she said. 'We wanted to give them a proper funeral at the summit of the Fell. Let the carrion birds clean their bones before they were buried. But we couldn't even do that much for them.'

When Ida's voice broke, Lymann took up her story. 'No one has left the barrier yet,' he said. 'But some are wondering why they should trap themselves in the hall if the outcome will be the same. They argue that we should spend our remaining time in our own homes.'

Kenrig nodded her head in understanding. 'If anyone wants to cross the barrier then send them my way,' she said. 'I need volunteers to help me set a trap.'

'A trap?' he asked. 'Do you intend to bring this Morgen creature here? You want to bring another monster to our doorstep?'

'I do. And I'm willing to bet your people will be glad to do something to help themselves.'

'What do you need from us?' Daglan asked before Lymann could protest.

'Killing a creature like him isn't easy. We need to decapitate him and burn his body. For that he'll need to be restrained.'

She turned and surveyed the flat ground in front of the hall. 'We'll need a pit and dry wood, plenty of it. Oil as well if you have it. Do you have bows? And anyone that can hit a moving target?'

'Aye,' Daglan said. 'A few of each, but what-'

She turned again and faced him. 'From you specifically I need something else. Dandall will help you heat your forge.'

Dandall seemed surprised to hear his name. 'I will?' he asked. 'Why?' He grunted as she pressed a pouch of silver coins to his chest. 'What-'

'I need to bury his head at a crossroads,' she said. 'And I don't think an ordinary one will suffice.'

Ida cleared her throat. 'The Parting Hill,' she said. 'South of here. It's where the first Karlan settlers eventually separated to found their holds. You could reach it in time, if you ride fast.'

'The Parting Hill it is then.'

Kenrig looked back toward Karstend's main gate. 'All that's left is bait and I know someone daft enough to volunteer.'

19

Decapitation

Dandall stepped across the barrier to join the villagers massed outside the hall. There was a pressure in the air as he crossed it, a slight resistance pushing against him like he was passing through a delicate curtain. The air on the other side was heavy and stale, the atmosphere of a room holding too many bodies.

The barrier did nothing to stop the gentle drizzle of rain, but inside its threshold the moisture was stifling. Within moments he could feel sweat clinging beneath his clothes from the humid warmth. He already felt disgusting after days in the saddle, but he wasn't prepared for the smell of unwashed bodies that greeted him inside the barrier.

Daglan followed him across. 'Oaft, that's ripe,' the smith said. 'My apologies. We've been short on water. And privacy.'

Dandall wrinkled his nose. 'No need to apologise. The thought of a hot bath is what's giving me courage.'

The smith managed a faint chuckle. 'You and me both.'

He stepped up beside Dandall and held out a cloth pouch. 'I hope your master is right about this.'

Dandall took the pouch and pulled open the drawstring. Inside it was a handful of silver balls, equally sized and weighted for his sling. The shots had been fashioned from the silver coins Kenrig had given him, melted down and mixed with steel into a harder alloy.

'If the Unseelie come after us,' Kenrig had said. 'They won't just be manifesting in an extension of their own world, they'll be manifesting here. Silver can sometimes weaken a spirit's hold, so maybe it will weaken their presence here as well. I wish I didn't have to guess.'

He removed one of the shots and held it up to the light of the grey evening. 'I hope so too,' he said.

Despite the rain, the villagers taking part in the trap had gathered outside of the hall to be ready at a moment's notice. He and Kenrig hadn't been sure how many people it would take to overpower Morgen, so they'd gathered the strongest men and women together. There were eighteen of them, armed with crude spears and ropes tied into lassoes. Behind them on the hall's front steps, five men stood fidgeting with short hunting bows.

Dandall turned away from the group and stood by the barrier. He was uncomfortable with the way that they looked at him. With Kenrig absent they relied on him to answer their questions or offer reassurances about her plan and his inability to do either of those things made him feel like an imposter.

The gap between his experience and hers was enormous, vast enough that he didn't think he'd ever be able to equal her knowledge. Earlier, he'd wanted freedom from her to prove that he was still worthy of trust, but with the eyes of the village boring into his back he just wanted her to stand beside him and remove any burden of responsibility.

It was her knowledge and her plan that they relied on. If she didn't return, if Morgen caught her before she could reach the village, he was certain that he couldn't do anything to banish the Unseelie in her stead. He hadn't even seen the Unseelie. He didn't know what they were capable of.

If they appeared before him to take the villagers, would he be able to do anything against them or would he be forced to watch as the villagers were dragged away to be tortured and killed? Would he see Lissi again before she died, or had his mistake already cost her life?

He kept his back turned to the hall and rolled two of the silver shots around in his hand to try and hide how scared he felt. The clack of metal against metal did a little to soothe his fears, but he could feel the beginning of a breathless panic growing in his chest.

He paced for a time, then thought better of it knowing the villagers were watching him. He glanced back at them and saw some of his own fear reflected in their nervous shifting.

Above them the summit of the Fell looked entirely ordinary, a sight that didn't reassure him. If there was some obvious sign of the Unseelie's presence, a clear marker to show that something unnatural had made its way into their world, he believed that would be a greater comfort than no sign at all. It unnerved him to think of creatures like them going so easily unnoticed.

He had to force himself not to shift his weight or tap his feet. He held his hands under his arms to keep them from fidgeting and flexed his feet to keep them from them tapping out an irregular rhythm. He wanted to seem confident to the villagers, but was sure they saw how much he was shaking, even when he tried to hold himself still.

He knew how they must see him. He was a boy, barely old enough to be a man, who wanted to stay hidden in his master's shadow.

He knelt when the trembling of his legs was too much. He stayed a few feet from the barrier, not wanting to come close enough to clearly see the pattern melted into the earth.

The symbols strained at their iron forms and he knew that if he allowed himself he could free them without second thought. Even out of sight he knew its pattern in a way that he couldn't have understood if he studied it by sight alone. The air was charged with their power and he heard their meanings like the hum of conversation within a crowd.

He couldn't compose his own spells from unstructured script, but he could feel how each symbol worked in cooperation with its neighbours, how they were divided into groups to coordinate their effects. It was like listening to a language he understood, but couldn't speak.

He was so focused on tuning out the noise of the magic that he nearly missed the signal from someone behind him.

'There!' they shouted. 'Look, there she is!'

He scanned the western fields, surprised that he could fail to spot anyone in the flat expanse. Movement eventually caught his eye and he watched as Kenrig rode hard for the village. When she reached the gate she wheeled Stoic around and stared back along her path.

He followed her line of sight, straining his eyes to find any sign of Morgen. His approach was obscured beneath the heavy cloud ringing the horizon, but there was no mistaking him. The shadow of a man, loping on all fours like an animal.

Kenrig didn't pause as she drove Stoic up the steps to the hall. The heavy beast barely slowed as he mounted the slope and his momentum carried them over the barrier.

Kenrig eased herself from the saddle, as breathless as if she had run the entire distance on foot. While someone tied Stoic alongside Kelpie at the hall's eastern end she drew her falchion and joined Dandall. Her face was flushed and glistening with sweat.

'Did you enjoy the fresh air?' he asked.

'It was invigorating,' she said between breaths. 'The past few days have done wonders for my health.'

Morgen sprinted through the gate only a few minutes behind her. He slowed his pace as he crossed the threshold and rose to his full height. From the villagers Dandall heard muttered oaths.

When he didn't move to approach the hall, Kenrig walked toward the barrier.

'Come on,' she said, pausing behind the iron symbols. 'I'm right here.'

He paced just inside the door, head cocked as he scented the air. He moved cautiously into the village, searching among the dark homes with mirror-bright eyes.

'The barrier,' Dandall said. 'Maybe he can't sense us?'

Testing his theory, Kenrig stepped outside of the barrier. For a moment, she went unnoticed. Morgen's head turned slowly in their direction, twitching as it followed Kenrig's scent. When he caught sight of her stood on the hill he dropped to all fours again and charged, pounding the earth beneath his knuckles.

'You were right!' she shouted over her shoulder.

She waited until he'd reached the base of the stairs, baiting him, before she retreated across the barrier. She stood facing him down with her falchion drawn, the blade steady in her hands.

Dandall wanted to emulate her confidence, but the iron symbols etched into the ground seemed like scant protection against the charging monster. He could feel power filling the air around him and yet he couldn't help feeling they'd corralled themselves together for Morgen to slaughter at leisure. The villagers who'd trusted the barrier for days but never seen it tested must have shared his fear. As the undead king cleared the stairs, they retreated towards the hall.

Dandall braced himself as best he could, but couldn't help taking a step backward as Morgen struck the barrier head on, a handspan from the end of Kenrig's blade. He expected to see the king pass clear over the iron symbols and bear her to the ground, but the barrier held. His ears filled with deafening pressure as the air ahead of them suddenly grew dense enough that even Morgen's immense strength couldn't push through.

The king pushed against the invisible force holding him back, leaning his entire body against it. His feet pressed deep into the sodden ground, robbing him of purchase.

The barrier muffled his frustrated roar. Rain soaked his clothes, pressing them against his immense frame. The burns Dandall had inflicted hadn't healed and knotted in his neck and face like pale roots, tightening and twisting as he roared.

Kenrig side-stepped and shouted to the archers in the hall. 'Loose!'

Though he was only a few feet distant her voice sounded dull through the pressure in his ears. When no arrows followed her order she turned toward the hall and swept her falchion in an arc toward the king.

'Loose!'

Dandall didn't hear the first arrow pass him. In the time it took him to blink the arrow had embedded itself in the meat above Morgen's hip. The king didn't recoil, but straightened and looked down at the missile as though he didn't understand what he was seeing.

His apparent confusion lasted only a moment and he squared up facing the hall, clawed hands bared at his sides. The first shot broke any hesitation from the other archers and more arrows followed. Many of them missed, but enough found their marks deep in the muscle of his limbs.

'Bind him!' Kenrig shouted.

The villagers moved quickly to surround Morgen, hemming him in with spears as others threw ropes to bind his limbs.

Even pinned with arrows Morgen stayed on his feet and fought like a cornered animal. He caught the first lasso as it spun for his head and dragged its wielder from the circle. The man released the rope too late to stop his own stumbling momentum from carrying him onto Morgen's claws.

Dandall's clay shot struck Morgen high on the skull, staggering him. The man he'd pulled from the circle fell back, hands clutched to his side, and retreated past the line of villagers as they pressed forward. They punctured him with spears and looped ropes around his wrists and neck.

'Hold him steady!'

The villagers holding spears dropped their weapons and rushed to join their strength to the ropes. Three lines formed to hold the king in place, two stretching his arms wide and a third behind him pulling the rope tightening like a noose around his neck. Inch-by-inch the king drew his arms closer to his body, dragging half a dozen men and women toward him.

Dandall loosed clay shots into Morgen's knees, driving the king's legs out from under him. More villagers joined the ropes and steadily they drew the kneeling king's arms straight again.

Kenrig stalked around behind him and the villagers drew apart enough to give her room to swing. Morgen howled his outrage as she raised her blade high over her shoulder, the rope around his neck doing nothing to still his voice. He howled even as his head rolled to the ground.

*

Kenrig looped a gag through Morgen's mouth, muffling his head's continued screams. The tightly-rolled cloth didn't silence him, but it kept him quiet enough that Stoic didn't shy from the head.

'That's a relief,' Dandall muttered. 'Is he really going to scream the whole way?'

She shrugged. 'Maybe he'll get tired.'

The turf and wooden boards covering the pit outside the hall fell away with a dull thump. After some initial hesitation at seeing Morgen's headless body continue to fight, the villagers worked quickly to prepare the body for burning. Like the head, its strength hadn't been diminished after decapitation, but deprived of its senses it flailed without direction.

Even so, the villagers kept their distance, dragging the body at the end of their ropes. It dug its heels into the ground and lashed out at anyone that came close enough to touch it, but its efforts did nothing to save it from the pit.

Rain fell in a light drizzle, too weak to quench the fire already raging deep within the ground. The villagers dragging the body split into two teams on either side of the pit and lowered the body toward the climbing flames.

'Don't stop until the body is ash!' Kenrig shouted as she mounted Stoic. 'Tear down every house in the village if you have to!'

Dandall was already mounted on Kelpie and led the way down the hill and toward the gate.

'That was the hard part, right?' he shouted over his shoulder.

'There's still a long way to go,' she said, patting Stoic's neck.

They cleared the gate and she urged Stoic to greater speed in the open ground, his long stride helping him to keep pace with the fresher mare. Morgen's head jostled her shin as their pace increased and she wrinkled her nose at the eyes still moving in their sockets. They watched the road, following the turns, then settled staring toward the Dullie Fell.

Kenrig craned her head to look at the hill, some instinct warning her of danger. The hill was already half a mile distant after only a few minutes of riding, but it dominated the bare landscape, high enough to cut the clouds as they passed above it. A rift opened in the clouds, splitting wide as the wind drove them against the hill's summit. Silver light dripped from the opening, spilling across the hill as the moon, swollen almost to fullness, pushed its way closer to the earth.

Drumbeats shivered the air, so low and steady at first that she thought it was her own heart beating. New drums joined with every beat, each one adding its own discordant rhythm to the mass of music emerging over the hill. Horns, bells and whistles forced their way into the tuneless din, heralding the whoop and holler of inhuman voices.

As she watched the moon wax over the hill, its light brightening in pale imitation of dawn, she saw shapes emerge where the light pooled. They were too far for her to see their shapes clearly, shining as if they were formed from molten silver, but she heard the tortured cries of animals accompany their arrival. The screaming of horses and the baying of dogs pierced the terrible cacophony of instruments.

The Unseelie had sounded the hunt.

20

Burn the Body

The Wild Hunt caught them at the edge of a forest. Horns signalled the hunt wherever they were discovered and drums drove bloodless hounds in frenzied pursuit so that they could neither hide nor escape.

The forms the spectres had possessed in life were half-visible behind veils of moonlight, the remnants of human features demented by the madness of the hunt. Armour of silver so thin it was translucent flowed over their shifting bodies like cloth and in their hands they carried weapons which waxed and waned with the shadows.

Dandall and Kenrig rode without stopping, their path dictated by the hunters as every route was closed to them. They couldn't outpace the spectres who rode on steeds of silver mist unhindered by the trees, tireless as only the dead could be. The wings of the hunt drew in to encircle them, ranks of spectres blurring into shapeless fog.

His granny had told him stories of the Wild Hunt and his boyhood dreams had turned those stories into nightmares. He'd lain awake on nights of the full moon in fear of the Pale Riders stealing him from his bed, forcing him to join their hunt. He'd imagined himself driven ahead of their immortal steeds until he expired from exhaustion, only to rise as a spirit forever enslaved to the hunt, doomed to dole out the same fate to others.

His nightmares had become so terrible that he'd begged his father to block up the narrow west-facing window in the roof of their home. His father had told him there was nothing to fear, that the old stories of spectres riding out with the full moon were just stories, but had relented with little argument. All Cadogan carried an ancestral fear of such creatures.

Dandall had put his nightmares behind him eventually and believed he'd outgrown them. He'd never believed he would find himself trapped in one years later.

Despite their speed the hunt never approached close enough to touch their quarry. Individual riders broke from their ranks, becoming more solid the further they rode from the others. They darted close and cut across whatever path Dandall and Kenrig had been forced onto. With the tips of their spears they goaded Kelpie and Stoic to reckless speed and rode alongside the living mounts in easy mockery of their pace.

Dandall flinched whenever a rider approached, each time fearing the attack which would surely kill him. Yet no attack ever came, the weapons of the spectres only ever falling near enough to taunt him before their wielders fell back, laughing and whooping as they rejoined their ranks.

Why are they waiting? he thought. *Are they toying with us?* Were they holding back until they'd grown bored of the chase before finally ending the hunt? He watched the spectres pass through trees as if the forest around them were no more solid than the surface of water and he wondered if their weapons could actually harm him, though he didn't want to test the theory.

Morgen's head was bounced around by Stoic's movements, but its gaze was steady. Whenever Dandall caught sight of it he could swear it was tracking the paths they took, watching for the turns as the spectres drove them in a new direction. Black blood glistened at the severed neck, but still its jaw worked in an effort to chew through the gag muffling it.

Kenrig's theory about the king drawing the Unseelie to the Middle March had proven true, but that was no comfort as the hunt closed around them. If they could reach the Parting Hill and bury the head then they might banish the spectres, but their route south was cut off at every turn.

Kelpie tired rapidly beneath him and with every turn they were forced to make he found it harder to push her onward. He'd never ridden so far for so long and the effort was telling. His muscles had gone beyond aching. Blood oozed over his shoulder and he'd had to loop Kelpie's reins around his wrists as his grip failed.

Kenrig didn't slow their pace, but he knew her own

injuries were telling. She hunched in the saddle, sweat slick across her face and neck, knuckles white where she held Stoic's reins. She may have been the single toughest person he knew, but even she had limits.

How long can we keep doing this? How long will they let us run before they end this?

Answers came to him sooner than expected. The sounds of the hunt died all at once. Drums stilled and horns emptied. Shouts and cries drifted away in the wind. The spectres continued their pursuit in unearthly silence. Their steeds rode without touching the ground, their arms and armour too immaterial to clash and rattle. Only the wind accompanied their grim procession.

A new voice cried out from their ranks. Not the laughter and holler of hunters cornering their prey, but the screams of a frightened child.

The spectres closed their lines and blocked all escape. Dandall stopped and turned Kelpie all around, searching for a new path, any way that they might ride, but the spectres stood in an unbroken circle.

Kenrig made no effort to seek an escape. She turned Stoic to face back along their path, toward the source of the screams. The narrow track they'd followed extended straight for nearly half a mile and the pale glow of the spectres lit the forest all around them.

Lissi clung to the neck of a piebald horse, her short legs clutching its shoulders in the absence of a saddle. The horse was wild with fear, running in fits and starts without any direction of its own. Seven riders herded it along, boxing it in with a close formation. When it tried to break left or right for the trees one of them moved to block its escape.

The riders were worse than anything Dandall had seen in his nightmares. They were long-limbed and willow-thin, their strange bodies clothed in rags and scraps of skin. Grisly ornaments flew behind them and their weapons were cruel, promising a slow and painful death. *The sluagh.* The vanguard of the Wild Hunt.

He understood then why the hunt hadn't simply run them down and ended the chase. They were waiting to reveal a final cruelty before the kill.

Lissi had no hope of evading the sluagh on the maddened horse. Clinging to its back she was steered straight toward Dandall and Kenrig who could only watch, as trapped and helpless as she was. The girl still wore Kenrig's pendant around her neck, but its protection wouldn't spare her if she fell from the horse or if fear and exhaustion overcame her.

In the corner of his eye he saw Kenrig's hand move to rest on her falchion. He fumbled for one of Daglan's silver shots to load his sling and dropped it to the road. His hands shook as he reached for another but he clamped it tight against his palm.

'What do we do?' he gasped, breathless from the ride.

He looked to Kenrig and saw her eyes narrow to study the approaching sluagh, but she had no answers for him. Her jaw worked and her fingers flexed over the grip of her falchion. He knew she wanted to fight, but didn't see any way they could win.

They could only win by banishing the Unseelie and sending the sluagh and Wild Hunt back to the Otherworld with their masters. Which meant Kenrig needed to reach the Parting Hill with the head.

He scanned the steady ranks of silent spectres for a weakness, but saw none. They ignored the obstacles of the forest to close a seamless circle. Their forms overlapped and blurred together, seeming no more substantial than fog, but as long as he was afraid to test them they may as well have been flesh and blood.

His mind chased one half-formed thought after another, never able to catch anything that might give them a chance of escape. He knew that if he stopped believing there was a way out he would panic, but he couldn't see how they would both make it past the hunters. *Unless, we don't both need to escape.*

He looked from Kenrig to the king's head. They didn't both need to escape the hunt, only she did. His racing mind leapt and settled with a grim clarity on the realisation.

'Go,' he said. When she didn't respond he repeated himself louder. 'Go!'

She turned and he could see her eyes searching for meaning in his face. 'Go. Bury the head. I'll distract them.'

'No,' she said. 'We stay together.'

He could hear the weakness of her protest. 'You know I'm right. This won't end until that thing is buried.'

She was shaking her head, but he knew she had no argument against him. 'I'll get Lissi. It's my fault she was caught. You go and make sure we have a chance.'

He didn't watch for her agreement. To convince his body to throw itself at the enemy he charged without thinking. His heels kicked into Kelpie's flanks and for once the horse obeyed him without complaint.

The spectres surrounding them rippled as he began to move, their silent composure shifting as their quarry resumed the chase. They were hunters so he would give them something to hunt again.

'Come and get me!' he yelled. 'Come and get me!'

He gathered his fear into his lungs and emptied it into the air with every shout. It almost felt good to charge. The distance between him and the sluagh disappeared as he raced toward them and he could feel laughter building where his fear used to be.

His sling whistled as he spun it high overhead and he let out his laughter in turn. If he'd been able to hear himself he'd have thought he'd gone mad, but his laughter disappeared beneath cries of alarm and the sporadic blare of horns. The spectres broke ranks around him to give chase and he smiled knowing that at the very least he was a good distraction.

He charged even as a new figure joined the road ahead, mounted on a horse that dwarfed all others. Skin like charcoal armoured the giant and in one hand it held a sword long enough to touch the ground from the back of the enormous horse.

It lifted the sword point from the ground and levelled the blade at him.

*

Against all instinct Kenrig forced herself to run. Dandall was right and in that moment she hated him for it. She couldn't look back. She couldn't bear to watch him charge headlong into the sluagh. She didn't want to waste the chance he'd given her.

If he was to have any hope she had to reach the hill and bury the head, ending the hold that Morgen had given the Unseelie. That was all she could do for him. She had to trust and hope that he could help Lissi and keep them both alive long enough for her to do it.

As he charged the spectres broke their formation to follow and she used the opening they left to ride as hard as she could in the opposite direction. The spectres were swift in their pursuit of Dandall and she passed them before any could realise what she intended.

The discordant music of the hunt began again, too loud and chaotic for her to know if any had turned to pursue her as well, but she spurred Stoic to run as if they were at his heels. She leaned forward over his neck to keep her balance as she kept her falchion drawn.

'Your breeder told me you were his slowest horse,' she whispered. 'Time to prove him wrong.'

When the road turned she followed the bend, though she wasn't sure it was the right way. The spectres had done their part to disorient her and cut off any route south. Without them surrounding her the forest was dark, lit only by the faint traces of moonlight that crept in through the dense canopy. The tracks she followed ran in a dizzying series of directions and it was only by some lucky accident that she emerged onto a wide road clear enough to see the sky above.

The clouds had been pushed to the horizon by the moon which had swelled in the emptying sky. The stars seemed to lean away from it, their light stretching into distended lines. A halo of darkness grew alongside the moon, clinging to its edges and bulging outward as though the moon were stretching the night sky like fabric. She could only imagine what the people in Karstend witnessed under its shadow.

Stoic bore the worst of their journey, but she was almost breathless with pain and sweat filmed her skin like she was in the midst of fever. Again and again she was sure that she couldn't muster any more strength to hold herself up in the saddle, wanting nothing more than to let herself fall and rest wherever she landed.

She couldn't remember a time when she'd been so exhausted. So close to breaking and being unable to keep moving.

Every step she took. Every time she climbed into the saddle. Every blow struck and injury sustained. They were each more difficult than the one before and with a weariness that felt like it had been dragged across miles of distance, she realised her exhaustion had been years in the making.

In the time since she'd met Dandall and they'd killed the creature that took his father's life she hadn't stopped. Not for long enough to matter. She'd ridden the length of the Marches, resting only long enough to recover from the latest injury. The latest ordeal. The latest threat that had almost cost her life.

Thinking about her fatigue only worsened it and she tightened her grip around the falchion's hilt until the discomfort brought alertness. She had to keep going, to push through fatigue and injury. There was more at stake than her own life. There was Dandall. Lissi. The people of Karstend, like the people of all the villages and towns that had come before them.

'Maybe we'll stay in Karstend a while,' she said. 'Rest properly-'

The sounds of the hunt had dulled behind her and she'd let the rhythm of Stoic's movement make her complacent. A shadow hurtled from the trees to their left, too fast for her to bring her blade around. It collided with Stoic, leaping against his shoulder and knocking his front legs out from under him.

She was spilled from the saddle, thrown forward over Stoic's neck and hitting the ground. She tumbled over her shoulder as she hit the ground, dispelling some of her momentum. She stopped hard against her hip, but the impact could have been worse.

Stoic's screams sounded and she craned her neck to see he'd regained his feet and was backing away from the creature that hit him. He tossed his head and stamped the ground, but retreated from the path into the cover of the forest.

Between them stood the shadow of a man, given substance by the mass of moonlight behind him. On one half of his body the clothes had been burned away to reveal warped skin glistening red beneath a black char like dying embers. His frame was broad and powerful, but ended at the neck.

How? she thought. *How is his body here?*

As if sensing her thoughts Morgen's body turned. The broken shafts of arrows still pierced the body and severed ropes hung around its wrists. His tunic hung open across its chest, revealing how far his body had burned before it had escaped the pit. The damage done to it was staggering but silhouetted against the growing moon its strength seemed undiminished.

Headless as it was it had no trouble in sensing her. Before she could rise it dropped into a crouch and leapt, crossing the space between them in an instant. It fell across her, kneeling over her stomach to pin her down. Its claws were broken and cracked, but sharp enough to cut easily across her arms as she curled them around her head.

The padded cloth of her sleeves dulled the worst of the cuts, but they did nothing to blunt the force of its blows. Numbness spread through her forearms and her shoulders shook with the effort of keeping her arms raised. She rocked back and forth as much as she could under its crushing weight, trying to angle her arms so each strike glanced over them, but its attacks were monstrously fast.

She twisted, rocking from shoulder to shoulder under it and making space to kick herself along the ground little-by-little. The body was far heavier than she was, but its movements were wild and its balance shifted rapidly. Once she'd wriggled enough space to bring her hips underneath it she planted her feet and bucked her hips upward.

The attacks stopped as its hands flew forward to arrest its fall and she used the opening to bring her legs between them. Before it could recover its balance she brought her forearms down into the crooks of its elbows and trapped its arms against her chest.

Its strength was incredible, but she didn't give it a chance to overpower her. She pulled her leg across its chest, hooking the top of one foot into the crease of its hip and with the other foot kicked one of its knees out from under it. As its weight dropped away she followed through with the movement, pulling with the foot hooked into its hip and throwing herself into a roll.

With their positions reversed she adopted a crouch, pressing her knee into its gut as she planted her other foot over one of its wrists. It swung its free arm up to dislodge her but she caught the arm, trapping it against her chest. She buried her fingers into its sleeve to grip the fabric and felt oil under her hand.

Where the fire hadn't touched them its clothes and skin were still coated with unburned oil. It writhed under her, its strength great enough that it didn't need technique to free itself. She drew a dagger into her free hand before she lost her position and plunged it into the shoulder of the trapped arm.

Magic steel met the undead flesh and flames burst in the wound. The fire needed no encouragement to spread, catching quickly in the oil-soaked rags that remained of its clothes. With a final effort it whipped its arm back toward itself and she was thrown clear, but the fire had already grown quickly to engulf its shoulder.

She hit the ground and fell onto her side. Her cloak wrapped itself around her as she rolled, tangling itself in her legs. Above her Morgen's body stood and thrashed at the spreading flames as it stamped its foot down toward her. Trapped in her cloak she could do nothing but roll to avoid the attacks.

It followed her across the ground, not stopping until the flames surged down one of its legs. While it hesitated she reached for the clasp across her neck and tore it open, letting the cloak fall as she rolled free to regain her feet. The body turned to face her no matter how she moved to sidestep around it and she wondered how it knew where she was without eyes.

The head. The head had continued to move its eyes long after she'd cleaved it from the body. Morgen had been watching their route the entire time, following every turn they'd taken and leading his body back toward his head.

She found the head lying in the road where Stoic had fallen, the straps that had secured it roughly severed by his claws. Its eyes shone silver with reflected moonlight and they were fixed unerringly on her. The eyes twitched to one side and just in time she threw herself out of the way as the body lunged for her.

It fell to its hands beside her, blazing uncontrollably. Black smoke poured from it and she ran choking through the acrid cloud. The body abandoned any effort to stifle the flames as they both raced for the head. On all fours the body was faster, but she'd given herself the lead.

She crouched down as the body leapt for her and it flew overhead, stumbling at the edge of the road and tumbling between the trees. Burying her fingers into his hair she pressed Morgen's head to the ground and drew her other dagger. The blade passed easily through the delicate film of his eye, searing the eye socket clean in moments.

Morgen howled through the gag as she pressed the dagger to his other eye, blinding him as his body tried to crawl from the trees. The flames had done their work quickly, engulfing his body completely. His formidable size was gone, the flames having gladly consumed his skin and muscle almost to the bone.

Not yet satisfied, the flames moved into the brush under him and caught amongst the lowest branches. Despite the steady fall of rain the flames spread quickly between the trees, turning the undergrowth into a funeral pyre. She watched the body make a last feeble effort to drag itself onto the road, claws digging into the soft earth, before it collapsed, its flesh scorched away entirely.

She turned the head over in both hands and stared into its ruined eyes. 'One last thing.'

21

Bury the Head

Dandall cursed as his first shot went wide. The sluagh were nimble and they moved with the nervous swiftness of birds. His target rode closest to Lissi's horse, steering it straight down the road's centre. Desperation lent him the speed he needed to reload and his second shot found its mark in a mask of metal scraps.

The shot passed through the mask like a stone through glass. The sluagh slumped back, smoke trailing from the side of its head where the shot had exited. The dark fabric of its hood stretched away from the impact, ragged strips trailing in the wind until they were no more substantial than the smoke. When the sluagh reeled forward, he saw the mask rippling where it was punctured.

Directionless, the sluagh's horse turned from the formation as its rider's weight tipped across its shoulders. The other sluagh chittered and keened, the sounds piercing the Wild Hunt's music and driving a bolt of pain into Dandall's ears. The next rider in their line turned to follow the insensible sluagh and Lissi's horse swerved from the road.

Wincing, Dandall steered Kelpie an instant before he hit the sluagh's broken formation. So close to them their high-pitched cries felt like fingers scraping the inside of his skull and he rode into the trees half-blind with tears.

The sounds of the hunt dulled below the ringing of his ears, but he saw the spectres overtaking him once more. Through his tears they were distorted into searing streaks of white light. Only Kelpie's instincts kept them from crashing headlong into the trees.

He blinked and urged her onward, surprised that she was still able to quicken her pace and hadn't thrown him off long ago. Lissi's horse was hemmed in by the spectres just as he was and it ran in a clear path, following the wide clearings where the trees had been felled by human hands.

Lissi's horse had no reins and the girl had her hands buried deep in its tangled mane. Her face was pressed to its neck, her eyes screwed shut so that she didn't notice Dandall draw alongside.

She'd been ragged when he and Kenrig had met her at the crossroads, but days in the Unseelie's captivity hadn't been kind to her. Dark hollows ringed her eyes and the pallor of sickness was visible in the spectral light surrounding them. She looked smaller, not simply thinner but diminished from the brash child he'd found so irritating days ago.

'Lissi!' he shouted.

His voice was lost beneath the noise of the hunt. He led Kelpie closer to the other horse, until his leg scraped against its flank.

'Lissi!' he shouted again.

Her eyes crept open to look back at him, then widened in surprise.

'When I tell you, you have to let go!'

She shook her head, eyes closing again as tears started to fly across her cheeks.

'I'll hold on to you, I promise! But you'll have to let go!'

He had to steer Kelpie to avoid a tree as it rose up between her and the other horse. More trees forced him to travel wide and when he was able to draw alongside again the ground sloped upward, narrowing their path and forcing him to fall behind. They climbed quickly onto a wide mound, rising above the hunt.

The spectres climbed after them, pushing upward on empty air to ride high overhead. Their harsh light banished all shadows beneath them as their lines blurred together, gathering like the luminous clouds of a strange sky.

The path widened ahead, only briefly, and he urged Kelpie alongside the other horse. Not waiting for Lissi's cooperation he leaned over and grabbed her. When she didn't slacken her grip on the horse's mane he began to slip in his saddle, but after a moment she let go and he pulled her in front of him.

Kelpie pushed forward ahead of the other horse, narrowly overtaking it as the trees closed their path. The mound dropped away and they slipped down slick mud, landing hard on more stable ground. Kelpie stumbled, throwing them forward. He had to clamp his legs tight against Kelpie's flanks to keep himself and Lissi in the saddle and sat back hard as Kelpie righted herself.

He worried that she wouldn't carry them any further but only moments behind them the other horse crashed to the ground, scaring her into a sudden sprint. He had no control and let her run, focusing on just staying on her back.

With one arm clutching Lissi to his chest and the other clinging to the reins he had no free hands to shoot the gaining sluagh. His sling was still in his hand, crushed in his grip against the reins, but it was little use.

'I hope you dreamt of a way we survive this,' he said.

Kelpie responded to her reins again and he led them under the line of spectres. He knew they couldn't stay ahead of the hunt, but without options he needed to do something. If nothing else, he gave Kenrig more time to reach the Parting Hill.

Come on, Kenrig. We can't do this all night.

The spectres continued to ride above them, leaving a clear path ahead even if they couldn't outpace the hunt. Too late he understood why.

Above the endless din of hundreds of instruments he heard the roar of water moments before the forest opened and they spilled from the trees. Kelpie's speed carried them clear across the bank and they fell into the swollen belly of a river gorged on the recent rains.

Water rose up to swallow them. The muffled roar of the river flooded into his ears. Lissi thrashed in his grip and he had to fight to keep his mouth closed as her elbows dug into his stomach.

Years spent diving the loch around his home kept him calm against the searing panic spreading through his breathless chest. He held himself against the saddle, trusting Kelpie to push them above the surface.

The water was thick with mud and blocked out all light from above. Silt stung his eyes, but he kept them open as they surfaced. Within the darkness of the river he could believe that they'd escaped the hunt and he savoured that fleeting peace.

Noise greeted him first when his head emerged, overwhelming the sounds of his own gasping. The spectres had descended from the air and lined themselves in two columns along the river's banks, heedless of mud and water. They marched easily along the river's course, setting their pace to its currents, their ranks doubled in its murky reflection.

He felt rather than heard Lissi coughing and eased his grip as the current stopped trying to rip them apart. They were both shaking, half-submerged as Kelpie barely kept her head clear of the river. *Be like your namesake and swim,* he urged.

She was a stronger swimmer than him by far, but she was still helpless to oppose the weight of water bearing them along. She angled herself to swim for the nearest bank, back toward the side of the forest they'd emerged from. He pulled on her reins, trying to steer her toward the opposite bank, but she pulled the reins from his grip.

Through the shining column of spectres he watched the sluagh race across the stable ground deeper in the forest. In the ghost light they were distorted blurs glittering with bright trophies. They howled and whooped, their frantic glee almost enough to distract from the enormous shadow that trailed them.

Dandall fumbled for Kelpie's reins, catching nothing as they floated out of reach. He tried to drive her away from the bank with his knees, but the water robbed him of any leverage.

He watched certain death approach as the giant warrior resolved itself from the forest's gloom to overtake the sluagh. Everything about it seemed too massive to move between the close press of the trees, but its size was matched with impossible grace. Its steed ran without a single missed step, the thunder of its hooves clear amidst the drums.

'Don't let go of me,' he shouted.

Without waiting for Lissi to answer he twisted out of the saddle and threw them into the river's currents. Without Kelpie to steady them they were pushed along faster, unable to resist the flow of water. All he could do was angle himself to push Lissi out of the water and keep his head above the surface.

The river carried them ahead of the sluagh and the giant, but the spectres followed relentlessly. The two columns flowed toward the centre of the river into reach of their spears. Slivers of shadow blazed against their bright forms, lancing the water around him. Mist curled from the river where they'd struck and patches of ice pressed against him.

He shivered as the water froze, cold enough that he felt as if his skin was burning. The spears left no wounds, but he felt the chill of their edges slice into his muscles as if they'd carved him to the bone. Hot breath froze in the air above him as he gasped and hissed with the pain.

Riders broke from the columns and swooped over them, swinging their spears in pendulous arcs that came mockingly close to striking him. All around him spears nipped at his limbs, but from above they never touched. Slowly, he remembered the pendant around Lissi's neck.

The metal was pressed against his ribs, just above his heart. Thinking of it brought the characters and pattern of its magic shining into his awareness. There was warmth in the pattern, a fragment of the sun's heat radiating from each character held in its golden filaments.

Something urged him to reach into the pattern. He knew now that he could tear it apart without effort and let the characters burn free of the pattern's tempering guidance. The characters wanted to flare, brilliant and searing just for an instant and only the pattern held them in check, halting their brilliant decline.

He almost obliged them, imagining their heat driving away the cold, but he contented himself with the little warmth that seeped through his sodden shirt.

The water dropped sharply over a low fall and spilled them onto a narrow beach of smooth pebbles. He released Lissi and she crawled further up the beach as he dragged himself fully from the water. The warmth of the pendant left him as Lissi moved away and he curled around his knees, crushed under the weight of his wet clothes.

He shook so violently he disturbed the pebbles under him though he could barely feel them through spreading numbness. Out of the water he felt colder still and he knew he ought to move, but he couldn't muster the strength to do anything except huddle against his legs. The spectres began to feel like a distant concern.

'Get up!' a voice urged and dimly he realised it belonged to Lissi. 'Get up!'

She was shaking him. *Get up*, he urged himself. *Get up*. Her fingers dug into the tender flesh of his wounded shoulder. The pain was dull, but it drew his focus away from the cold.

'Get up!'

He gritted his teeth as he rolled onto his knees. His body felt like it had grown twice as heavy and he moved like he'd lain still for years. He fell when he tried to climb to his feet and crawled across the beach. The movement brought feeling seeping back into his limbs and beneath him the pebbles felt like they'd sprouted needles.

He crawled to the edge of the forest and wrapped his arms around a tree to drag himself upwards. He listed from one tree to the next, but he was moving and every step was easier than the last.

On foot, half-drowned and exhausted they had no hope of escaping the spectres. The Wild Hunt ambled alongside them, mocking their feeble progress with the sonorous drumbeat of a funeral march. Lissi clutched his arm with one hand and in the other she brandished the pendant, twisting it left and right to confront the spectres.

With clumsy fingers Dandall untied the sling that had twisted itself around his wrist. He reached for a shot and found the pouch had opened in the river, spilling all but two of the precious shots. He crushed one of them feebly against his palm, willing blood back into his hand.

He tried to ignore the pendant but it glowed like a lantern in the corner of his mind. He craved the warmth it offered, he wanted to let the characters free from the metal and chase out the cold that clung to his bones.

The pendant was their only protection, but every moment they walked with it he came closer to giving in and tearing its pattern apart. He wondered if he could use it to drive the spectres away. If he flared its magic, used it all in one desperate effort, could he create an opening for them to escape?

Despair snuffed the dim hope. Even if they had an opening, where would they escape to? How far could they get before the Wild Hunt caught them again and found them without even the pendant's scant protection?

They wandered aimlessly away from the river, squinting against the blinding light of the spectres that washed the forest clean of shadow. Dandall's head throbbed with bright pain. When the light dimmed it was such a relief that he failed to see it as a warning.

The spectres spread themselves through the forest, widening their circle. Their forms softened into shapeless mist and flowed together into bleary ranks radiating out of sight.

The sluagh leapt into the circle, spindle-limbed silhouettes against the shining ranks. They howled as they rode around the circle with disorienting speed, brandishing weapons whose shapes he could only guess at. He heard a whip crack in the air and the scrape of blades sliding against each other.

Their circling heralded the giant's arrival. It rode without ceremony, charging for Dandall and Lissi with the weight of the forest behind it. Dandall tensed, ready to leap aside.

Holdainn. The name came to him from Kenrig's account of the feast. After all the strangeness he'd witnessed he couldn't suppress a shiver of fear at seeing one of the Unseelie.

The giant leapt from his horse and shoved it away, sending it running for the distant edge of the circle. He planted his sword into the ground and stood, clawed hands resting on its antler hilt. Armoured in scales of bark and crowned with woven branches he looked as though he'd been grown from the forest.

'You gave decent sport,' Holdainn said. 'But the chase is done.'

The giant's voice echoed with the splintering of wood and the rumble of thunder. His words came slowly and he sounded almost bored by what he said.

'Surrender and your deaths will be quick. You have suffered and struggled long enough. Your final rest is well-earned.'

Holdainn's fractured face seemed impassive, as though the hunt had meant little to him. Dandall swayed. Without moving to keep his muscles warm he felt the cold seeping further into his body. He was tired. If he shut his eyes for more than a moment he thought he would collapse where he stood.

The offer of a quick death sounded entirely reasonable to him.

'He's a liar!' Lissi spat. 'They're all liars!'

Her outburst startled him from his fatal stupor. Holdainn's face split into a snarl and his hands twisted around the hilt of his sword. Armoured skin cracked across his knuckles under the sudden strain. Dandall stepped backward, pushing Lissi behind him.

'Your master will fail,' he growled. 'She is weak and alone. She thought she was clever to trick us, but she will soon learn how my father deals with those that bargain against us.'

Dandall loaded his sling as he kept backing away. Holdainn turned his head to address the Wild Hunt.

'Go! Find the woman! When my father is done with her bring her to me!'

The sluagh whistled and chirruped as they wheeled away through the ranks of spectres. He watched them pass Holdainn's monstrous horse standing far from its master's reach. *We won't have a better chance.*

Holdainn's eyes were lost in shadow as he stared at Dandall. 'You will see her broken and know what awaits you all. You will suffer. You will beg me to end your lives, but death will not come easily.'

He levelled his sword at them, easily bearing its weight in one hand. 'Even beyond death, you will suffer.'

Dandall leaned down to Lissi. 'Run,' he whispered.

When she didn't move he shouted and pushed her toward the edge of the circle. She ran, pendant raised ahead of her as she reached the line of spectres. He watched her go just long enough to follow her direction and turned back toward Holdainn.

The giant advanced, his strides long and slow. With a snap of his wrist he slapped out with the flat of the blade. The strike was slow, swung at the limit of his reach, but sent a bolt of pain through Dandall's injured shoulder. The attack was an insult, to show him he was outmatched.

If Holdainn wanted him dead he'd be dead already.

'Your spirits belong to us,' the giant said.

Dandall twisted his shoulder away from a second strike and gasped as the sword whipped around to catch his knee.

'I will drag you to the Otherworld as a prize. I will parade you before the souls in my charge so they will not forget the cost of insolence.'

His leg was too numb to step out of the way of another hit and he almost collapsed over the blow that struck his thigh.

'There will be no rest for you after death. You will not join your ancestors. You will not see your mother. Nor your father.'

His leg buckled under his weight. Holdainn's free hand lashed out and grabbed him around the collar. His legs flailed under him as he was lifted from the ground and his sling fell as his hands rose to pry at Holdainn's grip.

'I will let you glimpse the Mother's paradise so that you will understand what your arrogance has denied you. Past the Veil there will be no death to end your pain.'

The tip of the sword rose between them and pressed against his cheek. His skin parted easily against the edge and he understood a sliver of the promised agony.

The cut was shallow but he had to clench his teeth to stop himself from screaming. The blade felt wrong, as though it shouldn't be possible for it to touch him. It bore a cold greater than the chill he'd carried from the river, a fragment of what awaited spirits crossing into the Otherworld, threads of the Veil woven together into metal.

He didn't understand how he knew that, but he could feel the pattern that gave the blade substance in his world. It was wild, a tangled mass of fibres overlapping in ways that he couldn't have predicted. It was more complex than anything he'd sensed in mystic objects, but he didn't need to understand it to break it.

He pressed his hands against the pitted blade, gasping as the cold burned his palms. The pattern was dense and resisted his efforts to unravel it, but it didn't truly belong in his world and once he'd loosened a single thread more of them followed. With Kenrig's dagger he'd plucked apart the pattern like pulling on spider silk, but the Unseelie blade felt more like he was trying to tear cloth.

Iron softened under his fingers and clumps of magic came away in his hands as he tore the blade open. Without the pattern to hold it together metal vanished as if it had never existed.

Holdainn threw him to the ground and he landed hard against a patch of roots. He lurched to his feet like he was drunk.

His efforts to break the blade had shortened the weapon, leaving a ragged edge where there was once solid metal. Holdainn growled and hefted what remained of the weapon in a high two-handed grip. As Dandall ran for his sling the sword came down in a lethal arc.

Only stumbling took him out of the blade's path. Feeling hadn't returned to his leg and it skidded on the wet ground, throwing him past Holdainn's reach.

He landed on his hands and turned as he stood. The shot he'd loaded into the sling was gone and the last silver ball nearly slipped from his burned hand as he fitted it into place. He limped backwards as he spun the sling around his body, earning him precious moments to shoot.

Holdainn snapped around to face him, face cracked into an expression that promised murder. Dandall's aim was off, but the shot whistled as it left the sling and struck Holdainn's ribs just below one of his shoulders. Scales fractured and splinters exploded from the impact. The splinters spun in the air like shards of silver, then drifted away in the wind as shimmering dust.

The giant's hand clamped over the wound and his sword arm fell at his side. He roared loud enough to silence the drums and Dandall ran before he could give chase.

The ranks of spectres were unmoving as Dandall approached. Their faces were lost in the brilliant mass of their own light, any expression they might have had unreadable as he dipped his head to avoid losing his vision. Dark spears drifted up to meet him, but he charged without stopping.

He hit the first rank and staggered. The spectres were no more substantial than fog, but the shock of hitting them was like plunging through the river's surface again. He emerged from the circle hunched over, hands clutched to his chest. The darkness beyond the spectres was impenetrable and he ran blindly.

*

The Parting Hill stood low above the forest, the highest of a range of short hills clustered at the centre of the March. Paths of white stones, their edges made rough by centuries of travellers, crawled across it, each one marking the direction chosen by the first generation of Karlan clans to settle the Middle March.

Chalk figures and clan markings were cut into the hillside at the start of each path, identifying the clans that had created them. Under the moonlight the chalk shone, but the figures and markings had been made indistinct as the forest had grown to reclaim the base of the hill.

Stoic's strength was spent and she left him tied in the forest, taking down a spade from his saddle as she slung Morgen's head over her shoulder on the cord she'd tied around it. The gag kept it from biting her, but it still made her skin crawl where it wriggled against her back.

Parting stones crowned the hill, not flat like the one outside of Karstend but squat monoliths raised in a ring where the paths met and diverged. Under the swollen moon their mottled faces were luminous, the eroded carvings etched into them blurred by the brilliant light. At first she thought some trick of the light seemed to angle the shadows so that all of them met in the exact centre of the circle, but as she walked closer she realised it was no trick.

'Yours is the face I least wanted to see today,' she said, trying hard to mask her fear.

Gloam Ogda stood where the shadows met, the fabric of their robes only distinguishable as Kenrig moved around the stones, bringing Ogda into stark focus against the brilliant rock. The moonlight made no impression on them except in the delicate angles of their face and the silver threads that lined their hood.

'You ought not to have told us your name, Kenrig Ebermann,' they said. 'You would not have given it if you knew the power it held.'

What choice did I have? Kenrig thought that they sounded almost sad as they spoke, intoning their words with the mournful drone of a eulogy.

'Your efforts are at an end,' they continued. 'You provided entertainment to us as you promised, but we've allowed your *adventure* to reach its natural conclusion.'

They pointed to Morgen's head now hanging at her side. 'Lay down your burden. You need not struggle against us anymore. You are tired. Injured. Older than when you began your journey all those years ago. Surrender, and your cares could all be taken from you.'

Kenrig felt the infectious sorrow pass between them, dragging at her with a despair not her own. Pain, doubt and fatigue all seemed harder to bear while Ogda spoke, the weight of them made heavy by the immortal's grief.

The feeling of the Unseelie lord's emotions affecting her were familiar from her time in the feast, but the power it held seemed weaker in her world. She stopped outside of the stone circle and shook her head to clear it.

'You look tired,' Ogda said. 'Why not kneel and take the weight off your legs?'

Kenrig felt her leg twitch and bow at the knee. The sensation was brief and she straightened her leg as soon as she felt it, but the movement was not her choice.

'I prefer to stand,' she said. 'I don't intend to stay here long.'

'Kneel, Kenrig Ebermann,' Ogda said. '*Kneel.*'

Stones dug into her knee as her left leg buckled under her. Her right foot remained planted, but the harder she tried to push herself up the harder her knee ground against the path.

Ogda was smiling when Kenrig looked up at them. 'Unburden yourself. *Give that wretched thing to me.*'

She resisted as best she could, but found herself holding Morgen's head toward them. She tossed the head into the circle and watched it disappear into the substance of Ogda's robe. They didn't stoop to pick it up, but the next moment it was in their hands.

'Such a disgusting, feral thing to have drawn us here,' they said, looking into its blind sockets. 'Yet I cannot doubt its power. This land is rich with the potential to breed such creatures.'

'What do you want with it?'

They held it out by its hair. 'With this? Nothing.'

The head fell from their grip and rolled to a stop against a parting stone. 'I needed it only to end your feeble attempt to oppose us.'

'Feeble? I doubt you'd have come personally to stop a feeble attempt. Nor sent your Wild Hunt to pursue me across the entire March.'

'Quiet!'

Her jaw clenched shut, but Ogda's power over her wasn't absolute. With effort she was able to speak.

'What did you mean, about this land's potential?'

If they were annoyed that Kenrig was still able to speak their face betrayed nothing. 'I'm surprised even your dull senses cannot perceive the power here.'

'Here? On this hill?'

Their laugh was without mirth. 'Here in your Marches. In every crack and corner that darkness gathers. The Veil hangs close over this land. It is thinnest here. The Otherworld spills through its weave, flooding the ancient shadows with power.'

Their eyes gleamed as they stared down at her. 'I know something of your path, *Kenrig Ebermann*. Have you never questioned why these petty kingdoms should be so populated with misfortunes? Why so many monsters stalk their people? Why mortal souls should lose their way so often and linger so long without rest?'

Kenrig's jaw tightened around her words. 'Tell me.'

Their eyes grew hazy as they looked south. 'This land is old, yet something older still has taken root here. Old enough to draw the Otherworld closer. It is at the heart of your woes. The woes of all your people.'

She tried to keep her face neutral, but Ogda's words spoke directly to her fears. 'Why tell me this?'

Their smile returned. 'Consider it a final kindness.'

Kenrig watched them unblinking, but in an instant Ogda stood over her. Their shadow trailed them to the circle's centre, stretched thin by the distance they'd travelled. They too seemed to have thinned, their edges wavering where they caught the moonlight.

Their hand cupped Kenrig's chin and she flinched as much as the magic holding her allowed.

'Your efforts to banish us were amusing, as your bargain promised. That ought to be recognised. Your existence will soon be one of utter agony. You should enjoy this small mercy.'

Everything in Kenrig rebelled against Ogda's touch and she managed to pull her face from their grip. A flicker of annoyance disturbed their serene face.

'*Be still.*'

Her muscles grew taut so suddenly she felt joints pop and crack everywhere in her body. She grimaced against the pain, but after a few moments she was able to relax enough to ease it. She held herself as still as she could, fighting the need to stretch the numbness from her kneeling leg. She didn't want to betray the magic's weakening hold on her, not until she knew how far she could resist it.

'I am not ungrateful to you,' Ogda said. 'You have brought me the only means by which you could have banished us.'

In another instant they'd returned to the circle's centre and held Morgen's head again. 'Soon it will not matter. We will no longer have need for such things as this *beast* and its bloodletting. Our presence here in your world will not depend upon the wax and wane of mortal lives to draw us across the Veil.'

While they were distracted Kenrig flexed muscles across her body, testing how far she was able to push against their control. It felt like hooks had been sunk into her flesh to hold her still, but her muscles obeyed.

Morgen's head writhed as Ogda's grip tightened around its skull. 'We will never be tied to such as this again. The ancient power of the Marches grows without pause. With it we will never be subject to mortal interference. Never be bound by the constraints of our nature. This land will host our feast without end and all its people will be our guests. They will come to us gladly and their reward will be endless revelry!'

Their grip on the head relaxed and they straightened to stare northward. 'Your escort is here.'

Kenrig didn't turn her head to look back along her path, but she heard the high cries of the sluagh carried clear by the cold air. *Dandall*, she thought. *Lissi.*

Her legs were weak under her, but they held as she forced herself from the ground. She hunched as she stood, feeling like she fought the weight of chains draped over her shoulders. Ogda looked up from the head.

'I told you to kneel!'

The command staggered her and she stumbled as her legs bent to obey. She almost bowed as she fought to stay upright, but she held her ground and drove her legs straight.

'Kneel!'

The rumble of hooves on the hill behind her joined the thunder of blood in her ears.

'Kneel!'

Her legs twitched and trembled under her, but with every command she resisted the magic weakened. She gritted her teeth until she was sure they'd crack and drew blood from her palms as her nails dug into her skin, but she stood until she was able to straighten to her full height.

'I have your name, *Kenrig Ebermann.* You will obey!'

'I need to be honest,' Kenrig gasped. 'I adopted the name. My real name caused me too much trouble.'

She had never seen Ogda lose their composure and the sight terrified her. Whatever brief triumph she felt was quickly snuffed.

'Adopted name or not,' they screamed. 'It is yours. It was chosen or it was given. Now *kneel.*'

She was prepared, but the force of the command nearly sent her crashing to her knees. She snatched up the shovel as her legs bent and planted it in the path to push herself up again.

The sluagh crested the hill and swirled around the stone circle like a sudden storm. Trinkets and weapons flashed across her vision, leaving dazzling trails of blindness.

Kenrig tried to follow the sluagh as they spun around her, but she was slow, too slow to track which of them would come for her first. She hefted the shovel in both hands ahead of her, unsure what use it would be against the howling spirits no matter how physical they seemed.

Her daggers and falchion hung around her like iron weights, the thought of drawing them enough to exhaust her. She was outnumbered, on foot against seven mounted warriors. Properly armed and rested she knew she wouldn't have been able to fight them all.

She was close enough that she could have reached the circle's centre in a few paces, but she might as well have been miles away. Not knowing what else to do she took a step forward, her stiff leg barely moving a few inches before her foot crashed back down.

Ogda held out Morgen's head, their fury dispelled by a look of something approaching pity. 'You ought to save your strength. You and your apprentice will be the first guests of honour at our next feast.'

So he's alive. Her lips twitched into a thin smile. *Maybe I'm not too late.*

'Bind her!' Ogda shouted to the sluagh. 'Drag her behind your horses! Break her body against the ground and parade her before the people she thought to save from us!'

She recognised Crow-feeder at the head of the sluagh. Its mask of scraps was distorted around a wide hole and its head trailed silver smoke, but its frenzy wasn't diminished. *Nice shot anyway, Dandall.*

She thought it a strange coincidence that it was the first of the sluagh to receive a name from her that rode ahead of all the others, but she remembered the way it had bested its kin for the honour of binding her in chains. Something that Ogda had said came back to her then. *It was chosen or it was given.*

'Crow-feeder!' she shouted over the howling riders. 'I gave you that name.'

Her body might be slow, but her mind raced. Could she even command them? What could she say to them if she could?

'Crow-feeder! Halt!'

She tried to throw her will into the words, speaking with a confidence she didn't feel. She braced herself for the effort to fail, certain that that she would hear Ogda's mocking laughter as the sluagh forced her into chains.

Crow-Feeder pulled back on the reins of its horse so suddenly that the beast reared up, front hooves kicking into the empty air. The other sluagh whistled in alarm, breaking around the rearing horse. One of them veered into the circle, charging for her, and she thought desperately to remember the name she'd given it.

'Thread-cutter! Halt!'

The sluagh's horse skidded across the circle, coming to a stop beside Ogda. Thread-cutter trembled and twitched, but it sat limp on the horse's back, long arms slack at its sides. Ogda's hand shot out and grabbed its wrist.

'I told you to bind her!'

The sluagh's arm spasmed in their grip and it whined, but made no move to obey.

Ogda turned to the rest of the sluagh fighting for control of their horses outside the circle.

'Bind her now!'

Five of the sluagh struggled to follow their order, but Kenrig was ready.

'Courage-taker!' she roared. *'Shade-lurker and Wind-stepper! Lidless-watcher and Grim-hailer! Crow-feeder and Thread-cutter!'*

Their names brought keening wails from each of them and they reeled as she addressed them. *'Bind your master! Bind the lord and lady Gloam Ogda!'*

For a moment the sluagh hesitated and she feared that her commands had failed, that she'd pushed her control too far in commanding them to threaten their real master. Then they began to dismount, one-by-one in the order she'd named them.

Ogda stood their ground as the sluagh advanced into the circle. *'I am your master, not her.'*

With their attention off her, the magic holding Kenrig was lifted. She staggered forward as she felt suddenly weightless. She walked freely into the circle, keeping her distance from the line of sluagh.

'You were so certain I'd fail your challenge,' she said. 'So sure that I couldn't uncover what brought you here. You made your own servants vulnerable to my control.'

Ogda began to retreat, drifting backward as the sluagh staggered toward them. 'Stay where you are! Do you hear me?'

Morgen's head fell from their grip and rolled, kicked and stomped by the heedless feet of the sluagh.

'I told you to stay! Damn you all, obey me! I am your master, I gave you life! I fashioned you from the formless fabric of the Otherworld! Without me you are nothing!'

The sluagh began to slow and Kenrig rushed for the head before they could slip from her control. Ogda lunged for her, moving with the same impossible speed they'd shown before, but the sluagh barred their path. They tried to pull away from the hands that seized them and sink into the shadows, but they were held fast.

The soil of the crossroads had been made soft by rainfall and yielded easily to her shovel.

'You will suffer for this!' Ogda screamed and Kenrig was sure that they were addressing her. 'You do not know what horrors you bring upon yourself!'

Kenrig dug without stopping. Nothing else mattered. Every ache and injury made themselves known as she worked, but she was fuelled by a fatal resolve.

'We are immortal, *Kenrig Ebermann!* I promise you will not escape us!'

Kenrig kicked Morgen's head into the hole. Even after all it had suffered it still struggled, wriggling with what little muscle it had left to it, scattering the dirt that she piled on it.

'There is power in these kingdoms you do not understand! If we do not claim it then others will! Your efforts here will avail you nothing! There will be no end to the monsters these lands will birth! No end to the procession of wayward souls!'

Kenrig stared down into Morgen's eye sockets as they filled with dirt.

'You will die someday, Kenrig Ebermann! The time you have left is the blink of an eye to us! We will watch for your spirit's arrival and you will find no peace in death!'

Kenrig had wondered what might happen when the night was done. She'd imagined her plan failing. Tormented herself in idle moments and dragged herself from the cusp of sleep with the thought that she and Dandall had struggled in vain. That the Unseelie would refuse banishment and resume their feast anew with two fresh guests.

She'd also wondered what might happen if they did succeed. How the Unseelie might be dragged roaring across the Veil. Would there be some sign that it had happened? Would she see something in the sky, some disturbance in the moon's surface to show that finally their struggle was over?

She hadn't expected the sudden silence. Nor the empty night that surrounded her. When the Unseelie were banished they were banished with blessed quiet and a waning moon.

Epilogue

Dandall's sneeze startled a flight of pigeons from a tree. The snap of their wings sent ripples through the cold fog hanging over the road.

'We can turn back, stay longer if you're not recovered yet?' Kenrig offered.

Dandall steadied his new horse and stifled another sneeze with a finger under his nose. 'Last one, I promise.'

The boy was paler than usual, but he was the picture of health compared to the shivering wreck she'd stumbled across on her return from the Parting Hill. He'd been as white as the spectres and shivering so violently he couldn't stand or even speak. He'd walked, how far she didn't know, and managed to collapse directly in her path. Without Lissi he wouldn't have survived the night.

'I knew where we needed to be,' she'd said. 'I dreamt it.'

Kenrig had no more reason to doubt Lissi's abilities and needed no more explanation. She'd built a fire right where Dandall had fallen and brought Stoic to lie down beside the boy. After that she'd stripped Dandall of his wet shirt and cloak, wrapped him in blankets and stayed up through the night rubbing warmth into his feet.

By the morning he was recovered enough to ride and she let him and Lissi sit in the saddle while she led Stoic on foot. She'd recounted everything that had happened since they'd parted and forced him to do the same in an effort to keep him awake. Lissi had been happy to kick him whenever he'd trailed off toward sleep.

He'd spent the next days in bed piled with blankets, tended by Etholie and Daglan who took every opportunity to remind him how grateful they were for Lissi's return. Kenrig was sure the heat of his embarrassment was what finally broke his fever.

She'd returned to Orveng while he rested and searched among the dead fort for the dagger lost in her flight from the longhouse. The storm had broken on her journey west and the longhouse had dried enough to burn once she'd found oil to start a fire. The flames had raged through the night and by dawn it was a blackened shell, its ashes the best burial she could offer Morgen's victims.

She'd taken her own chance to recover after that. There'd been barely an inch of her that wasn't injured and she'd been all too happy to sleep under a roof as winter set in around them. Life in Karstend had been quiet, its people grateful to be free but slow to recover from their ordeal.

The pace of life in those weeks was what all of them needed to heal, but eventually it had grated on her and her thoughts had turned back toward the road. Frost had bloomed in the empty fields and she didn't want to be trapped anywhere when the first snow arrived. Her restless mind dwelled on Ogda's parting words and fear settled in like an itch.

'Well if you're sure,' she said.

'Another night in a warm bed and I won't be strong enough to leave.'

'Warm beds, hot baths, regular meals. Sure you don't want to turn back?'

He yawned. 'Don't tempt me.'

When he met her gaze there was a smile on his face, wide and genuine. *He betrayed you.*

She returned his smile as best she could. 'Alright then, onto the next job.'

Their path brought them inevitably back to the crossroads under the apple tree, to the sight of Lissi dancing across the parting stone. Her breathless song carried strangely in the fog, at once sounding muffled and as clear as if she sang it right beside them.

She stopped dancing when she spotted them and her face fell. 'I dreamt yous sneaking away without saying bye.'

'We knew we'd never be able to escape your gifts,' Kenrig said. 'We thought it would be easier to say our goodbyes on the road.'

She pondered that for a while then shrugged.

'Do you want us to take you back?' Dandall asked.

She shook her head. 'Daglan will come get me.'

Kenrig urged Stoic into the crossroads. 'You won't try and follow us, right? Daglan and Etholie have worried enough for one lifetime.'

The girl kicked her toes against the ground. 'I've to stay here for a while. I'll leave when I'm ready.'

Kenrig exchanged a look with Dandall. 'I've no doubt,' she said, turning back to Lissi. 'Whatever you've dreamt, I'm sure will happen. You have a true gift.'

The girl returned her gaze. 'Some won't believe you,' she continued. 'And others might fear what you see. But if you keep using your gift as you have, I think you'll do great things with it.'

She smiled as she asked her question, but feared what Lissi might say in answer. 'Any final prophecies for me before I go?'

The words of the girl's last prophecy echoed in her mind, ringing anew with Ogda's final warning. *A feast will come, of carrion all, where murder rests 'neath funeral pall. A thread to unravel, a thread to weave. A pattern to wind, a pattern to cleave. Traitor to one and hero to none. The fate of the kingdoms unjustly won.*

Dandall had told her what he'd done to Holdainn's sword to save himself. How he'd broken the magic shaping it the same way he'd broken the mysticism in her dagger. How had he described it, as they'd rode back through the blighted farms?

'It was like...pulling on a thread, or...tearing a pattern.'

Threads and *patterns*. What did it mean? Why did he have that power?

Lissi craned her neck to look at Dandall. She studied him with a frown, staring until his pale cheeks had regained some colour. Kenrig could see the confusion plain in his face and wondered if Lissi might repeat her prophecy, but instead she shook her head again.

'You already know what you need to,' she said.

An awkward silence hung between them until Kenrig cleared her throat. 'Well, Lissi, I believe you have something of mine. I'm sorry to have to ask for it back.'

The girl looked down at the dagger tucked through her belt. Kenrig had already retrieved the pendant from her, but she had slept more soundly with the dagger in easy reach. She'd complained of nightmares since the night of the Wild Hunt and the dagger had helped to ease her fear of sleep.

She drew the little blade and held it close as though reluctant to part with it, but after a moment she held it up.

'Don't be sorry,' she said. 'I'll see it again. Only-'

Kenrig leaned down to take it from her. 'Only?'

The girl chewed the inside of her cheek and looked down at her feet. 'Only, you won't be the one holding it.'

Kenrig slid the dagger into its sheath. She was quiet for a time, unsure what to say in the face of the meaning those words carried.

She forced another smile onto her face. 'Then I hope whoever does carry it will take good care of it.'

She thought she saw Lissi's eyes dart towards Dandall again, but the girl twirled abruptly and skipped over the parting stone, her voice picking up the words of her song where she'd left them. Kenrig opened her mouth to say a final goodbye, but Lissi was already running for home, carrying her strange song with her.

Acknowledgements

First of all, I'd like to thank anyone who's read this far. Thank you for indulging me and I hope that you enjoyed my debut novel.

Since I wrote my first book of short stories in 2021 I feel like I have even more reasons to be thankful to the people that have helped this novel come into being. As always the Simms family deserves recognition for dedicating time to searching my early drafts for spelling mistakes, punctuation errors and logical inconsistencies, even knowing I still expect them to buy a copy of the final book. I also have to thank my mum and dad for filling my childhood with books and starting me on a lifelong obsession for fantasy and sci-fi. Without that I wouldn't be writing this now.

I want to thank every member of my DND group (named in alphabetical surname order to prevent bias): Jack Coutts, Katelyn Holmes, Amy Murdie, Iain Simms, the brothers Wright, Ben and Jamie, and Craig Young. Over the past few years playing DND with you all has been a source of constant joy across hundreds of hours of fantasy escapism. Thanks for the laughs, the tears (from laughing) and for bearing witness to my cursed dice rolls.

It's hard to know where to begin thanking my partner Charlotte. I feel like I should begin thanking you for your incredible patience. Without your support I wouldn't have been able to dedicate half as much time to writing this book. You more than anyone have to bear the brunt of my sudden daydreaming, mumbled ideas, odd bouts of writing at unpredictable hours and complete inability to focus. You're my first line of defence against doubts and every day I think about how lucky I am to have you in my life.

Finally I have to thank my two co-authors Dante and Diego. Somehow the random strings of characters you typed with your paws always coincided with a section I needed to edit.

If you've enjoyed reading this please feel free to write a review or leave a rating on your site of choice. Amazon, Instagram, Twitter, Goodreads, Bookish, LibraryThing, LoveReading...there are too many to name, but wherever they are, all reviews help the books of aspiring writers find their way into the libraries of readers like you. Help wayward books find a home and share the stories you enjoy.

See where it all began in this free excerpt of

the short story 'Water'

I

'Do you want to know why it's called Finegan's Way?'

'No.'

Kenrig sighed when the boy, whose name she struggled to remember, finally stopped talking. She wriggled in the back of the wagon with a creak of leather armour and settled as best she could under her cloak. She intended to sleep away the rest of the journey nestled between two rows of barrels. It was a shame the boy and his father farmed mussels, but she was growing used to the smell.

The boy didn't stay quiet for long. 'It's a good story,' he said.

Kenrig didn't respond. She closed off her ears and hoped the boy would grow bored. He did not.

'Finegan was a great warrior,' he said. 'The best Cadogan warrior ever seen. Strong as five men together, and so big he had to ride an ox into battle. Well, he-'

'She doesn't want to hear your story, Dandall,' his father said.

Tanach had a pleasant voice, gruff but not harsh and sounded almost as good as he looked. He wore a wedding band around his left wrist. *A widower,* she thought as she fell asleep.

She woke later with difficulty. Judging by the light burning red through her eyelids she hadn't slept for long. Daylight, weak as it was in that part of the world, kept her from falling asleep again, but she was reluctant to open her eyes and resume the monotony of travelling.

Like most Marchers she didn't know much about the Bann beyond what was recorded on maps, and her first impression didn't inspire her interest. Flooded woods, shallow lochs and miles of marshland bordered roads fashioned more by the passage of feet than any deliberate engineering.

Previously she would have avoided the place, but her new role demanded she travel in the dark corners of the world. That's where the work could be found.

Dandall and his father were arguing. She listened, though not with any great interest.

'But I want to see the beast, dad,' Dandall said.

'No,' Tanach said. 'You really don't.'

'But you're showing her where to find it, and she's just a woman. I'm going to be a man soon, you have to show me.'

'You think you're nearly a man at eleven?'

'Madan said he was more of a man than any of the other boys, and he's twelve.'

'Madan is full of nonsense. If he was a man already he would help bring in the harvest, not sit on his lazy arse.'

'Madan said he's seen the beast.'

'What did I just say about Madan being full of nonsense? Besides the beast's only been seen near Barrow Law and Madan is too fear't to leave the village.'

Dandall sounded triumphant. 'Ha, the beast is near Barrow Law?'

Tanach groaned. 'That was a mistake. You're not to go there, understood?'

'But-'

'Understood?'

'Yes, father.'

Kenrig yawned and that seemed to alert the pair of them that she was awake.

'Mistress Kenrig, are you awake?' Tanach said.

There would be no chance of more sleep. 'Yes. And don't call me mistress.'

'As you wish. I'd call you Father, only-'

'Only I'm not a man,' she said, sitting up. 'I'm also not a priest.'

'But you carry-'

'Symbols of office and holy relics, I know. So do most roadside peddlers, but that doesn't make them priests.'

'I dare say yours will be more genuine than theirs.'

She sat with her eyes closed for a while. 'I hope so, otherwise this beast of yours will eat well.'

'It doesn't eat people,' Dandall said, with a hint of morbid delight. 'It drowns them.'

Kenrig opened her eyes and turned to rest her back against a barrel. She looked round to the front of the wagon where Dandall and Tanach sat on the raised bench. Both of them had the scrawny, underfed look of the other people she'd seen in the Bann, but as Cadogan they took care to maintain their dark hair in neat braids.

'Drowns them? And leaves them untouched otherwise?' she asked.

Both of them stared ahead along the narrow track, but Tanach inclined his head slightly toward her whenever he spoke.

'Aye,' he said. 'The folk we've found have all had water in their lungs.'

'No chance they just drowned in a conventional fashion?'

Tanach shook his head. 'The Cadogan round here have to be good divers, and we only swim when the waters are calm.'

'People have accidents.'

'That would be a lot of accidents. No, they were drowned and their necks were crushed. You'll hear the same story in every village.'

'And you said this beast resembles a bloated corpse?'

Tanach nodded. 'You don't live here without seeing at least one body swollen with water. The beast resembled them, only-'

'Yes?'

'Well I didn't see it clearly, I'd not be talking to you if I had, but it seemed like it wasn't quite there. Not solid if you catch my meaning?'

Kenrig didn't really know what he meant, but she wanted to keep Tanach talking about the creature. She had neglected to gather many details when she'd hastily agreed to deal with whatever it was.

'More or less,' she said. 'You said the beast is near Barrow Law, any bodies of water nearby?'

'Not nearby exactly. But that whole area is marshland except for the hill and the fort on top.'

'Any battles happen near there?'

Tanach was silent for a while. 'Not for a long time. Maybe two hundred years or more, when the Karlans came.'

'Could be a water elemental.'

She spoke casually, feigning a confidence she definitely didn't feel. Tanach's descriptions of the creature and its victims fit with what she'd read about water elementals, but her knowledge of them was purely theoretical. If something went wrong, and she survived, then she might admit that to her new employers.

'You'll know better than I what it is,' Tanach said. 'Could one of these elementals live for two hundred years?'

'They're not alive so I suppose there aren't really any limits,' she said.

'But why has it only shown up now?' Dandall asked.

'Well, someone might have stumbled into its territory,' Kenrig said. 'Water elementals aren't very active and they can sleep for a long time before some poor soul wakes them up.'

She wished she could believe her own words the way the Cadogan seemed to, but she felt a gnawing anxiety in her chest as she realised the perils of a theoretical education. She was trusting her life to books written by old men who'd likely never seen the creatures they described.

They rode in silence for a while after that. Dandall finally ran out of energy and fell asleep in the early evening, and Tanach was content to let Kenrig keep to her own thoughts.

The wagon was pulled by a single, thin horse and their progress was slow. The track that they followed was remarkable only because it was a rare trail of dry ground amongst the sodden muck either side. Trees grew uncomfortably close to the track, the shadows between them impenetrable in the twilight gloom.

Kenrig found it impossible not to stare into the shadows, feeling breathlessness tighten around her ribs as the trees seemed to sway closer in a faint wind. She felt an urge to cough to relieve the pressure swelling in her lungs, yet didn't dare to make a sound. She wished that Tanach would speak, or that Dandall would wake up and tell her a story, anything to drive off the oppressive quiet.

The only sounds that warded away absolute silence were the grinding of the wagon wheels and the sullen clatter of the horse's hooves. Then even those noises stopped.

The horse snorted. Kenrig's head twitched round and she peered between Tanach and the sleeping Dandall. The animal was shaking its head high in the air and pawing at the ground. Tanach whipped at it gently with the reins, and when that didn't goad it into movement he struck it harder.

'Mother's sake,' Tanach said, his voice sounding dim.

He stood on the bench and jumped from the wagon, landing with a low thud. He grumbled as he moved round to the front of the horse. It shied as he approached, backing into the wagon. He muttered something and it let him in close enough to touch its neck.

Kenrig's mind was full of thoughts of the beast as she stood in the back of the wagon. The gloom darkened and her eyes were too dull to see anything between the trees.

A branch snapped and the horse jolted backwards. The wagon shuddered under Kenrig's feet and she was thrown forward, her fall stopped by a barrel. The horse reared and its front leg struck Tanach in the chest. He was knocked from his feet and staggered backward off the track, falling into the forest.

'Tanach?' Kenrig shouted after him.

He didn't answer. Kenrig jumped from the cart, fearing Tanach had been seriously hurt. Dandall stirred and groaned in his sleep as she passed the front of the wagon.

She walked to the spot where Tanach had fallen. At the edge of the road his feet had churned up a patch of mud. Two deep ruts led into the forest. There was nothing visible of him in the gathering fog.

'Tanach?' she shouted, less certain that time.

She held her breath, straining to hear over the sound of her heart. She inhaled to call out again until Tanach's choked screams echoed from the trees.

Read the rest in 'Elementals: Stories of the Four Elements' *available from Amazon in eBook and paperback formats*